Nuclear Winter Wonderland

Adam Weiss' twin sister, Anna, is kidnapped by Ebbetts, an unpleasant and possibly cancer-ridden man who might have plans that involve a nuclear device. Desperately searching for Anna, Adam acquires a couple of sidekicks: Filbert, a man of small stature who used to do something brutal for the Mob, and Cherry Sundae, a Croatian female clown who only speaks Spanish. If that isn't enough to make you dive right into the novel, consider this: it is remarkably polished and stylishly written (remarkably, because the author hasn't been doing this for years: this is his first novel.) It is richly comic, surreal without being silly—except where it intends to be silly—and playful in its use of language. Christopher Moore writes this way, and so does Robert Rankin, although it would be a serious mistake to assume that Corin is imitating them or anyone else in any way. If you can judge a writer's future output based on his first novel, Corin is one of those writers who, years from now, other newcomers will be imitating.

— David Pitt/*Booklist*

Nuclear Winter Wonderland

Joshua Corin

KÜNATI

LARGO, USA

For information, contact Kunati Inc., Book Publishers in both USA and Canada.
In USA: 6901 Bryan Dairy Road, Suite 150, Largo, FL 33777 USA
In Canada: 75 First Street, Suite 128, Orangeville, ON L9W 5B6 CANADA,
or e-mail to info@kunati.com.

FIRST EDITION

Designed by Kam Wai Yu
Persona Corp. | www.personaco.com

ISBN-13: 978-1-60164-160-1   EAN 9781601641601
FIC000000 FICTION/General

Published by Kunati Inc. (USA) and Kunati Inc. (Canada).
Provocative. Bold. Controversial.™

http://www.kunati.com

TM—Kunati and Kunati Trailer are trademarks
owned by Kunati Inc. Persona is a trademark owned by Persona Corp.
All other trademarks are the property of their respective owners.

Library of Congress Cataloging-in-Publication Data

Corin, Joshua.
  Nuclear winter wonderland / Joshua Corin. -- 1st ed.
    p. cm.
  ISBN 978-1-60164-160-1 (alk. paper)
  1. College students--Fiction. 2. Brothers and sisters--Fiction. 3. Terrorists--
Fiction. 4. Nuclear terrorism--Prevention--Fiction. 5. Cancer--Patients--Fiction. I.
Title.
  PS3603.O74N83 2008
  813'.6--dc22
                    2008014009

D e d i c a t i o n

To my wife (whoever she may be)

Acknowledgements

The author would like to take this opportunity to thank the many people who helped
shepherd this book from manuscript to publication: his parents Alan & Sharon;
his siblings Heather, Seth, & Noah; his sisters-in-law Kelly & Michele; his stalwart
champion Kristy Hamer; his early readers Amber Hutchison & Jordan D. White;
his manager Jim Strader; his agent Josie Freedman; his editor James McKinnon;
his cover artist Kam Wai Yu; his publisher Derek Armstrong; and his supportive
colleagues at Georgia Perimeter College, most notably David Cromer & Alan Jackson.

He also would like to thank you for buying his book. He hopes you enjoy the journey.

Now please buckle up. The tank is full, the roads are narrow, and the driver has a
mischievous gleam in his eye.

Chapter One

"Adam, I've got some rotten news. Your Uncle Dexter is dead."

"That sucks, Mom." Adam chomped off an inch of banana and chewed. "Who's Uncle Dexter?"

"Look, how many times do I have to—Jesus, Adam, I—you do not talk on the phone with your mouth full. It makes it difficult for people to understand you, and it's rude. Either finish whatever you're eating or hang up the—"

Adam clicked off his phone and swallowed down some more soft, sweet banana. Once finished, he carried the phone and peel out of his room and into the quiet, wood-paneled corridor. The house was empty; the rest of his fraternity brothers were using their physics textbooks to sled down a local hill. Adam had promised to join them after he finished studying for his physiology final. Sledding = joyous. Physiology = soporific. Life = unfair.

His phone emitted a series of farting noises.

"Hello?"

"You hung up on me."

"Hi, Mom." He wandered back into the hall. "So who was Uncle Dexter?"

"You know who he was."

As his mother offered an account of nutty dead Uncle Dexter, whom he had never met and who apparently had fancied himself the exiled king of Mars, Adam jogged down the steps to the house's first level and plopped in front of the fraternity's sixty-inch flat-screen TV. He hoped Garth had left the Xbox plugged in.

"... so we expect to see you there on Thursday."

Adam sifted through the pile of discs for his MVP baseball game. On its highest difficulty setting, his Orioles had made it into the playoffs.

He was very proud of this achievement.

"Adam, are you listening to me?"

"Sure, Mom. You expect to see me there on Thursday. Where is there?"

"Rhode Island."

"Yeah, Mom, I don't think that's going to happen. I'm still at school here in Michigan for another week."

"I thought tomorrow was your last final."

None of the twenty-three discs heaped in front of the TV was his baseball game. Adam, panicking, gazed around the room: couches, chairs, shelves, foosball table. He paced to the foosball table and investigated its crevasses for his game.

"Adam ..."

"Tomorrow is my last final, Mom, but then we have stuff here at the house for another week." They had the end-of-semester party, and then the party to celebrate the end-of-semester party ... then the Alpha Phi Kappa annual eggnog chug-a-thon for charity, which he was going to win this year, damn it ... "After that I'm coming straight home. I promise."

He moved aside the toys and bongs on the room's white wooden shelves. No game disc, although he did find a soggy condom.

"Okay," said his mother a thousand miles away, "your choice. I can't force you to come pay your respects. I need to pack my suitcase now. Take care."

Adam slid his phone into his sweatpants and headed for the couch cushions. If his baseball game could not be found there, he would have to start going through his brothers' rooms. His Orioles were in the playoffs! On the highest difficulty!

The room's two plaid polyester couches, acquired at a yard sale at the beginning of the semester, were nicknamed Lauren and Yvonne, after two freshmen who had lost their virginity (Lauren to Garth and Yvonne to Craig "Salamander" Watson) on the respective pieces of furniture. Adam ransacked Lauren first, yanking off her cushions and burying his hands into her many nooks. He found $2.32 in change, a sodden paperback novel, a stainless steel spoon (its bottom scorched), and a blue g-string that smelled exactly like Velveeta … but no game, no Orioles.

"Fuck," he decided.

His phone farted.

"Hello?" He heard a condescending sigh on the other end and knew it was his sister Anna. "What's up, Anna?"

"So why aren't you going to the funeral, Captain Caveman?"

Anna was his twin sister. Both she and Adam were blue-eyed, blond-haired, tall, athletic and tan; by most counts, a pair of Aryan wet dreams. But Adam was a pre-med (by default) frat boy at the University of Michigan, Ann Arbor, population 40,583, while Anna studied the cello at the Oberlin Conservatory of Music, population 602.

Adam plunked down on one of Lauren's cushions. "How am I supposed to get there?"

"You have a car. Use it."

"I'm busy this week. And anyway, we never met him. And Mom says he was a loon."

"Maybe so," replied Anna, "but he was Dad's oldest brother. You don't think Dad wouldn't want us to go?"

"I can't believe you're playing the Dad card."

"Well I am, Adam, and I'm right, and you know I'm right. And I think we should be there. And if you leave tomorrow after your exam and pick me up we can be there in time for the service."

He kicked the collection of Xbox discs, scattering them across the rug.

"I have plans," he said.

"They're flexible," she said.

"What I do is no less important than what you do," he said.

"I never said it was," she said. "I had plans too, you know. I'm canceling them."

He picked up the spoon off Lauren's bare body and stared at his stretched, blurry reflection in its metal bowl. All he had to do was say no. Simple word, one breath, done. He would still see most of his family next week anyway. It's not like any of them were going to withhold his Christmas gifts if he didn't attend this meaningless funeral. The worst they would be was disappointed. Just as from Anna they expected achievement and aspiration, surely by now from him they had come to expect disappointment …

The next morning, after bombing his physiology final exam, Adam stuffed his suitcase into the trunk of his 80,000-mile-plus green Escort, cleared out the Bud Lite empties and snack cake wrappers from the car's backseat, and hit the road. Depending on traffic—and he did not expect much on a Wednesday morning—Oberlin was a two-hour drive. As he revved onto the highway, Adam mused on his Xbox Orioles and the impossible heights he and they would reach after Christmas break.

He tapped a live Led Zeppelin album into his CD player (wired into the car's old tape deck, ah sweet rejuvenation) and cruised south at a breezy eighty-five miles per hour. The Escort filled with howling guitars, gunshot drumbeats, and the occasional billowing mist of Adam's breath; ever since a minor collision last winter with an implacable moose, the car's heater had been nonfunctional (and its transmission had become crotchety). Adam's fists, encased in green mittens, pounded staccato rhythms on the steering wheel. An hour into the trip, he crossed into Ohio. He switched out Zeppelin for The Who.

Michigan in December was cold and white. Ohio in December was cold and white. The whole Midwest in the winter months became a gigantic, pale, indiscriminate corpse.

"If you hate the cold so much, Adam," his sister would often say, "why didn't you go to school in Florida?"

"If he went to school in Florida," his mother would reply, "he would just complain about the heat."

Ha-ha. So funny they could be. But he put up with the teasing and the mockery. As long as they were harassing him, their minds were off Dad.

Adam shivered inside his dark green fleece coat. Thirty minutes until Oberlin, and then a hot lunch. All he had eaten for breakfast was a three-day-old slice of pepperoni pizza (also found in the pizza box, coincidentally, was his game disc) and downed the slice with a mug of powdery hot cocoa. He had a box of Twinkies keeping him company on the passenger seat, but what he needed as the temperature reached the single digits, was fire for his veins, not sugar for his nerves. Perhaps a hamburger, or a steaming bowl of chili.

Ten minutes outside Oberlin, the Escort's engine light flashed on the dash. Adam gave it a good flick and it blinked off. He turned off the exit ramp and headed for Maple Willow Drive. Anna lived in one of two first-floor apartments with her best friends Jasmine (pianist with gorgeous blue eyes and burn scars across her arms and legs from a *verboten* childhood trauma) and Hope (flutist).

Making sure all the doors to his Escort were locked, and keeping one watchful eye on the neighborhood crack house, Adam approached his sister's front door and fingered her doorbell, trilling a metallic Ode to Joy throughout her apartment.

"Anna," yelled Hope from the other side of the door, "he's here!"

The door remained shut.

A Canadian wind washed across the front yard, tossing dead leaves to Adam's sneakers and biting at his bare ears. He shuffled his feet to keep warm and tucked his gloved hands in his jeans pockets.

"Have you seen my hairdryer?" bellowed Anna.

"Check the kitchen!" replied Hope.

Sick of this bullshit, Adam pressed the doorbell again.

While waiting: another icy breeze. Adam turned his back to the current.

The door opened two inches. Hope peered out at him with a mascara-circled eyeball. "She'll be right out."

The door shut.

"Wait!" Adam thumped the doorframe with his fist. "Can I at least wait inside?"

"No," she answered, "sorry. This is an asshole-free zone."

The two inches snapped shut. Never had a human being been so ineptly named as his sister's roommate Hope.

Two long, cold minutes passed and then the front door yawned wide. Anna clutched the gargantuan black case for her cello. Two more bags, much smaller, sat at her feet.

"Ready?" she asked.

As expected, the cello occupied the entire backseat. They managed to squeeze one of Anna's bags into the trunk; the other she kept on her lap.

"I'm keeping my window open," said Anna. "It will help air out your car."

"Whatever."

They pulled into a Denny's near the interstate and were seated in a booth by a window. The outside chill penetrated the thick glass and coiled itself around their bodies. Adam ordered a bowl of chili, a hamburger, onion rings and a hot cocoa. Anna ordered a Caesar salad and a diet Coke.

"Aren't you cold?" he asked.

"It's winter," she replied.

Adam gobbled up his chili in heaping spoonfuls. It was bland and watery, but hot. Oh so joyfully hot! When his hamburger and rings arrived a few minutes later, he launched into them too.

"Eat much, Captain Caveman?" she asked.

"Anorexic much?" he replied. In the time it took him to scarf down his chili and half his quarter-pounder, she had barely attacked her hill of salad. Adam and Anna, identical and inverted.

The waitress brought their separate bills.

Adam watched his sister rifle through her tiny, kidney-shaped purse.

"Do you need any change?" he asked.

"No. Yes. Yes. Twenty cents."

Adam checked his pockets, removed a gob of lint, two pennies, and no dimes.

"Sorry," he said.

"Neanderthal," she replied.

They each paid by check card and headed out to the car. A light snowfall had begun, and Anna's open window had allowed thousands of frozen flecks to melt on the front upholstery. Adam started up the Ford, leaned forcibly across his sister's chest, and rolled her window back up.

He slid a Black Sabbath album into his CD player, punched up the volume, and maneuvered back onto I-80E. In theory the distance from Oberlin to Newark was about five hundred miles, but Adam figured that if he gunned the accelerator, avoided all cops and maintained an adrenalized playlist on his stereo, they could arrive by sunset without stopping.

Contrary plans, however, were being hatched by the gastric team of chili + burger + onion rings + hot cocoa. Forty minutes down the stretch of smooth highway and Adam first felt something kick against his spleen. He frowned, wondered if he had any antacids in the glove compartment, realized he did not, frowned again, shrugged and continued driving. In the passenger seat, Anna dozed. Fifty minutes out of Oberlin, Ohio, and a spear ripped into the right side of his abdomen and wiggled about. Adam wiped the sweat from his upper lip. Sweat? At best, the inside temperature of the car was thirty-five degrees Fahrenheit. Sweat? Something was decidedly un-kosher.

Fifty-four minutes after leaving Denny's parking lot, Adam began looking for rest stops. The next big city was Scranton and that was hours away. His fingers clenched the steering wheel as if intestinal relief could be obtained from a ring of aged faux leather. The spear in his belly teased his liver, poked at his appendix. Adam bit down on his lower lip then abruptly stopped—even the idea of chewing made him nauseous.

Green sign, side of the road:

REST STOP THREE MILES

Adam pounded the roof in joy.

Anna seconded with a snore. A bubble of spit formed at her mouth.

He floored the gas pedal. Providence was but a breath away.

They passed a hitchhiking clown by the side of the road. Adam ignored the clown and floored the gas. To keep himself distracted from the jagged cramps, and from any errant thoughts of food, Adam muttered his multiplication tables. One times one is one. One times two is two. One times three is three. Ever since primary school, he had taken comfort in the reliability of numbers. One times four is four, always. One times five is five, every time. Numbers had buoyed him through tryouts for high school baseball. Numbers had carried him week to week as he waited to hear from the admission board at U of M. Numbers had been his sole salvation in dealing with his father's …

REST STOP NEXT RIGHT

Adam took the exit a bit too abruptly and jolted Anna from her slumber.

"What … where … are we there yet?"

The rest stop was a pair of tubby brick huts, one labeled in black paint MENS and one labeled in black paint WOMENS. Identical and inverted. Adam parked beside the lot's only other vehicle, a pickup truck flaking dark red paint, and hopped out of the car.

"I'll be right back," he said, snatching the keys from the ignition, and he jogged into the MENS room.

The time on his wristwatch read 1:52 P.M.

The roadside latrine was decorated. A chain of red and green tinsel snaked around each of the six urinals' rusted silver handles. A knee-high fir tree, probably uprooted from nearby woodland, drooped underneath the automated hand-dryer. Mistletoe dangled from one of the ceiling light fixtures, barely obscuring the collection of dead flies accumulated at the base of the fixture's clear plastic dome. The restroom smelled strongly of myrrh and Lysol.

Adam bolted straight for the corner cubicle. His jeans and boxers bunched at his ankles, his ass collapsed against the cold hard seat, and a small hot apocalypse rained into the toilet water. Relief—climactic, exhausting relief—lopsided his face with a goofy grin. The day was good. His quest was over.

"Nice sneakers," wheezed the man in the next stall.

Adam glanced to his right.

"I said nice sneakers. I like your sneakers." The man spoke in aching, breathy growls, like an aging grizzly ready for that last, long hibernation. "I see they're Nikes. I used to own a pair of Nikes but now (WHEEZE) all I have are these ugly things."

Below the flimsy wall separating the stalls, Adam spotted a pair of big brown boots splattered with dirt. No, not dirt. Dried blood.

"My name's Ebbets. Like the ballpark."

Don't respond, thought Adam, and the bozo will shut up.

"I grew up in Brooklyn and now I'm here (WHEEZE) with you. How about that?"

Adam unrolled a foot of toilet paper and cleaned himself up. It was time to leave.

"Forgive my wheezing, Nike. I'm a little cancerous. Trust me, it doesn't sound as bad as it feels. Anyway, lean back. I want to show you something."

BAM! Adam nearly fell off the toilet seat. The gunshot had punched a half-inch hole, about eye level, in the wall between them.

Two times one is two. Two times two is four. Two times three is six.

Adam reached for his jeans and boxers.

"Relax, Nike," Ebbets said, "you and I need to (COUGH) chat."

Adam looked at the wall. Out of the half-inch hole peered a dark brown eye.

"Give me your wallet," he wheezed, "I want to see your (WHEEZE) wallet."

Without hesitation, Adam slid his billfold under the stall. A pale hand, stunted and trembling, wrapped around it, picked it up. Patches of dried blood mottled his flesh like lesions.

"Well, it's a pleasure to make your acquaintance ... Adam Weiss. Let's see what we got. You're from New Jersey. I have a cousin who lives outside Hoboken. She (WHEEZE) works in fashion. Her name's Crystal. You know anyone named Crystal from outside Hoboken?"

Adam swallowed his breath.

His watch ticked by another minute.

"Yeah, okay," Ebbets said, "you don't have to talk. I like your photograph. You look like a good kid. A little dumb. Are you a little dumb? Did your teacher ever pick on you at school? I'm what they call (WHEEZE) freakishly smart. My teachers sure picked on me. They used to give me stuff—books, magazines—this one teacher gave me a paperweight with $E=MC^2$ printed on it in block letters. I tracked her down to her nice house on Long Island and I used the (WHEEZE) paperweight to smash in her windshield."

The eye reappeared in the hole.

"You look scared. You don't have to be scared, not of me, not yet. Sorry I fired my gun but it was just to (WHEEZE) get your attention. Didn't want you scampering off to Newark, New Jersey, without us getting to know one another."

Adam rubbed his moist palms against his bare thighs. "What do you want?"

"Could have been anyone, you know. First guy who came in. I've been hiding out here a long time and it turned out (WHEEZE) to be you. How about that? If you believe in God, you got to believe that God, for whatever reason, wanted it to be you, so let's talk, you and me, let's talk about (WHEEZE) the end of the world."

Three times one is three. Three times two is six. Three times three is nine.

"According to the New Testament, four horsemen will come and kill all the unfaithful, but I'm not a Christian. Muslims believe that a great beast will rise up and everyone will die of blisters on their armpits. I'm not a Muslim. And Buddhists and Hindus have us all becoming rapists. All these peaceful (WHEEZE) religions and all of them have the world ending with this violent buildup. They all share that in common. How about that? Would you believe me if I told you that I knew how the world was going to end? Because I do. And there isn't going to be any violent buildup. It's going to be sudden. People are going to be (WHEEZE) drinking their coffee and chatting with their buddies and cheating on their spouses and then poof: the end. That's how the (COUGH) world's going to end, and I'll tell you what else. I know when it's going to happen."

The brown boots shifted around. Ebbets was agitating himself. Adam recalled learning in some physics class that the average person used more force to scratch an itch on his backside than was required to pull the trigger on the average 9mm handgun. How easy it would be for this maniac to accidentally pull the trigger of his gun and suddenly end Adam's world.

That was when Adam thought about his sister, alone in the car, waiting for him. Probably wondering what was taking him so long. Oh God, would she come in to investigate? Would she pop her head in the restroom and call out his name?

"Next Wednesday is Christmas Eve," Ebbets continued. "That's when the world is going to end. The trigger's right here in my (WHEEZE) pocket. Just in case you were wondering."

Now a rustling sound, a slight movement of feet: the man stood up.

"I'm going to go take your car now. Mine's no good to me anymore, but you're welcome (COUGH) to use it, because I'm just a softie. I really am. I broke that goddamn teacher's windshield, but I felt so bad about it that I wrote her a letter. I wrote her a letter. How about that? I'm going to take your car now. It's been nice chatting with you. Why don't you count to a good high number like five hundred before you get up, okay? Otherwise, we might (WHEEZE) run into each other outside and then I might have to use my gun. Count to five hundred. Don't forget the Mississippis. You have yourself a nice day."

His toilet flushed. His door squeaked open. His boots stomped across the floor tiles.

And then he was gone.

Chapter Two

Four hundred ninety-eight Mississippi.

Four hundred ninety-nine Mississippi.

Five hundred.

Adam yanked up his jeans and boxers and bounded out of the restroom. All the time he sat in the stall counting, the only image in his mind—the only thought his brain allowed—was of Anna. His bratty overachieving sister. He rushed out into the December cold, not knowing what he would find but hoping, hoping ...

But his Escort was gone. Ebbets was gone. Anna was gone.

Adam took a step back. He collided against the brick wall of the MENS building.

"Anna!" he called out. "Anna!"

Her name rolled down the Ohio highway.

"Anna!"

Quickly he searched the old rest stop for something—a pay phone, a police callbox—but all he found was garbage, and all that remained with him in the snowy lot was Ebbets' dark red pickup truck.

Where was he taking her? Adam tugged open the driver's door and climbed into the cab to search for clues. Sure enough, he found them. Hundreds of them. Come Explore Historic Williamsburg! Meet Us in St. Louis! Road maps and travel brochures for every metropolitan area in the eastern United States carpeted the floor of the cab like oblong confetti. Make Cleveland Your Next Vacation Destination!

Adam again patted himself for his cell phone, but he knew he had left it in the Escort. So he waited. Two minutes. Five minutes. Eventually a traveler would have to pull into the rest stop and they would have to have a cell phone and they would have to call the police and the police would have to track down the Escort and arrest this deranged man and

Anna would have to be safe. That was what had to happen.

Fifteen minutes. Twenty minutes. Twenty-one. Twenty-two.

Adam ripped off his wristwatch and threw it against the dashboard, where it landed in a shadow next to a small silver key. A key! He just about jammed it into the ignition. The engine barked to life. Salvation! Now where was the gear shift? Where was the …

Oh. A stick shift.

Fuck.

Adam's father had been an accountant. On the weekends he could be found in the garage, tooling with his black Harley-Davidson FLH. Adam and Anna rode on the back of a Harley long before learning how to ride a Schwinn. When he offered to teach them how to ride it themselves, however, Adam refused. He was ten years old and believed anywhere worth going was worth going on a skateboard. By the time he and his sister were fifteen and taking driving lessons, the skateboard was cobwebbed in the basement and the Harley-Davidson sold for the Ford Escort that Adam and Anna would be sharing. Adam had insisted his father get a car with automatic transmission. Anna, having learned the basics of manual transmission on the Harley, did not care either way.

Their roles reversed, Anna would have been able to drive the pickup truck and track him down. Yet another example of his sister's superiority and his absolute uselessness. Adam battered out his fury onto Ebbets' steering wheel.

And he realized he was being watched.

Fifty feet away, near the off-ramp for the rest stop, stood the hitchhiking clown he'd passed earlier, now waving at him. He wore a billowy, patchwork garment of yellows and reds and blues that swirled in slow motion across his body. His hands and feet were encased in white—tiny white mitts and long white shoes. His face, too, was painted white, like a mime's, but with a mascara grin stretching ear to ear and peculiar green circles on his cheeks that matched the green bushy wig atop his head.

Adam darted out to meet him.

"Do you have a phone?"

The new arrival stared at him for a moment and then replied, her voice breathy and sweet, "¿Que?"

The hitchhiking clown was a woman. And Spanish. Okay …

"Do – you – have – a – phone?"

She smiled. A few snowflakes caught in her eyelashes. "¿Que?"

"PHONE!" Adam held his pinkie and thumb to his face in the universal sign for telephone (and hang-ten). "PHONE!"

She imitated his hand gesture and yelled back, "PHONE! PHONE!"

Adam paced. Every second that ticked by on his discarded wristwatch, his sister and that crazy son of a bitch were getting farther away.

"Look, I don't speak Spanish. I'm sorry. I don't even speak German and I took three years of it in high school. But I'm desperate. A psychopath has stolen my car and kidnapped my sister. Now please. Please! Can you help me? Can – you – help – me?"

She opened her arms and gave Adam a gentle hug. Her body felt strange, erratically bumpy, as if she had four or five toasters taped underneath her costume.

They parted. She pointed at herself and said slowly, "Cherry Sundae."

"Cherry Sundae?"

She smiled and nodded. "Cherry Sundae! *Si.*"

Adam threw up his hands in defeat. This was going nowhere. He waved goodbye to Cherry Sundae the Spanish clown and padded up the ramp to the highway. Perhaps if he flagged someone down, someone who spoke English, he might have a chance of saving Anna.

His feet crunched across the snow-crusted asphalt. Yes, it was the middle of the day and yes, he was in the middle of nowhere, but this still was a major interstate highway. He headed east. As he walked, his fingertips glanced across the icy guardrail. A tractor trailer drove by. Then a couple of sedans. Adam gesticulated for them to stop but no one did. Some even accelerated. Had he been one of those passersby, would he have stopped? Only an hour before, he had passed Cherry Sundae the hitchhiking clown, and instead of offering her a lift he had waved at her in arrogance.

Turns out I did the right thing anyway, he mused, 'cause she's a nutjob. Adam almost smiled, and then thought about his sister.

He tried to remember the last road sign they had passed before parking at the rest stop. Where exactly in Ohio were they? Had they crossed the border into Pennsylvania? The next metropolitan area off I-80E was Scranton and no matter how far they had traveled past the border, Scranton had to be a good two hundred miles away. Surely some of the tiny towns in between had to have police stations, but how much assistance could a sheriff/solicitor/mortician and his son/deputy provide?

He leaned back on the guardrail and for the first time since he was nine years old and his father had sent him to his room for cheating on a spelling test, Adam wept. Thick wet tears dribbled down his face; the wind caught each tear, one by one, and crystallized them. He stared blurry-eyed down at his sneakers, the knockoff Nikes he had found for twenty dollars at Target that Ebbets had so admired. If he had just taken them off and passed them under the stall, maybe—

HONK!

Adam looked up and to his left. A vehicle had stopped mere feet from where he stood. The dark red pickup truck.

From the driver's seat waved Cherry Sundae, the lunatic clown.

Adam hustled over to her window.

"What are you doing?" he asked.

She honked the horn again and her mascara smile stretched even wider. She motioned for him to join her in the cab.

As Adam wavered between accompanying this painted woman, with whom he could not communicate, and waiting for some unknown commuter to maybe stop and help him, thick snowflakes tumbled from the sky, as if from a bottomless reservoir. Soon the black highway would be a white river; soon the temperature would plummet; soon Anna would be gone for good.

Adam splashed the travel brochures to the foot of the cab and buckled himself into the passenger seat. Cherry gave him a thumbs-up, shifted into first, and rumbled back onto I-80E.

She clicked on the radio. Willie Nelson warbled about pot and lost love. Adam picked up a few of the pamphlets and searched them for Ebbets' handwriting. If anything, the man's fingerprints would be all over the pickup truck, and once the sheriff/solicitor/mortician called in the state police, they would have definite leads. And while waiting at the cop shop for the case to be solved, he would call his mother.

"Mom," he imagined himself saying, "I've got some rotten news." That was how she had informed him about Uncle Dexter's death. Had that been only yesterday? He wondered what she was doing now, what she was thinking. How well had she known Uncle Dexter? Had he always been delusional or at one time had he been sane? Had he danced at their wedding? Had he been the best man? Adam knew so little, mostly because he had never cared to ask, but now as he and Cherry Sundae raced across the freeway in a madman's pickup, his family history felt vital, and his ignorance of it absolutely foolish.

He was certain Anna knew.

They passed a tractor trailer stopped by the side of the road, the same tractor trailer that had zipped by only ten minutes ago. Now layered with snow and motionless, it resembled the flaccid, disembodied arm of a pale giant.

"Turn around," said Adam.

Cherry glanced in his direction.

"Turn around!" Adam pointed behind them at the trailer fading into the flake-filled distance. "Truckers have CB radios! We can get him to radio for—look, you need to turn around!"

Cherry smiled and pressed down on the gas pedal. The speedometer crept past eighty.

"No! Go back! Not forward! Back! Back! Oh, Christ. Never mind.

How can you live in America and not understand English? That's like living in Canada and not being able to understand … English. Okay, not the best example. I see you like to speed. That's nice. Are you sure you know how to drive?"

Eighty-two miles per hour. Eighty-five.

"You can't understand a word I'm saying so you don't know that I'm in trouble so that means you're trying to break the sound barrier because you're in a hurry to get somewhere. Where are you in a hurry to get to, Cherry? What are you running from?"

Hearing her name, Cherry patted him on the shoulder.

Then Adam spotted a state police car up ahead in the left lane. When they whizzed past it, they had to be going at least ninety.

Well, he thought, that's one way to contact the authorities.

The rear view mirror glowed red and blue.

"Uh-oh," said Cherry.

Adam looked over at his companion. "Guess 'uh-oh' is a universal expression, huh?"

She took her time drifting into the breakdown lane, dragging angled tire marks into the fresh snow. By the time she had turned off the ignition, they had been tailed by the police car and his flashing lights for an eighth of a mile.

"I don't know how to drive a stick," mumbled Adam, "but I'm pretty sure I can do it better than you."

Officer Neal, a twenty-two-year-old peach-fuzzed boy, rapped on Cherry's windowpane. Cherry fired up the ignition and depressed the electronic control for her window.

"¡Hola!"

"Please remove your key from the ignition."

Cherry replied with a frown, so Adam leaned over and complied with the request.

"Officer, I am so glad to see you. My name is Adam Weiss. My sister Anna has been kidnapped by a crazy-ass psycho with a gun and maybe something explosive in his pocket. He's got big brown boots and he's driving my car. I think they're headed east. Maybe. This is his car. He left it for me. So you think you can get on the radio and report the crime and you know, stop him?"

Officer Neal nodded, exhaled a plume of cold breath, stared at Adam a moment, and then turned his attention back to the clown in the driver's seat. "Sir, I'm going to need to see your license and registration."

"Oh, she's not a guy," said Adam. "She's a woman. I made the same mistake. And I think she only speaks Spanish."

Officer Neal nodded, exhaled a plume of cold breath, stared at Adam a moment, and then turned his attention back to the female clown in the driver's seat. "Ma'am, I'm going to need to see your license and registration. Now."

"I told you, she—"

"Sir," said Officer Neal, aiming an index finger, "you're going need to close your mouth."

"You're not—look, you're not listening to me! My sister is in danger!"

"I heard you, sir. Now please open the glove compartment and remove this vehicle's registration."

Adam sucked on his lower lip. Who knew what horrors a man like Ebbets buried in his glove compartment? Definitely not gloves. In the Escort's glove compartment, Adam usually stashed a pack of Newports (menthol), a Bic pen (red), a roll of Trojans (ribbed), and a Swiss Army knife from his brief, brief days as a Boy Scout. With a deep breath, he leaned forward and clicked open the pickup's glove compartment.

The chamber was empty. No bullets, no switchblade, no chopped-off fingernails. Not even a driver's manual.

Or an insurance card. Or a registration.

"Sir, I'm going to need to see your license right now."

"I ..." Adam glanced at the cop, whose ebbing patience was darkening his face. "See, Officer, this guy Ebbets, he made me give him my wallet and—"

"Okay, both of you. Out of the vehicle."

Not one to argue with an armed man, this being his second in an hour, Adam opened his door and quietly emerged from the pickup. Cherry Sundae, assessing the situation, did the same.

Officer Neal stuffed the pickup's key in his jacket pocket and led Adam and Cherry to the rear of their vehicle, where pulsing emergency lights colored each falling snowflake either police-blue or fire-red. "Remain here," he said, and returned to the warmth of his squad car to radio his colleagues.

"So," said Adam, fidgeting in the cold, "how long you been a clown?"

Cherry Sundae glanced at him. Her lips smiled; her eyes did not.

"When we were kids, my parents used to take me and my sister to this traveling circus that always came by in August. They would set up in the soccer field behind Governor High School, you know, with this big tent and all these booths. We always used to do the booths first and save the tent for the end. Well, wouldn't you know it, in the tent this one summer, as the opening act, here comes out the clowns. Seven clowns stuffed in a tiny car. It's a common act. I mean, I've told people this story and they've all said, 'yeah, my circus used to do that too,' so I know it's a common act. But the first time I see those clowns crawl out of that car, I am terrified. Give me a break. I was eight years old, right? And fear of clowns is even more common than that little piled-in-the-car act they did. Anyway, my sister sees the look on my face—my sister Anna, the one who's missing, my twin sister—she sees the look on my face and she reaches over and tickles me in the ribs. I mean, just goes at it. And our parents are there, loving it, thinking I'm laughing about the clowns. When the clowns are done and it's time for the trapeze act, Anna leans over and whispers in my ear. 'See,' she says, 'now you don't have to be scared. Clowns only eat you if you don't laugh.'"

Officer Neal emerged from his car, blocking the snow with his raised forearm and slowly approaching Adam and Cherry.

"What's under the tarp?" he asked.

Adam turned around. Until then, he had not even realized there was anything in the pickup truck's flatbed but sure enough, stretched out across its dark red aft was a sheet of old green canvas and underneath the canvas lay …

"I don't know," he replied.

"You don't know what's in the back of your truck."

"I told you, Officer, it's not my truck."

"Please remove the tarp."

Adam unhooked its clasps from the flatbed and peeled back the tarp. He half-expected to uncover a dead body, bloated and bullet-ridden, but instead revealed a lead crate the size of a baby grand. Stenciled letters across its hull read: WARNING RADIATION.

Jesus Christ, thought Adam, now what?

Chapter Three

The back of the squad car reeked of stale corn chips. Adam wrinkled his nose and investigated the source of the odor, but the grille separating the back seat, where he and Cherry Sundae were located, and the front seat, where Officer Neal sat sipping Styrofoam coffee, impeded adequate investigation. Then again, perhaps the smell came from the tiny old man in the gigantic leather overcoat.

This was Filbert.

Adam was planted in the middle, between Filbert and Cherry. Filbert, who was quietly asleep and possibly dead, had a tendency to lean his raisin of a head on Adam's shoulder. Adam leaned forward, dislodging the raisin, and said to Officer Neal, "Can you at least, you know, tell other officers to be on the lookout for my Ford Escort. Put out an APD or something?"

"Sir," replied Officer Neal, peering into the rearview, "you're going to need to be quiet."

Filbert had slumped down behind Adam, making it impossible for him to sit back. Cherry Sundae ran a finger across her face and traced her name in greasepaint on the upholstery. When she finished, she elbowed Adam and grinned.

Outside, the snow was really coming down. Adam estimated at least three inches on the ground already, maybe six by nightfall. He tried to check the time, but the car's dash was obscured by CB equipment, a holiday box of Kleenex, and a 12-gauge shotgun.

"How's your coffee? Is it good? I'll bet it's good. You know who likes coffee? My sister. Who's been kidnapped."

"Sir—"

"Adam Weiss! My name is Adam Weiss. Not 'sir.' Not 'mister.' Not 'buddy.' Adam Weiss. Look it up. No criminal record. No prior convictions. Well, except for that one time when I was twelve. But I was twelve and all that stuff gets thrown away when you turn eighteen, right?"

The policeman responded with a loud sip.

"Listen. I have a lot of respect for law enforcement. My cousin Ritchie is a cop. Sort of. So I understand that you need to follow procedure. I respect that too. I'm a member of a fraternity. We have procedures too. Tradition's important. The university is trying to outlaw hazing, but it serves an important historical purpose. Were you in a fraternity in college?"

The policeman responded with a loud sip.

Cherry Sundae, pretending her safety belt was a sitar, plucked her fingers up and down its frayed diagonal swath.

Adam cleared his throat and said: "Did I mention my uncle just died?"

Twenty intolerable minutes later, Officer Neal's backup finally showed. She was a burly Jamaican woman with dreadlocks bundled up inside her fedora. Neal downed the rest of his coffee, groomed his peach fuzz, and stepped out of his vehicle.

Adam slipped his hands underneath Filbert's itty-bitty head and propped him up against the door. Gooey spit dribbled out of the old man's mouth; he was awakening. Outside, Officer Neal and his colleague chatted very closely. Adam could imagine them trading gooey spit before the hour was up.

"Where's the john?" mumbled Filbert in cultured tones, and then he belched an eighty-proof cloud.

"You're in the back of a police car."

Filbert's eyes shifted right, shifted left, then, accompanied by a moist sigh, shifted down. "I hate it back here."

"Yeah," replied Adam, "it's no toilet."

Filbert's eyes shifted left again and fixed on Cherry Sundae. She waved at him and pleated her multicolor costume. Filbert leaned in to Adam's right ear and whispered, "There's a clown over there."

"Her name is Cherry Sundae," answered Adam.

"¡*Hola!*" echoed Cherry Sundae.

Adam grimaced. "She's a Spanish clown."

So for the next ten minutes, Filbert and Cherry conducted a gleeful, animated conversation in Spanish, trading language across Adam's lap. Adam, flabbergasted, attempted to interrupt, but was shushed twice by Filbert and then once by Cherry. Finally, when they seemed to be through, he turned to Filbert and asked:

"Are you Hispanic?"

"Me? No. But I love Taco Bell. And Cherry's not Hispanic either. She's Croatian."

"Croatian?" Adam frowned. "Then why is she speaking Spanish?"

"Do you understand Croatian?"

"No."

"Do many Americans understand Croatian?"

"No."

"That's why she learned Spanish."

"Why didn't she just learn English?"

"I don't know."

"Ask her," said Adam.

"For ten dollars," answered Filbert.

"Ten dollars?"

"My services aren't free, sport-o."

"I don't have ten dollars. My wallet was stolen. When I get it back, I'll pay you."

"Funny. My wallet was stolen too. It had ten thousand dollars. When I get it back, I'll pay you."

"Pay me for what?"

"For the headache you gave me."

Outside, the two state troopers fiddled with the device in the bed of the pick-up. Then Officer Neal fiddled with the zipper on his colleague's coat.

Filbert cleared his throat and spat on the toe of Adam's sneaker.

"Sorry," the old man said, "but I can't open the window."

"Uh-huh."

"What's that in the back of the truck?"

Adam shrugged.

"Maybe it's an atomic bomb."

Adam shrugged.

"Is it your atomic bomb?"

"No," replied Adam. "I'm just borrowing it. What makes you think it's a bomb?"

Filbert pushed his face against the grille and waited for Adam to do the same. Adam complied. Then Cherry, smiling, also pressed her face against the grille.

"Do you see the radiation warning there?" he asked.

"Yes."

Filbert smacked Adam upside the head and leaned back in the seat.

"What did you do that for, Filbert?"

"For stupid questions, sport. You see the label, lead box, and you wonder if it's maybe possibly an atomic bomb. Do you also need a map to find your cock?"

Filbert then babbled several Spanish sentences to Cherry, who giggled, pointed at Adam, then giggled some more. Having had enough of this nonsense, and desperate to reunite with his sister, Adam turned around in his seat and pounded with his fists on the car's back window.

"Anna!" he cried. "Anna!"

But the only dents he made were on the skin of his hands.

"Who's Anna?" asked Filbert.

"My sister," Adam said, and then, sitting upright once again, summarized the past few hours of his life to the ancient inebriate to his right. Mulling over the tale, Filbert pursed his lips, squinted his eyes, and replied with the wisdom of his years:

"Well. You're fucked."

"Thanks."

"That would explain the Nevada plates on your pickup truck. Would you like some advice?"

"Sure."

"Take a nap. The world is always better when you're sleeping."

At that moment, Officer Neal returned to the vehicle. He stooped into the driver's seat, started up the car, and without a word they drove past the pickup and the Jamaican and the atomic bomb and were on their way.

"Where are we going?" asked Adam.

"You're going to be detained at the Buchanan Station pending arraignment for your crimes."

"Crimes? What crimes? What did I do wrong, other than, you know, getting out of bed this morning?"

"Sir, you and your companion are being charged with driving thirty-six miles per hour over the posted speed limit, driving without a license, refusal to show registration or insurance, and for trafficking possible hazardous materials. You are under arrest. You have the right to remain silent."

"Great."

"Anything you say can and will be held against you in a court of law."

"Great."

"You also have the right to an attorney. If you cannot afford an attorney, one will be provided for you free of charge by the court."

"How generous of them."

"Do you understand these rights as I have explained them?"

"No," replied Adam. "Please repeat them a couple more times. It sounds like a long drive."

It was a long drive. Furthermore, it was a southern drive, far off the reliable path of Interstate 80. Adam could feel the distance between himself and his twin sister widen with each rural mile. If only he could use a phone, call his mother. She would rescue them both. That was her job.

As the roadway became steeper and the snowfall denser, Officer Neal called his quarry into his radio and advised HQ he would be a few minutes late. Visibility had become guesswork, and the road had long since transformed into a slippery white sheet. Cherry and Filbert gripped their respective door handles; Adam, not having a door handle to grip, interlocked fingers in the grille.

" 'Oh … the weather outside is frightful …' " whispered Adam nervously,

"'… and the fire is so delightful … since we've no place to go…'"

Filbert joined in: "'Let it snow, let it snow, let it snow.'"

In unison, cautiously: "'It doesn't show signs of stopping … and I've bought some corn for popping … the lights are turned way down low … let it snow, let it snow, let it snow.'"

The vehicle sluiced sharply to the port. Officer Neal hugged the wheel and expertly maneuvered back on track, such as it was. They continued to ascend whatever slick mountain the asphalt circumnavigated.

" 'When we finally kiss good night …' " murmured Adam and Filbert,

"'how I hate going out in the storm … but if you really hold me tight … all the way home I'll be warm.'"

The rear tires shimmied once more, this time to the starboard.

Cherry crossed herself—*el padre, el hijo, el fantasma santo.*

Officer Neal steadied their traction.

Weaker now, a prayer: "'The fire is slowly dying … and my dear we're still goodbying … but as long as you love me so … let it snow, let it snow, let it snow.'"

End of prayer.

Silence.

Then the car spun again to the portside, and this time off the side of the mountain.

"Shit!" cried Adam.

"Shit!" cried Filbert.

"¡*Mierda!*" cried Cherry.

The front end of the squad car teetered over the cliff edge like a dizzy drunk. Officer Neal pushed open his door. Looked down. Way down. Pulled shut his door. Wiped the sweat from his fuzzy upper lip.

"Shit," he sputtered. "Shit."

Cherry and Filbert yanked at their door handles, pounded at their doors, but the back seat doors of police vehicles did not open from the inside, not for anyone, not ever. Adam thumped again at the rear window, but there was no escape. He felt his bladder sprinkle his pants with a few drops of pre-death pee.

The car slid an inch forward, the snow underneath it beginning to give.

"Get out," yelled Adam to the front seat, "and open these doors!"

Officer Neal stared at him. His eyes had gone crimson with adrenaline and fear. He shook his head and croaked, short of breath, "I can't. I'm sorry."

"It's okay," said Filbert, smoothing out the creases in his overcoat. "I've seen Paris. I'm ready to die."

"Well I haven't seen Paris," replied Adam, "and I don't want to see Paris and I do not want to die!"

Suddenly Cherry clapped her hands and blurted out: "Boom!"

All eyes aimed at her.

She smiled.

"Oh, Paris is lovely," resumed Filbert.

"Great. You can show it to me as soon as we get out of this car."

Cherry again clapped her hands and boomed. This time she did not smile. She pointed. At Neal's shotgun in the front seat.

Then she pointed at the rear window.

Neal nodded, and reached for his weapon.

"What are you doing?" asked Adam.

"You're going to want to get on the floor now, sport," said Filbert, getting on the floor.

Cherry grabbed Adam by his coat and dragged him down to the floor on top of her. The distribution of weight rocked the vehicle back and forth. "Hello," he said to her. "*Hola*," she replied. Their necks were necking.

"Cover your ears!" cried Filbert.

"Why?" Adam sat back up. "Why should—?"

BOOM! The shotgun spat its load through the grille and against the rear windshield, raining glass shards all across the back seat and opening a nice wide hole for Adam, Cherry, and Filbert to scramble out through. Cherry and Filbert were already clawing their way toward freedom, but Adam, half-deaf from the shotgun blast and covered in shards, just glared at them all and threw up his fists and bellowed:

"WHY DO PEOPLE KEEP SHOOTING AT ME?!"

"Some men are hunters," said Filbert, "and some men are targets. You said you don't want to die? Get your ass into gear, sport."

As they clambered out the back of the car, Adam looked back at Officer Neal. The trooper remained jailed behind the grille, and knew it. The red in his eyes had dimmed to blue. His cheeks were wet. He held a gloved hand against the grille as if to wave goodbye.

"Wait," Adam said to his two fellow escapees, "don't get off the car."

Cherry and Filbert, perched on the vehicle's trunk, stopped.

"I've changed my mind, sport. I'd rather not go down with the ship."

"If we all get off the car, there won't be any weight keeping it from toppling off the mountain."

"So? We'll still be up here."

Adam thumbed at Officer Neal. "He won't."

"He's doomed."

"I'm not doomed!" whimpered Officer Neal. Weeping, trembling, he looked just shy of twelve years old.

"Can you open the door and pull yourself onto the roof?"

Officer Neal opened the door and tried to pull himself onto the roof, but the snow-capped roof proved too slippery, and the drop too precarious, for him to exert much of an effort.

"What we need is a rope," said Filbert, "and we don't have a rope."

"How about bunjee cords?" asked Adam. "Officer, do you have bunjee cords?"

Neal shook his head.

"Kid, why would he have bunjee cords?"

"I don't know ..."

"And anyway, we need something that's firm. Something long that he can grip. Please insert penis joke here."

Metal groaned as the car dipped another degree toward bottom. Filbert suddenly turned to Cherry and rattled off a few Spanish sentences. She nodded, smiled, and stuffed her right hand up her left sleeve. In seconds, she was drawing out of her sleeve a banana-yellow handkerchief, and then an apple-red one, and then a kiwi-brown one, all knotted together. Peach followed plum, orange followed peach, lime followed orange. By the time she was through, she had six feet of firm, long cloth. She whipped the yellow end to the left side of the car; Neal caught it on the first try.

"Are you sure this will hold me?"

Filbert translated the cop's inquiry for Cherry.

She countered with a nonchalant shrug.

Adam, Filbert and Cherry, poised on the wet trunk of the vehicle, gripped the orange end of the line. Officer Neal wound the yellow handkerchief around his left forearm, carried on a brief discussion with his Maker, and launched himself out of the car. His body vanished from view and thumped into the snowy slope.

"Climb!" yelled Adam.

Hand over hand, breath on top of breath, Officer Neal ascended Cherry's color-coded magic trick. The three on the trunk finally spotted his head, then his shoulders, torso, waist. He was halfway to purchase.

The car angled down another inch. Despite the weight of several human beings on its backside, it would not maintain balance for long. Officer Neal saw it dip and scaled faster, legs kicking and arms yanking.

Adam heard fabric tear.

"Hurry!" he said, and just in time too. The colorful rope rent in half, right down the center of the peach handkerchief. But Officer Neal was already pressing himself horizontal on the white earth, kissing snow. He had made it. He was safe.

Adam and Cherry and Filbert cheered.

Officer Neal looked up at them, eyes alive and full of merriment.

And the white earth beneath him—not really earth at all but precariously piled snow—gave way, emptying the cop down the side of the mountain.

"No!" cried Adam, and he rushed to the side of the cliff. Cherry and Filbert joined him, and they gazed down into the deep darkness. Where had he fallen? Was he alive?

"I'm okay," came Neal's voice, weak but still full of merriment. "I'm all right."

Adam spotted Neal's hand waving, and he waved back. They all cheered again; they had battled death and defeated her. Then the automobile, no longer counterbalanced by weight on its trunk, tipped over the edge of the road and plummeted down the abyss, crashing two tons of steel onto the merry state trooper.

Chapter Four

The Commonwealth of Pennsylvania had been replaced by snow. Mounds of snow, heaps of snow, streets and rivers and cities of snow. Snow snow snow snow snow snow snow. Except for fuzzy-lipped Officer Neal, who was covered by the wreck of his car. And snow.

Adam, Cherry and Filbert slid down the hill. Slowly they approached the twisted rubble.

"I think he's dead," said Adam.

In lieu of sarcastic comment, Filbert coughed up some phlegm. Cherry wiped a tear from a painted cheek. Adam plopped down on a sodden stump.

The three mourners meandered in the pale clearing. The trees were gone; only snow-starched skeletons remained. Anna was gone. This policeman was gone. Adam slicked his hands through his blond hair and wished he were gone too.

About five heavy minutes later, a snowball thudded the back of his skull. Somewhere behind him, Cherry giggled.

"Are you psychotic?" He stood up and faced her. She held out another snowball, presumably for him to take and throw at her. "No, really, Cherry, are you? I'm curious. Because I've already met one psychopath today and he shot at me in the bathroom, stole my car and kidnapped my sister. But why should one psychopath in my life be enough when I can have two?"

He stared into her glassy green eyes. He wondered if she wore contacts. He tried to peer into her soul but saw only his own reflection.

Filbert grabbed him by the arm. "She can't understand you, you know."

"She knows what I'm saying," replied Adam, shrugging off the old man. "She got the gist. Didn't you?"

Cherry let the snowball, his snowball, fall to the ground. She joined it, sitting cross-legged, head low.

"Now look what you've done, sport. You've made her sad. Nothing worse in this world than a sad clown."

"Really, Filbert? Nothing? Nothing in this world is worse than a sad clown? How about an atomic bomb, for one, on the back of a pickup truck? How about the three of us stranded out here in the middle of nowhere? God only knows what time in the night it is. How long do you think it will be before Officer Car-crash's buddies come looking for him in this weather?"

Filbert studied him for a moment, then walked over to Cherry, knelt beside her and whispered phrases into her ear. At first she waved him off but soon his words, whatever they were, seemed to calm her spirits. He helped her to her feet, and the two of them strolled into the forest.

"Where are you going?" Adam asked.

"What does it matter, sport?" The old man kept walking away. "We're all doomed anyway. You said so yourself. So get comfortable. Maybe you can start a nice fire with that car's ruptured fuel tank and have some roast pig for dinner."

Filbert and Cherry were disappearing into the forest.

"But where are you going?" he called after them. "What's this way?"

"I'll tell you when we get there," Filbert replied, and he and Cherry were gone.

Remaining at the crash site, Adam futzed to and fro. Part of him wanted to stay there. Despite his protestations, eventually Officer Car-crash's buddies would come looking and if he remained near the smoldering wreckage, he would be found and he would tell them about Anna and she would be found and they would finish the drive out to Rhode Island and take a long nap on some cousin's furniture. Maybe their cousin even had an Xbox.

But another part of him wanted to rush into the woods to meet his loony tunes acquaintances. When lost, he recalled, it's safest to remain in one place, but there's also safety in numbers. Yes, the old man and the strange clown made for unsteady company, but they were company, and on this cold dark night in rural Pennsylvania …

Snowflakes whipped by his bare face. He touched his nose and ears to prove they were still attached. Only once before in his life had he been this irrevocably lost and alone: inside the local Wal-Mart, when he was four years old. His mother had spotted some friends and left him in the cereals aisle.

"I'll be right back," she had said, "so don't go anywhere."

He had volunteered to accompany his mother on the shopping trip; Anna had stayed home with Dad, watching him fiddle in the garage with his Harley-Davidson. Being left alone in the grocery store was a big-boy responsibility, and as his mother tracked down her girlfriends, little Adam beamed with pride. He walked up and down the aisle, tapping each cereal box he wanted (Captain Crunch, Lucky Charms, Count Chocula—oh Count Chocula!) and making sure to skip over the disgusting brands he loathed (Raisin Bran, Cheerios, Corn Flakes). He must have made twelve sorties, back and forth, before he began to wonder if his mother was ever going to return.

He envisioned himself growing up there in the cereal aisle, eating nothing but cereal all day. Nearby aisles had soup and spaghetti and candy, but he had promised to stick there by the breakfast foods, so there by the breakfast foods he would stick. He would outgrow his shoes and have to make new ones out of cardboard cereal boxes. The plastic bags inside the boxes would serve as shirts. Adam planned out the next ten years of his life while he awaited his mother's delayed return from gabbing.

He wondered if she had just forgotten him and gone home. They had Anna. They did not need him. He crayoned the walls and refused to eat his macaroni and cheese. He plucked flowers out of the garden and stained his new pants with dirt. They had Anna. They did not need him.

As four-year-old Adam began to sob (and twenty-year-old Adam, remembering the turmoil, welled up), his mother reappeared, the cavalry over the hill, pushing her wobbly cart.

"Why are you crying?" she asked, and wiped away his tears and snot with a Kleenex from her pocketbook. "Everything's okay now, Adam. Mommy's here. Mommy's here."

She added a box of Count Chocula to the cart; they spent the rest of the time in the store holding hands.

Adam suddenly realized that he was not waiting at the crash site for the troopers to rescue him; he was waiting for his mother.

He followed Cherry and Filbert's tracks into the woods. The meager starlight barely illuminated the snow-coated trees, much less the ground, but through patience and perseverance, Adam managed to lose the path only twice. Before long the crash site had vanished from view, if not from mind. Adam ambled through the unnamed Pennsylvania forestland, occasionally calling out "Filbert!" or "Cherry!" and made sure to keep moving. Stopping meant death.

Each step poured more frozen water into his porous Nikes. His saturated socks were becoming barbells and the muscles in his thighs and calves were cramping, but he continued. Stopping meant death.

"Filbert! Cherry!"

His lungs ached for warm oxygen, not the deep-freeze molecules currently circulating through his mouth and down his straining trachea.

"Filbert! Cherry!"

How had this happened to him? Why was this happening to him? Had his Xbox addiction offended God? Adam cycled through satisfactory answers; none lit the way for him out of this maze of wood and ice.

He looked down at the ground and saw no tracks save his own.

He realized he was going to die. He had no ID on him, no wallet. Days from now, some backwoods hunter would find his blue-skinned popsicle corpse and, out of respect, bury it. His face would appear on a milk carton and four-year-olds across America would eat their cereal while staring at his forlorn face.

Falling to his knees into the foot-deep snow, Adam craved a bowl of Count Chocula. And a glass of OJ, extra pulp. And a few slices of bacon. And maybe a pancake, apple cinnamon if possible. And also a—slap on the face from an ornery old man.

"Wake up, you brick-brained child," said Filbert, still smelling like stale corn chips. "This isn't your bedroom in the suburbs."

"How long was I out?"

"An hour. Thirty seconds. How should I know?" He helped Adam to his feet. "We heard you calling our names and I drew the short straw and went looking for you. Come on."

Adam traipsed after him into the arctic darkness.

"Do you know where we're going?" he asked after about a minute.

Filbert halted. Pirouetted toward the inquisitive boy. Flashed some yellow teeth. Thumped Adam repeatedly in the skull with his bony knuckles. Pirouetted again. Continued on his way.

Adam, rubbing his bruised skull, followed.

Shortly thereafter:

"Thank you, by the way," Adam said, "for coming back."

Filbert harrumphed. "Don't mention it. And I mean that, by the way. Don't mention it. Please."

"I was wondering something, though."

"Yes?"

"What were you doing in the back of that car?"

"Napping."

"Yes, no, I know that. What I mean is, you know, why were you in the back of his car? What did he arrest you for?"

"Beating up college kids. Look up."

"What?"

"Look up."

Adam looked up. Saw snow and stars. "Yeah?"

"See that bright star over there?"

"That star?"

"No, that's an airplane. You can tell because it's moving, sport." Filbert propped up Adam's arm and traced his finger across a constellation. "Okay, elementary school science class. That is the Pole Star. Always in the same place, even if you're not. North. That's how you can always know where you're going. No matter what, eventually you arrive somewhere. Lesson over. Come on. We're almost there."

"Where's there?"

They emerged into a small copse. Cherry was doing jumping jacks, presumably to keep warm. She saw them and immediately ran and embraced Adam, smearing greasepaint over his cheek.

"We found a bear trap here by this stump," said Filbert. He indicated a bear trap by a stump. "I think it's a new trap and Cherry agrees. So is this some hunting ground in the middle of nowhere or are we near someone's residence? Also, the woods are thinning out and there are more bushes here. I don't know. Either way, I've been needing to take a dump forever."

He slogged off into a thicket.

The black sky spat down a few more snowflakes, sputtered, then ceased production altogether. Adam glanced up, found the Pole Star, and thought about his sister.

Cherry tapped him on the shoulder.

Adam turned around.

Cherry covered his head with a bushy wig, identical to hers except fluorescent pink.

"Thanks," he said.

She mimed taking a snapshot and giggled.

"I don't suppose you have a cup of coffee in that costume? Or maybe an electric blanket?"

She switched their wigs and took another snapshot. Gave him a thumbs-up.

"Yeah, I always did look better in green."

She took off her pink wig. A cellophane skullcap matted down her brown hair. Cherry held the upturned pink wig out in front of her, waved a hand over it like a magic wand, and then held it out for Adam to see.

Adam peered into the wig. He saw a magic eight ball.

"How cool is that," he said, and took the toy.

She beamed at his glee.

"Is my sister okay?" asked Adam of the magic eight ball.

He shook it.

The magic eight ball prophesied, in watery block letters: "*Usted no es listo saber.*"

"Much help you are," Adam answered and handed the toy back to Cherry.

Filbert rustled his way out of the bush. "I feel much lighter now," he said. "Got to avoid those pecan pies. My intestines are not what they used to be. Nice wig, sport. Suits you. Anyway, come on. We've got miles to go before we sleep."

Adam returned his wig to Cherry and they moved out. Occasionally Adam would look up and check their status with Filbert's star, each time becoming more and more dismayed by his conclusions. Finally, he stopped and said:

"We are not heading north."

Filbert and Cherry stopped too.

"What?" asked Filbert.

"We're not heading north."

Filbert nodded. "We're not heading north."

"You said the Pole Star, the North Star—whatever—we were following it for navigation. Well, we're not heading north."

"We're not heading north. We're heading west." Filbert tucked his hands underneath his armpits. "Look, I made a small mistake earlier. We should have just stayed by the road. But we didn't and now we're here, so I made a decision to head west because, well, it seemed the thing to do."

"It seemed the thing to do?"

"Hey, I never claimed to be Rand fucking McNally!"

Cherry reached into her outfit and removed a spare pair of white kid gloves for Filbert but he shooed them away and stomped westward. Cherry hurried after him, and Adam, ready to scream, hurried after her. The snow may have stopped, but the winds were gaining strength and cruelty.

Soon they came upon a barn; beyond it on a distant hill lay a farmhouse. Despite the soupy blur of snow and ice, some of the barn's oaken structure remained visible, including its giant red door. Cherry, Adam and Filbert plodded through the white, knee-deep in some areas, and approached the door. An angry-looking two-by-four, bristling with bent nails and jagged splinters, barred it shut.

Adam and Filbert lifted the bar. The doors rasped open.

A scream of wind immediately caught one of the doors and it whipped open, slapping Cherry off her feet.

"Cherry!" cried Adam. "Cherry!"

He leaned beside her face. The door's kiss had left a nasty red splotch above her left eye. Her lungs bleated wet, wounded noises.

"Grab her ankles," he told Filbert.

They carried her into the barn and several horses whinnied hello; this wasn't a barn at all, but a stable. Adam almost tripped over a kerosene lamp. He and Filbert put Cherry down, lit the lamp, picked her back up, and lay her on a hay bed in a nearby stall, carefully avoiding a hillock of dung. Adam sat with her, holding her hand, while Filbert ran back to the door and struggled to shut the giant gate.

As icy air bellowed through the stable, its three horses complained. One stomped her hooves. Another banged his body against his stall.

"Kid!" yelled Filbert. "I need your help!"

"Cherry needs me!" Adam yelled back.

"She really doesn't!"

Cherry's eyes were closed. She was either asleep or unconscious. Adam, for the life of him, did not know the difference. He patted her hand, delicately placed it on her chest and rushed out to help the old man battle the wind and the swinging red doors.

They each grabbed a door and shoved them shut, but the wind

fought against their efforts. Filbert picked up the two-by-four, which he had wisely kicked inside, and with all of Adam's weight against the doors, managed to secure them with the bar.

"Damn," he said, sucking on his thumb. "Tetanus."

The horses calmed down. In her stall, Cherry lightly snored.

Adam and Filbert reclined on their respective bales. "Well," said Adam. "Yeah," answered Filbert.

"This is comfortable," said Adam.

"It's not bad," answered Filbert.

"It's a little itchy," said Adam.

"What you need to do," answered Filbert, "is—"

BAM! The two-by-four exploded into countless splinters, and the red doors bounced open, and into the stables strolled a seven-year-old girl in a one-piece red pajama (with little green horses on it). She carried a fat black pistol.

"If you hear my voice and you ain't a horse," she declared, "say your prayers 'cause you're about to be dead."

Arms raised in surrender, Adam stepped out into the open. Reluctantly, Filbert joined him.

"You here to steal the horses?" she asked.

"No," said Filbert.

"No," said Adam.

"'Cause if you're here to steal the horses, I'm going to kill you."

Filbert and Adam, in unison: "We're not here to steal the horses."

"Then what are you doing in our barn?"

Adam took a respectful step forward. The little girl, holding the gun in both hands, angled the barrel to meet his forehead. Adam stepped back.

"We're just seeking shelter from the storm," replied Filbert.

She eyed him, then Adam, then spotted Cherry the clown.

"Are you circus folk? Is that why you want our horses?"

"No. We don't want your horses. The clown is our friend," said Adam. "She got hit by the door and hurt her head. She needs to rest.

We would be more than happy to ask your parents for their permission. Do you know where your parents are?"

"My mama's dead and my dad's stuck in town. Where are your parents?"

"My dad's dead and my mom's at a funeral in Rhode Island."

"How did your dad die?"

"None of your business. How did your mom die?"

"None of your business."

"If we promise—promise—not to touch the horses, can we spend the night here? We don't even have to come up to the house if you want."

Adam tried again to take a step forward. This time, the gun barrel lowered.

"My name is Martha," said the little girl, "but everyone calls me Bug."

"Why does everyone call you Bug?"

Martha shrugged.

"Well, Bug, my name is Adam, and this is Filbert, and the clown's name is Cherry."

"I'm allergic to carrots."

"Okay."

"I'm going to sleep here with you. It's too quiet in my bedroom."

"Okay."

Together they bolted shut the stable doors with another two-by-four. Bug then dragged out a scratchy burlap sleeping bag from its hiding place in a barrel near the doors, and smoothed out the bag beside Cherry in the stall. Adam wondered just how often Bug slept in here with the horses, and why.

"The horses' names are Violet, Chocolate and Glue. If you steal any of them, I'm going to shoot you until you bleed and die."

Adam and Filbert lay back down on their respective bales. Filbert turned down the kerosene lamp. Before long everyone in the stables was asleep, even the horses.

Chapter Five

Adam awoke with hay in his mouth, a crick in his neck and a burly Amish man staring down at him with anger. Cherry and Filbert and Martha/Bug were all still asleep.

The Amish man motioned for Adam to meet him outside.

Adam did not want to meet him outside.

Quietly the man walked to the stable door. He did not turn around to make sure Adam followed. Reluctantly, Adam followed.

Outside, the cold morning sun lashed at Adam's eyeballs. He brought a forearm to his face and squinted through blurred vision at the Amish man, who smoked a Marlboro.

Smoked a Marlboro?

"My name is David," he said, "and I really don't care for an explanation."

David reached into the pocket of his black coat, pulled out a pair of cheap sunglasses and handed them to Adam.

"Thanks," said Adam. He put them on. They helped.

"I've got a job to do today. It's not a job I'm looking forward to doing and it's not a job that I want to do alone. When your friends wake up, we'll have breakfast at the house and then we'll do what needs doing. Then I'll take you to where you need to go. Which is not here."

David flicked the cigarette butt into the breeze and stomped up the snowy path to the farmhouse on the hill. Adam pinched himself, decided yes, he was awake and reentered the stables.

The horses too were awake. Adam wandered over to one of the stalls and peered into a pale mare's giant eyes. She peered back with the carefree indifference of an animal able, with a well-placed hoof, to thwap whatever it wanted. Slowly, nervously, Adam raised a hand to her long milky-white nose. He had never touched a horse before, not even at the Newark Zoo. Would she mind? Would she bite? His fingertips dangled above her nose and forelock. The mare's nostrils billowed warm breath against his neck. He petted her, and she allowed him.

"That's Glue," said Bug, suddenly standing beside them. "She's my favorite."

"She's mine too," replied Adam. For the first time in twenty long hours, he could feel the knots in his neck and shoulder loosen. He slid the backs of his fingers up and down Glue's rangy countenance.

Bug handed Adam a bruised red apple.

"How do I …?"

"Just put it near her mouth. She'll do the rest."

Adam put the apple near her mouth. The mare's lips curled back, revealing teeth the size of small fists.

"Relax," said Bug. "She only bites you if you want her to."

Glue closed her mouth around the apple, gently yanked it from Adam's grip, and crunched it into breakfast.

"Your father came by earlier," said Adam, "and he—"

Bug shoved open the doors and scampered out of the stables. Her racket awoke Adam's slumbering companions.

"Ow," yawned Cherry. Her head wound had progressed into a blood blister above her left eye, and she delicately dabbed at it with a gloved finger, wincing with every touch.

Filbert removed his overcoat and, to clean it of hay and insects, proceeded to beat it against a post. The horses responded with bleats of irritation. Filbert, not one to argue with bleats, desisted.

"Where's the girl?" asked Filbert; Adam offered a rundown of the past few minutes, which the old man then translated, sleepily, for Cherry.

"So my guess," said Adam, "is this Amish guy David is waiting for us up at the house."

"Great. I'm heading in the opposite direction."

"Why?"

"I've got places to go, sport. Somewhere around here is a road. I'm going to find it and follow it."

"But—"

"It's been a pleasure knowing you. And if you believe that, I've got this golden egg–laying goose I'd love to sell you. Good luck finding your sister. Check the local morgues."

"Wait!"

Filbert moseyed out into the morning crisp. Adam and Cherry exchanged empty glances and rushed out after him.

The only visible path in the vast expanse of white was the footprints in the snow that trailed up to the farmhouse on the hill.

"Well," Filbert sighed, "isn't that always the way."

He hocked up a gob of phlegm and spat at the earth. A quick breeze slapped his mucus back into his willowy beard.

"You're so lovable, Filbert," said Adam. "Let's go."

Ascending the path proved a challenge. Adam and Filbert and Cherry attempted to follow in David's footsteps so as not to punch new holes in the snow and get stuck knee-deep, but David's gait was so wide that the boy, man and clown had to hop just to keep pace. By their tenth hop, all three had slipped at least once, falling face-first into the flaky frost. Egos bruised and faces scraped, they staggered up the steep slope to the two-story oaken farmhouse. Spirals of smoke curled up from a stone chimney. Adam, shivering, could not wait to share in some of that heat.

The thick front door wore a brass knocker molded to resemble the chubby head of a cherub. Adam rapped it once, twice, and waited.

"I once made a house like this," he said, "out of Lincoln Logs."

"Remind me later to pee in your shoe," replied Filbert.

The door swung open, revealing David the Goliath. He nodded at them, turned around and ambled his way back into the kitchen. Whatever manner of beast was frying on the stove top, it smelled glorious. Adam, Cherry and Filbert silently occupied three of the massive kitchen table's massive wooden chairs. Beer steins full of milk were already set at their spots.

"I feel a bit like Goldilocks," Adam murmured.

"You look a bit like her too," Filbert retorted.

David handed them each a steaming plate full of sausage links and hashed potatoes. The Amish man thumped down in the empty seat and began devouring. His three guests followed suit.

The rubbery sausages were nearly as difficult to chew as the slope had been to climb. Adam struggled to bite into one and it shot out of his mouth and struck David in the eye. Filbert, unable to chop his up with his utensils, took to popping them whole into his mouth and swallowing them one at a time. Seeing her comrades' failure, Cherry avoided her sausages altogether and concentrated on her potatoes, which she quickly discovered had the same consistency and taste as slushed snow.

Filbert pushed forward his plate, glared at their gigantic host, and said, "What is this garbage?"

David glanced at the old man, then down at the plate, then back at the old man.

"What Filbert means," stammered Adam, "is—"

David rose (up and up).

Hefted Filbert's plate.

Filbert ducked underneath the table.

David nodded, shrugged, dumped the plate into a basin of water on the counter and wandered out of the room, vanishing from sight. Adam thought he spotted two thin orange boxes that looked very familiar next to the water basin.

Filbert rapped Adam on the knee. "Is he gone?"

Adam walked over to the water basin and examined the boxes.

HandiFood Instant Sausages. Five for a dollar. How many of these orange boxes had he bought in his dorm room days, stuffed by the gross into the floor's freezer, and then nuked at three A.M. to aid in an all-nighter? He then noticed the orange cardboard cylinder of HandiFood Potatoes in a Minute, still half full with freeze-dried potato flakes (which, when ground into powder by a hammer or textbook and then snorted, produced a mild high).

No wonder the food had been so abysmal; David had attempted to cook cheap frozen dinners in an oak wood stove. But more to the point: what was an Amish man doing with cheap frozen dinners? Or a pack of Marlboro Reds? What task did he have set up for them to perform?

"Let's get out of here," Adam said. "Right now."

"That's what I've been saying all along," seconded Filbert, scurrying out from underneath the table.

Cherry slurped down her stein. Her milk mustache perfectly matched her greasepaint. She grinned at her two gallant gentlemen.

"Cherry," said Filbert, "vaya—"

David returned with two rusted shovels.

"Bug's staying in her room," he told them. "She doesn't need to see this."

"See ... what?"

David handed one shovel to Adam, paused for a moment and handed the other to Cherry. Filbert, indignant, snatched Adam's out of his grip.

"You don't even know what the shovels are for," said Adam.

David led them to the front door. "The old man and the clown will dig the hole outside. The boy and I will join you in a moment."

"Listen, David," replied Adam, "they're not going to just leave me alone with—"

Filbert scrambled out the door, dragging Cherry with him.

David turned around and slowly clopped the stairs to the farmhouse's second level. From the top of the stairs, in the darkness of the shadows, he called, "Let's go, boy. We've got work to attend."

"I'm not ... look, I've had a bad ... before I take one step, I demand to know ... listen, David, here's the thing." Adam gripped the sandy banister so tightly that all the blood receded from his knuckles. He gazed up into the shadowy darkness, at the outline of the man at the top of the stairs, the broad brim of the hat and the wide shoulders and the tall fatherly frame. Adam managed a complete sentence, choked in fourteen different emotions: "My sister has been kidnapped."

David grunted, shrugged those wide shoulders and that tall fatherly frame, and answered, "That's not your concern right now. This is. Move."

Adam moved, pulling himself by the railing up the steep brown steps. His whole body felt cumbersome, as if his bones had turned to lead. He wanted to lie down on a stair, any stair, and sleep. He made it up to the second floor and David led him to a locked door at the end of the narrow corridor.

David removed a key from his pocket.

Then he put a hand on Adam's shoulder.

"I can't help you," said the big man, "but when we're through, I'll take you and your friends to people who can."

As Adam pondered this unexpected humane gesture, David turned the key in the lock and opened the heavy wooden door. At first the room's contents were difficult to see; its only light source was a small oval window made opaque by snow and ice. Slowly Adam's eyes adjusted to the dimness and managed to discern some mundane shapes: a bed, a dresser, a bookcase. A menagerie of handmade cloth dolls decorated the dresser and bookcase. Adam took a step toward the bed. Queen-size, white cotton sheets, dour wool blanket. A lump underneath the sheets, in the center of the bed, immobile. Like a mischievous child playing possum. Mischievous or frightened.

"This," said David, "is my wife."

David pulled back the blanket and sheets and revealed a short pale woman, mid-thirties, clad in a modest nightgown. Long brown hair pooled behind her narrow head. Her small blue lips were pursed, as if mid-sentence. Hazel eyes peered at the ceiling. Three feet from where David's heart beat lay another heart that had gone cold. David's wife had become an object, a thing, as lifeless as the mattress on which it lay.

"She has been like that for three days," David added. "Her name was Anna."

Adam felt an ice cube slide down his spine.

"What ... do you need ... me to do?"

"Lift her by her shoulders. I will hold her ankles. We'll carry her outside, where your friends are digging the hole, and we'll bury her in the earth."

Silently Adam complied with David's request, bending down beside the corpse's upper torso. He slid his hands underneath its shoulder blades. The body felt light, more like a box of crackers. He easily hefted his end and David hefted his and the two gentlemen carried the corpse out of the bedroom, through the corridor, and down the wooden staircase. Through it all, Adam forced himself to think about David's feisty daughter Bug, sobbing in her room somewhere in this old farmhouse. He forced himself to think about her to keep himself from thinking about his sister.

Outside, Filbert and Cherry had barely dented the topsoil.

"It's frozen," said Filbert as the door opened, and then he noticed the body and clamped shut his mouth. Cherry gasped. Adam and David placed the body on the landing, quietly received the shovels from Filbert and Cherry and took over the digging operation. Sweat chased out of their pores and soaked their winter garments. Arms and backs vibrated with ache. As he bent and lifted and gripped the shovel in his hands, Adam experienced the strangest muscle memory: clearing the driveway on a snow day. He had only done it once, when he was twelve years old and his father was suddenly no longer around, and he decided it was his responsibility to clear the driveway of nature's mess, and so he slipped into his boots and went into the garage and found his father's shovel (wide face, orange neck) and began his business, not expecting snow to be so heavy or clearing the driveway to require so much work. He sortied four times to the kitchen for a cup of Swiss Miss hot cocoa (no marshmallows) but by the end of ninety minutes, he had vanquished the white beasty and unveiled their two-car strip of grey Jersey asphalt. Adam ran back into the house to get his father and show off his accomplishment, but his dad was dead, had been for months. The shovel disappeared shortly thereafter, and after the next snowstorm, Adam's mother hired Chuck Logan, a fireman down the block who owned a loud, large snow blower, to take care of their driveway.

"All right," said David, resting on his shovel. "This is enough."

The hole they had dug could not have been more than three feet deep, but every inch had been an agony and Adam was grateful for it all to end. He just wanted to go home.

Without having to be told, Cherry and Filbert carried the body of David's wife to the grave and ever so gently rested her into the shallow hole. Filbert crossed its wrists one over the other. The corpse appeared at peace, but surely such a state could not be achieved by an inanimate object.

"Do you want to say anything?" Adam asked David.

The Amish man lit up a cigarette, stared down at his wife's husk, exhaled a plume and replied softly, "Nope."

So Filbert and Cherry took the shovels and performed the relatively simple task of filling in the hole. David finished his cigarette, discarded it, adjusted the brim on his hat, and started off toward the stables.

"Let's go," he said. "Time to take you to town."

As they ambled down the path, Adam glanced back at the house, checking for a face in a window of a little girl looking for her mother, but saw only glass. The descent was much easier than the climb, and before long they all stood by the stable doors. David handed out snowshoes, one pair to Filbert and one pair to Adam. Cherry declined the pair handed to her; the large floppy booties, white as the snow on which they sank, were adequate. Then they trekked eastward, traversing a slender gap in forestland that maybe, in warmer climes, served as a road.

"So how far away is town?" asked Filbert.

David shrugged.

Filbert caught his breath, kept it close, and replied, "Now by that do you mean it's not that far or you just don't care?"

David shrugged.

"Nice talking with you, man."

As the day warmed, the skeletal branches of the surrounding elms shed their snowy skins, plopping deposits on heads and hands and down the collars of coats. Adam longed again for the green wig, if only to protect him from the sly, wet elements. He also wondered whatever happened to the hood that originally came with his coat; it probably was hiding out with his copy of Xbox baseball.

Forty minutes into their trip, David suddenly stopped, lit up another cigarette and said to them, "I used to be Mennonite. Old Order. We had our community. We never were happy but always content. My wife got sick. One day this old couple came to visit. We always have visitors in these parts. Tourists. This old couple came to visit, and the old man used to be a doctor, and he saw my wife was sick and asked if he could take a look. I said no. We had our community. We were content. He seemed to understand and bid us farewell, and they went on their way. A few months passed. My wife became sicker. She could no longer work. Our daughter took over her chores. She's seven years old. One day the old couple came back. The old woman gave us daisies. The old man saw how my wife had deteriorated and once again asked if he could help. He begged me. I said no. We had our community. We were content. The old couple left. Then my wife began to die. The community prayed. Friends came to visit. My wife lost the ability to speak. She needed assistance to eat, to sit, to use the privy. The old couple returned one final time. The old woman gave us roses. The old man pleaded with me, told me that there was a hospital only thirty miles away that could control my wife's suffering. Didn't I want her to be at peace? But we were at peace. We had our community. The old man shook my hand and wished us well and said that he and his wife were not going to return. That night I held my wife's hand. She had been playing with her dolls. She liked to knit dolls out of fabric. I held my wife's hand and I asked her if there was anything I could do for her. But she had lost the ability to speak and I knew she couldn't answer me. Maybe that's why I asked the question."

He snuffed out his cigarette and continued on his way.

"What happened after that?" asked Adam.

Without stopping, David answered him, "We just buried her body. What do you think happened?"

Shortly thereafter, they emerged from the path and were now in town limits, standing mere yards from a brick wall and the ice-glazed insignia for Buchanan Station, Pennsylvania State Police.

Chapter Six

"Well," said Filbert, nervously eyeballing the police station, "that's my cue to vamoose."

"Where are you going to go?" Adam asked him.

"Anywhere but here."

"Are you going to take Cherry with you?"

Filbert wrapped an arm around her waist, flashed some yellow teeth and replied, "Not a chance."

He scuttled down the semi-cleared road, arms flapping and legs pumping, but his coat was so huge on his bony frame that he looked not like a man on the run but like an overcoat off the rack, magically bounding down Main Street in some West Pennsylvania town. Then he slid on a slippery patch and fell on his ass.

Cherry ran to his aid, but David put a hand on Adam's arm and they remained put.

"I appreciated your help," said David.

"I'm sorry about your wife," replied Adam.

David reached into his black jacket, removed something small, unzipped Adam's jacket and stuffed whatever totem his palm concealed into the inner pocket of Adam's jacket. He patted the boy on the shoulder, turned and walked away.

Adam waited until the man was gone before checking his pocket's contents. David had given him one of his wife's handmade cloth dolls. It had yellow yarn for hair, blue buttons for eyes, a tiny stitched mouth and a black dress no larger than his hand. He replaced the doll in his pocket as Cherry returned with Filbert in tow. She sat him on the station's concrete steps and tried to comfort him like a child, but the old man shrugged her off.

"I'm fine, damn it, okay?" he growled. "But I won't be as long as I stay here. You think I was in the back of that cop car for my health?"

Adam passed them and reached for the front door. "Stay here or leave. I don't care. Thank you for everything you've done. Both of you. I'm going to tell them about my sister."

He abandoned them on the front stoop and entered the police station.

As soon as the door shut behind him, a golden retriever bounded out of nowhere and tackled him into a Christmas tree.

"Ajax, no!"

Ajax lapped his slimy tongue over and over Adam's face, as if trying to lick off his skin. The dog's apparent owner, a dwarfish desk sergeant name-tagged Alexis, reached down to Ajax's collar and yanked him off Adam's chest.

"Sorry about that," she said. "Ajax just loves strangers. Especially today."

Adam unwrapped himself from the tree's tinsel and pine cones. "Why especially today?" With his sleeve, he wiped the dog's slime off his nose and cheeks.

"Oh, well, we lost one of our own last night," sighed the midget. "Brett Neal. Rookie. Great ass. Someone will be with you in a few minutes to help you out, but right now everyone's in the conference room getting briefed on the case. Why don't you have a seat over there?" She indicated an alcove of crappy wooden chairs. "I'm Alexis. If you want, I'll get you a cup of coffee."

"Sure."

Adam sat down in the waiting area. So they knew Officer Neal was dead. As soon as their meeting adjourned, he would inform the first officer he saw of what had happened, what he had witnessed, and after filling out whatever paperwork was deemed necessary, he would then get them to find his sister. His ordeal was finally reaching its terminus. No more clowns, no more guns, no more kidnappers, no more—

Down the hall he spotted a bank of pay phones. He got an idea.

As Alexis the friendly midget returned with a steaming Styrofoam cup, Adam smiled warmly, thanked her for the coffee and politely asked for a quarter.

"Sure thing, honey."

She handed him two, one for good luck.

He ambled up to a pay phone, picked up a receiver, and dialed the number for his cell.

Sipped his coffee. Scalded his upper lip.

One ring.

He put the cup down next to the phone.

Two rings.

Had he even left his phone on? Who would pick it up?

Three rings.

Adam was not about to leave a message on his own—

"Hello?" It was Ebbets. Damn it. "May I help you?"

Adam took a deep breath. "Where are you, you son of a bitch?"

"Hello! How are you? My truck (WHEEZE) isn't causing you any troubles, is she? She is a rental. I'm not sure what I did with the paperwork."

"Where's my sister?"

"Would you like to speak with her?"

Adam gripped the phone receiver so tightly it bruised his palm. "Yes."

"Wish I could accommodate. I'm afraid she's a bit unconscious. She tried to attack me while I was driving and had a tiny accident with your windshield. Sorry about that. I promise not to lay a finger on her while she's out. I'm just really pissed off at the world. Like your father was."

Adam felt the color drain from his face.

"Yeah, your sister told me all about him. What he did. So you know what I'm talking about. You understand why in seven days I'm going to press my little trigger and blow everything up."

"I'm going to kill you," said Adam.

"That's nice. Anyway, don't forget: midnight, Christmas Eve. Greenwich Mean Time, by the way. I assume you found the package in the back of the truck? Hell of a thing, huh? Would you believe there are (WHEEZE) eleven other packages just like it, all over the world? London, Paris, Moscow, Jerusalem. You name it. I didn't put them there. I'm not the guilty party. But I am going to put an end to it. Christmas Eve. Six days."

"I'm going to find you and I'm going to kill you."

"How are you going to find me? Where are you going to look? Is the FBI doing a trace right now on your cell phone? Are they on the other line, listening in? My guess is they're not. Not yet. My guess is you haven't even found their (WHEEZE) field office yet, not with this weather we've been having. I hope you're wearing gloves. I didn't find any in your car, although I did find a pack of smokes in the glove compartment. I hope you're not a smoker."

"No."

"Then who are the cigarettes for? Are they your sister's?"

"They're for whoever wants them."

"Oh, I see. Well, I already have cancer."

Near her desk, Alexis toyed with Ajax. The patrolmen were still in their damned meeting. "Look, Ebbets, I want my sister back. I want my car back. I want you to leave us alone. I don't care about your cancer."

Ebbets released a long, sad sigh. "Oh, don't be such a selfish baby. After all, I—"

CLICK PLEASE INSERT TWENTY-FIVE CENTS TO CONTINUE THIS CALL CLICK.

Adam shoved his second quarter into the machine.

"Jeez, where are you calling me from? A diner? You're not still at that rest stop, are you? I didn't even know places had pay phones anymore, what with cell phones and pagers and email. I like your cell phone, by the way. Don't worry, I haven't used it too much. I did order a pizza, though. Every city has a Domino's. Your sister didn't seem too hungry. I think she really hurt her head on the windshield. She's not a hemophiliac, is she?"

"No. Are you?"

"No, although I once got knifed in the belly and I (WHEEZE) bled out like you wouldn't believe. I got stuck by this punk over a Buick. He stuck me over an American car! He claimed it was his and I claimed it was mine, finders keepers and all, and he took out this hunting knife—where he got this hunting knife from I'll never know, this guy wouldn't know a tent from a tourniquet—and he jammed it right into my gut. Man, I must have bled four pints. I was in the hospital for weeks. That's where they found me. On my hospital bed. How about that. Not that I'm trying to defend what I did for them. I knew every step of the way what was going on. You can't feign ignorance when you're building nuclear weapons."

"All I want is my sister back." Adam stared through tears at the digits on the payphone. "What can I do to get her back?"

"Well, that's easy. Find me and stop me. You've got six days. She's got six days. We all do. Find me and stop me. Give it your best shot. I'm going to hang up now, and I probably won't have this phone on me the next time you call, so if we don't get to speak again, it's been (WHEEZE) a real pleasure. And take good care of my truck, will you? It is a rental."

Click.

Dead air.

Adam hung up the receiver. A thunderclap of nausea rumbled through his body, and he bolted to the restroom, found the nearest cubicle, shut the door behind him, fell to his knees and threw up into the toilet. Panted like a dog. Wiped the slime from his face. Exhaled acid. Threw up again. A marching band pounded against his skull.

"What have I gotten myself into?" he whispered. "Oh God, Anna, what have I done?"

He looked around. So appropriate his epiphany of hopelessness should come, he mused, in a lavatory only twenty-four hours after a similar lavatory and Ebbets and the beginning of it all. The state police wouldn't be able to find him. No one would be able to find him. This was a man who may or may not have had an actual atomic bomb in the back of his truck that he just left on the side of the road.

A breeze from a small casement window above his stall—some moron had left it open—wafted the icy reek of his puke into his nose. Adam flushed the toilet but remained on his knees, watching the water swirl. How did he get himself into this? He used a rest stop. He had a meal at Denny's and then used a rest stop. He picked up his sister and they had a meal at Denny's and then he used a rest stop. His mother called him, demanded he pick up his sister; he drove to Oberlin, picked her up, they had a meal at Denny's, and then he used a rest stop.

His uncle Dexter died.

This was his fault.

Uncle Dexter, who fancied himself the exiled king of Mars. Who not only lived in Rhode Island but had the indecency to die there. Uncle Dexter, whose face Adam could not even envision. Had they ever met? Had his father even mentioned him, aside from a crack about his delusions?

Uncle Dexter. Damn him to hell.

The lavatory door opened and two policemen, A and B, shuffled in. Adam, kneeling in his cubicle like a parishioner at confession, was inconspicuous.

"Fucking tragedy," said A.

"Fucking right it is," said B.

They appropriated separate urinals, unzipped and hosed some porcelain. "A cop like that."

"I know."

"His age."

"Yeah."

"Never gave us a chance to stop ribbing him. Just last week, Anders left that plastic bag in his locker."

"What plastic bag?"

"You know, with the dogshit. From Ajax. And you know what kind of dumps that dog takes."

"Anders left a plastic bag of dogshit in the rookie's locker?"

"You knew that."

"Did I?"

Zipped up. "My point is, it's a fucking tragedy."

"Oh, I totally agree. You think that bomb in the back of that truck is real?"

"The fuck should I know? Mark my words, though." A flushed his urinal. "We're going to catch the guy."

"Damn straight we're going to catch him."

"I mean, what kind of stupid does it take for a kid to give us his name and address before killing a cop?"

Adam blinked: huh?

"A whole lot of stupid. Unless, you know, the car just slid out of control. Unless, you know, it all was just an accident."

"If it was an accident, why was there only one body? By the time this day is through, every precinct in the state will have a picture of this Adam Weiss motherfucker in their hands."

Adam blinked again: huh?

"As soon as we find him," said A, "I'm going to personally go at his kneecaps with a power drill. And that'll just be the start of his punishment, let me tell you."

B zipped, flushed. The two patrolmen washed their hands, dried them, and casually wandered out of the lavatory.

Adam couldn't move. Too many thoughts raced through his brain, blocking the simple instruction for his muscles to operate his hands, arms and legs. "Killing a cop?" "This Adam Weiss motherfucker??" "Go at his kneecaps with a power drill???"

Was this a trick, a game, a practical joke? Maybe they found Anna and she had talked them into pulling this grotesque gag on her simple twin bro. Adam would march out of the men's room and standing there would be a gaggle of patrolmen, Anna and their mother, all wearing party hats. Officer Neal would be there too. He wasn't really dead. This was all just an elaborate, collaborative joke.

"This is really happening to me," whispered Adam to himself. "I am incredibly, incredibly fucked."

A chill rushed down his spine—literally—from that tiny open window above his toilet stall, and he knew what he had to do. He mounted the plastic toilet seat and reached up for the pane. His fingertips tapped against the angled glass but could not find purchase; he had to stretch, but the more he stretched the looser his balance became on the plastic toilet seat, which shimmied a bit on its own due to aging screws.

He inhaled, exhaled and extended his body as long and tight as his muscles allowed. His fingertips tapped again against the angled glass. His fingers curled around the frame. A few inches more and he would have enough leverage to lift himself up.

The lavatory door swung open, and in walked a bushy-haired patrolman whistling "God Rest Ye Merry Gentlemen." Adam instinctively let go of the window frame, but in doing so he lost his balance and his right foot dunked itself into the toilet bowl, ankle deep. His left foot remained safe and dry on the toilet seat; his arms stretched out to the cubicle walls to keep him from further tumbling.

Adam held his breath.

The patrolman clomped into the neighboring cubicle, dropped trou and went about his excretory business. Three feet to the left, toilet water seeped into Adam's sneaker, soaking down his sock and drenching his right foot. He wanted to lift his foot, shake it off, scream out loud, but he kept silent and still.

"Corn?" queried the patrolman. "When did I eat corn?"

His toilet flushed. His trousers rose. As he waddled out of the restroom, "God Rest Ye Merry Gentlemen" became "Jingle Bell Rock." The door closed behind him with a hiss.

Adam scampered up the lavatory wall. His right foot weighed him down, but he managed to pull himself up to the window. He poked his head out. Good news: the window overlooked the rear of the building. Bad news: the ground, wet with melting snow, lay ten feet below. In an ideal world, in FantasyLand, he would have been able to climb out the window feet-first, and thus land safely, but as he had been reminded time and again over the past twenty-four hours, he did not live in FantasyLand.

And so when Adam pushed himself through the window, he tumbled earthward face-first. He tried to brace his fall with his hands, but ten feet was still ten feet and hands and arms thumped against planet. Mud smeared his coat and jeans. Bruises throbbed at the balls of his hands. He had escaped.

But now what?

Adam considered trying to return to David's farmhouse, but their tracks had already melted. No, he needed to contact Cherry and Filbert. They were his only allies now and he needed help. Adam skulked about the rear of the building, bracing against cold brick, and then turned the corner. No police. Good. He lowered himself into a crouch and continued along the wall. Cautiously, gingerly, he peeped around the front.

Cherry and Filbert were gone.

Chapter Seven

A brick stationhouse, a whitewashed Lutheran church, and between them an acre of paved parking space. Across the street: a diner/grocery store labeled (in giant stencil) Buchanan Eats and a windowless bar labeled (in blue neon) Buchanan Drinks. Down the road a ways: an ancient gas station.

These were the venues available. These were Adam's only sources of refuge. And the stationhouse was out. And the bar was closed. Adam made a beeline for the diner, trying to appear as casual and ordinary as a college kid on the run from the law in the middle of the road of a small rural town on the day after a blizzard could be.

He pushed open the diner door. A middle-aged waitress napped behind the counter, nibbling on a napkin. All of the ratty red booths were empty save the one in the back corner, furthest from the windows, occupied by none other than Cherry Sundae and Filbert.

"Oh thank God," said Adam, joining them. "I'm so glad to see you."

Filbert glanced up from his coffee. "Why?"

Adam condensed the past thirty minutes of his life into sixty seconds.

Filbert sipped the rest of his cup, sighed, and relayed Adam's story, in translation, to Cherry; his version took about twenty-five seconds and ended with the word, "*idiota.*"

The clock on the wall, featuring a portrait of a dapper President James Buchanan, read 12:30 P.M.

"What should I do?" asked Adam.

Filbert stared into his mug. A minute passed. Two minutes. The clock on the wall read 12:30 P.M. At the counter, the waitress snored awake, peeled the moist napkin from her lips, and lumbered over to their booth, where Cherry puppeteered the table's salt and pepper shakers, which were shaped (respectively) like a chess king and queen, in a reenactment of the ballet *Petrushka*.

"Another cup of coffee?" the waitress groveled.

"I'd like one," said Adam.

"How about you, cutie?" she asked Filbert.

Filbert waved her away. She lumbered back to the counter to pour Adam a mug of scalding caffeine.

"You have a plan," Adam said. He spotted it in the geezer's rheumy gaze.

"I do," Filbert answered and finally looked up from his cream-and-sugar ooze. "But it's going to cost you."

"Cost me? What are you talking about?"

"Kid, I told you last night. I don't work for free. Not ever. I can get you out of this jam, but I'm going to need to be paid for my troubles."

"Oh yeah? With what?" Adam emptied the lint from his jeans. "How's that?"

The waitress handed him his cup of coffee, frowned at the lint and left.

"I can accept payment after the fact. Look, I need you to agree to my terms, sport. I've got a plan but any minute now the cops across the street are going to be taking their lunch break and I'm guessing they're going to take it here. We either do things my way or you're on your own. Make a choice."

"Can I hear the plan first?"

"No."

"Why not?"

"Because."

"I feel like I'm selling my soul to the devil."

"I'm not the devil, sport," replied Filbert, finishing his coffee. "The devil has to play by someone else's rules. I don't. So what's it going to be?"

Adam stewed. Cherry manipulated her shakers into a dual pirouette. Filbert leaned back in his seat, coughed up a wad of lung and watched the college boy ruminate. It made for entertainment, even though its ending was certain.

"Okay," said Adam.

Filbert patted Adam on the shoulder, turned to Cherry and whispered rapid Spanish in her ear for about a minute. All the while she nodded, glanced a few times at Adam, frowned, shook her head, nodded again and finally shrugged her colorful shoulders, acquiescing to whatever Filbert had just suggested.

The old man rose to his feet.

"Where are you going?" Adam asked.

"I have to take care of my part of the plan. Don't worry, sport. Cherry knows what's what."

"Which is what?"

"Ask her."

Filbert strolled out of the diner.

"What an asshole," muttered Adam. "You know what I mean?" He glanced at his companion. She stuffed the royal shakers up her left sleeve.

Adam glanced out the window and watched Filbert make his way toward the weather-beaten Lutheran church. What kind of getaway plan involved a weather-beaten Lutheran Church? Adam suspected the old man was taking him for a ride.

Then Cherry snatched him by the collar of his coat and dragged him with the strength of ten men, five women and a baboon to the diner's unisex bathroom. She locked the plywood door behind them and emptied the copious contents of her outfit into the iron sink:

One salt shaker and one pepper shaker (recently acquired). A rainbow of handkerchiefs. A tiny tin of curiously strong mints. Four bushy monochromatic wigs (in green, blue, red and orange). A box of tampons. Four .22 monochromatic squirt guns (also in green, blue, red and orange). A pair of sequined ballet slippers. Two used decks of Hoyle playing cards (presumably with the jokers intact). One spare clown suit, mottled and pressed. One shiny piccolo. And a humongous plastic bag containing assorted jewelry, makeup, and prosthetics (noses, teeth, glasses, eyebrows, ears, rings, earrings, lipstick, mascara, blush, polish, polish remover, paint remover, paint applicator).

"Well. Looking for something?"

Cherry popped open the snaps on his coat and slid it off his arms.

"Wait, what are you—?"

She put a finger to his lips and smiled with hers.

"Okeydokey."

She lifted his U. of Michigan sweatshirt (Go Blue!) off his chest.

Adam reached over to kiss her but she gently pushed him away and, still smiling, shook her green-wigged, white-faced head, as her hands traveled down to his belt.

"Wait a second," Adam said. "Not that I'm complaining, but what exactly is going on here?"

She cocked her head, pondered a moment for the right word, and replied, "El plan."

"This is the plan? This? You take me back here and, you know, do whatever it is you're about to do?"

She whipped the belt out of its loops. The belt buckle clanked against the tiled floor. At this pace, Adam knew that in less than a minute his painted pal Cherry would be meeting his stretchable sidekick Joey P.

Adam attempted once again to plant a kiss, but Cherry shoved him down onto the toilet, hoisted up his ankles, and tugged off his Nikes and socks. They joined his belt, sweatshirt, and coat on the floor tiles.

Only his jeans and boxers remained.

Cherry, still holding his ankles, winked at him. Adam flinched, his back slapping against the cold piping behind the toilet. This experience had traversed from strange to sensual back to strange.

"Look, Cherry, I don't know what Filbert whispered in your ear, but I just want to get out of this town, find my sister and go home. And I don't want you to think I'm gay or anything. I mean, I'm in a fraternity. I once had sex with four girls in one night. Not simultaneously. Well, two were simultaneous. They were twins. Siamese twins, actually. Their names were Leftie and Rightie. Creative parents, huh? Anyway, my point is—what was my point?—oh, right. Clowns scare me. I think I told you that last night. I mean, you didn't understand it last night and I'm sure you're not understanding it now, but clowns scare me. You, with your green hair and all your makeup and colors, you scare me. Right now. A lot."

Cherry jerked at the cuffs of his jeans, but Adam held fast, clutching the waistband.

"Please stop."

Cherry jerked harder, but Adam held fast.

"What do you do, work out?"

She then wrenched the jeans right off his legs.

"Jesus!" he cried, as friction gobbled hair off his thighs and calves. He crisscrossed his wrists over his black cotton boxers and searched the room for a defensive weapon: perhaps a plunger or a dirty chunk of soap. He would protect Joey P. at all costs.

But Cherry did not lunge for Joey P. She instead reached into the sink, removed her spare costume from the hill of stuff and tossed it to him.

"What am I supposed to do with this?"

She crossed her arms and waited.

"Is this some kind of, you know, role-play fetish?"

She waited.

"Do you want me to put this on?"

She waited.

Adam put the costume on.

She handed him the big red funny shoes.

He put on the big red funny shoes.

She handed him the white gloves.

He put on the white gloves. Surprisingly, they fit.

Now she waved for him to join her by the mirror. He knew what was coming next and did not move. She smiled and waved again. He remained put.

She shrugged, took out her makeup kit and approached him. Adam tried to escape, but he was cornered, and she was armed with greasepaint.

The makeover took twenty-five minutes. Cherry seemed very pleased with the result, and led Adam by the hand to the bathroom mirror. In it he saw two clowns, almost identical save for height (he was a few inches taller) and the color of their wigs (hers: green, his: orange).

"This is a traumatic experience," Adam muttered. His belly felt gooey.

Leaving his clothes behind, but repacking her own belongings, Cherry opened the restroom door and walked Adam out into the diner. Eleven state patrolmen, enjoying their lunch break at Buchanan Eats, turned their heads and stared.

Adam suddenly understood and appreciated Filbert's plan.

Among the uniformed patrolmen sitting at the counter was the burly Jamaican from last night, the one who had been so friendly with Officer Neal. She also was the one who broke the spell of shocked silence and approached Adam and Cherry.

"The circus isn't in town," she said. Her eyes were bleary with sleep depravation and sorrow. The nametag on her brown uniform identified her as Sgt. Toms. "What's your story?"

Adam opened his mouth to speak, but Cherry beat him to it:

"¡Hola! Mi nombre es Helado de la Cereza y éste es mi cono de La Vainilla del Socio. Somos el pasar justo a través en nuestra manera a Philadelphia. Hay un circo de la familia en Philadelphia que amaríamos ensamblar. ¿Usted sabe cuándo llega el autobús siguiente del Greyhound?"

Sgt. Toms frowned, and then called a compatriot named Velaquez over to join them.

"You hear what she just said?" she asked.

Velaquez nodded.

"You understand what she just said?" she asked.

Velaquez nodded.

"What did she just say?"

Velaquez replied, quietly, "She wants to know when the next bus leaves for Philadelphia."

"Oh yeah? What's in Philadelphia? Ask her if in her travels she or her buddy have seen anyone matching the description of our fugitive."

Velaquez asked Cherry if she had seen anyone matching the description of their fugitive. Cherry kindly apologized and shook her head.

"I can't stand these foreigners," said Sgt. Toms, "coming into our country and seeking work in our country and refusing to learn our language. Makes me ill to my belly. Velaquez, what's Mexican for 'go back to where you came from, you sons of bitches?' Never mind. Walk them to the gas station."

The clock on the wall read 12:30.

Velaquez accompanied Adam and Cherry out of the diner. The morning thaw had churned Main Street into vanilla pudding. Adam, Cherry and Velaquez tramped across the road. As they passed between the stationhouse and the church, Adam glanced into the parking lot and recognized Ebbets' pick-up truck—sans munitions. He made a quick mental note of the Nevada license plate: DJX512.

They marched past the church. Velaquez rattled off a few sentences to Cherry. Cherry rattled off a few sentences to Velaquez. Adam tried to conjure up a few German phrases, but all he could conjure was: *mein Bleistift ist defect*—my pencil is broken."

The gas station loomed ahead. It appeared closed. Velaquez led them to the Greyhound sign, took out a pack of chewing gum and offered a piece to Adam and Cherry.

"Thank you," said Adam.

The patrolman frowned. "You speak English?"

Adam nearly swallowed his gum. He did not respond.

"What's your name?" asked Velaquez.

"Uh . . ."

"Is your name Adam Weiss?" Velaquez reached for his walkie-talkie. "Is that your name?"

"Uh …"

"Oh, good!" announced Filbert, approaching out of nowhere. "Officer, you've found my performers!"

Filbert put an arm around Cherry and Adam and then offered Velaquez the widest smile his cheeks could manage.

"Your performers?"

"Yes indeed. May I present Cherry Sundae and Vanilla Cone. Take a bow, people."

Adam bowed. Cherry bowed.

"Very good, very good. Would you like to see them do a trick?"

"They're your performers? In the diner they said they were on their way to Philadelphia."

"They are. We all are. Do you know, Officer, when the next bus to Philadelphia arrives?"

"It should be here any minute."

"Grand."

Velaquez took a hand off his walkie-talkie, narrowed his eyes. "These performers, are they any good?"

"They are indeed."

"Can they juggle?"

Adam gulped.

Filbert elbowed him in the spleen. "Of course they can juggle."

"When I was a kid, I used to juggle apples. Can they juggle apples?"

"Of course they can juggle apples. They could mount for you a demonstration, but alas, we're all out of apples today."

"Not a problem," said Velaquez. He reached into his pockets and withdrew his half-empty pack of gum, a half-empty pack of cigarettes, and a palm-sized notepad. He communicated his intentions, in Spanish, to Cherry.

Then the Greyhound bus, miraculously, began its rumble down Main Street.

"Oh well," Velaquez said. "Maybe next time."

The bus pulled to a slippery stop. Sgt. Toms, who had tracked it from the diner to the gas station, also pulled to a slippery stop. As the bus door hissed open, she and Velaquez marched past Adam and Cherry and Filbert and climbed aboard.

"What do you suppose they're doing?" whispered Adam.

"I don't know, sport, but if I were to guess," Filbert sneezed into the wind. "I'd guess they're looking for their cop-killer. Nice makeup, by the way."

Adam peered through the bus's windows. There could not have been more than six passengers on that bus, but Sgt. Toms and Officer Velaquez took their time. Adam took note of one passenger, a pimply man in a Santa Claus suit, appearing very unnerved by the sudden police presence. A large green swastika was tattooed across his forehead. Swastika Santa sat at the rear. Adam resolved then and there to sit near the front.

The driver joined them outside and lit up a pipe. She was a middle-aged woman with a long rope of grey hair and pendulous bags under her eyes the size of small children. The sight of two clowns standing at a rural stop on the Harrisburg-Pittsburgh-Philadelphia route did not faze her in the least. She puffed on her pipe and gazed up at the sky.

Sgt. Toms and Officer Velaquez descended the bus's steep steps.

"Good to go?" asked the driver.

Officer Velaquez waved goodbye to Adam and Cherry, and he and Sgt. Toms went on their way. So did the bus driver. She mounted the steps and fingered for Adam, Cherry and Filbert to follow her up.

"Where you headed to?" she asked.

"Three tickets to Philadelphia," replied Filbert.

"That will be thirty dollars."

Filbert smiled warmly, reached into his giant coat and flourished a ponderous wad of bills, from which he peeled off three soggy tens: one, two, three.

"Where did you get all that?" asked Adam once they took their seats near the front of the bus, Adam and Filbert on the left, Cherry alone on the right.

"All part of the plan, sport."

"Last thing I saw, you were walking into that church. What, did you pray for money?"

Filbert rested his back against stiff cushioning and sighed.

"Filbert, tell me you didn't rob a church."

"I didn't rob a church."

"Is that the truth?"

"Not at all. Shh. I need a nap."

The bus trundled on its merry way.

Adam noticed Swastika Santa rise from his seat but ignored him. He wanted answers from his elderly associate.

"You robbed a church?!"

"Things will be better in Philadelphia. They always are. I have a lot of friends in Philadelphia. You'll see. And there you'll be able to pay my planning fee. Now shush. Filbert needs a nappy."

The old man curled up in his seat like a stale corn chip and dropped his eyelids.

As Swastika Santa passed their row, Cherry reached over the aisle and handed Adam the queen-shaped pepper shaker. She held the corresponding salt king in her hand and raised it up in a toast.

"Did you know about this?" Adam asked her. "Stealing cash from a house of God in the middle of nowhere. Our path to hell just got very greasy."

She clinked shakers and pretended to drink.

Then the bus jerked right and came to a stop at the side of the road. All eyes turned to the head of the bus, where Swastika Santa, fake beard hanging half off his pockmarked jaw, pressed the tip of his bowie knife against the bus driver's throat.

He then addressed the passengers:

"I ain't gonna be caught by no state cops, so we're changing course. We're going across the border to Canada. And if I see a cell phone or a pager or anyone tries acting all heroic, there will be blood."

Chapter Eight

Twenty-four hours ago, something like being held hostage on a Greyhound bus would have really upset Adam. He might have even been frightened. But after the gunfire and the kidnapping and the Croatian-Spanish clown and some more gunfire and the nuclear bomb and the dead state patrolman and the blizzard in the forest and some more gunfire and the stoic ex-Mennonite and the bounty on his head and the fact that right now his face was painted white, his hair was an orange wig, and his clothes resembled a bowl of Trix, Adam reacted to Swastika Santa's threat the only way he could. He muttered, "Sit down," took off one giant red shoe and pitched it at the freak with the knife, beaning him square on his shaved head. The knife fell. Mr. Santa fell. The giant red shoe fell.

Adam walked to the front of the bus and slipped his shoe back on.

"Asshole," he noted and tromped back to his seat.

After most of the passengers expressed their gratitude (Filbert being the notably silent exception), the question then became what to do with their quarry. The following suggestions were offered:

Kick Swastika Santa off the bus.

Kick Swastika Santa off the bus and then drive over him.

Keep Swastika Santa on the bus and take turns bludgeoning him.

Turn the bus around and deliver Swastika Santa to the state police.

Turn the bus around and deliver Swastika Santa to the state police after everyone has taken turns bludgeoning him.

All parties involved waited for their hero to cast the deciding vote.

"It's not up to me," replied Adam. "I just need to get to Philadelphia."

As it turned out, everyone needed to get to Philadelphia. Or Harrisburg. Or Pittsburgh. So they stuffed the malcontent into an empty luggage compartment underneath the bus and continued on their scheduled route.

Barbara Cole from King of Prussia, age fifty-seven, insisted Adam sit beside her in the rear of the bus and share what she promised was a warm, pleasant drink. Adam saw in her a mother figure and agreed.

She handed him a thermos and he took a swig. He expected cider. He tasted bourbon. Hot bourbon.

"It's a toddy," she said. "I made it myself."

Adam coughed, choked, forced a grin. "It's lovely," he slurred. In seconds, the liquid had incinerated a layer of his tongue. He returned the thermos to matronly Mrs. Cole, who swigged down a pint without batting an eye.

"That was some thing you did for us." She capped her drink. "Very brave of you."

"Yeah, well ..."

"You must've learned courage like that in the circus."

Adam shrugged. "It's a tough business. You know ... dog eat dog, clown eat clown ..."

"I wish my son had your courage. He's a pansy."

At that moment the lavatory door slammed against the wall. Filbert stood in the small room, glaring at Adam, apparently waiting for the boy to join him.

"I'll be right back," Adam told Mrs. Cole, and he squeezed into the lavatory with the old man.

Filbert locked the door, pointed a shaky finger at Adam and spat out, "Are you a monkey child?"

"What?"

"Are you retarded or just immature?"

"That's not really a very nice thing to say."

Filbert smacked him upside the head.

"Ow!" Adam fixed his orange wig. "What did you do that for?"

"I come up with a plan to hide you in plain sight and then get you out of town and it's a good plan and what do you do? You almost get the whole bus turned around and the spotlight shining right in your face. Is it easy being so moronic or does it take a lot of effort?"

"At least I didn't burglarize a church."

"I did not burglarize a church!" Filbert huffed. "The doors were unlocked."

"Is that what Officer Neal picked you up for last night? Are you a thief?"

"I am a thief, but that's not what I was doing in the back of that car."

Filbert opened the lavatory door and ambled down the aisle, leaving Adam in the tiny room to mull his mystery. Adam then tried to pee, but the wobbling of the bus ride made proper aiming impossible. He decided to wait until their next stop, and sat back down next to Mrs. Cole. He suddenly needed more toddy.

The countryside grew concrete horns and metal teeth and became Pittsburgh. Mrs. Cole treated Adam to a Big Mac across the street from the bus station. Cherry spent the stopover on the bus, tranquilly snoring. Filbert left the bus and didn't return until moments before departure.

A few of the new passengers commented on the strange sounds coming from one of the luggage compartments underneath the bus, but everyone in the know remained tight-lipped. By dusk they had rejoined the freeway traffic and were motoring toward the keystone metropolis of Harrisburg, PA.

Adam stared at the passing trees and the Alleghenies and thought about Anna. What landscapes did her eyes behold? What sounds did her ears hear? Ebbets had suggested she was injured, that she had struck her head against the windshield. Was it true? Was she okay? According to the claims of a madman, Adam had six days to find his sister, but all he had to go on was the license number of a truck that may have been rented somewhere at some time by her kidnapper.

During their thirty-minute stopover in Harrisburg, Adam tried to track Filbert down and confront him about his earlier insinuations, but once again the old man had vanished. So instead Adam chaperoned

Mrs. Cole through the cold night air to a neon-lit liquor store down the block, where she refilled her thermos and he purchased a bag of cheap pretzels; in his experience, nothing balanced a thermos full of bourbon better than a bag of cheap pretzels.

By the time they hit the road for their final stop in the City of Brotherly Love, Adam was not especially sober. So when Filbert once again glared at him from the bus's lavatory stall, arms crossed, well …

"If you need me to hold your penis," chuckled Adam, "I might first need to drink some more."

"I need to talk with you."

"We are talking." Adam glanced at Mrs. Cole, who was conked out, and then back at Filbert. "We should probably talk somewhere else, though. We don't want to wake her."

He joined the old man in the stall. Filbert locked the door.

"I've made arrangements for tomorrow," said Filbert. "Tonight you'll be—are you listening to me?"

Adam was transfixed by his own reflection in the lavatory mirror. The orange hair, the greasepaint, the outfit—he had forgotten he was dressed like a clown. He waved a hand; his reflection waved a hand. He smiled; his reflection smiled. He stuck out his tongue; his reflection stuck out its tongue.

"Wow," said Adam. "I'm a clown."

"Yeah, the clothes make the man. Listen, I got you a room tonight at a motel."

"Do you like clowns?"

"No. Are you listening to me?"

"Yes."

"Then what did I just say?"

"'Are you listening to me?'"

Filbert slapped him upside the head.

"Ow!" Adam winced. "Stop doing that!"

"I got you a room tonight at a motel. You need to be in the lobby tomorrow at eight o'clock. Got it?"

"You got me a room in a motel?"

"Yes."

"That's so nice of you!"

Adam gave the old man a hug.

"I need you in the lobby tomorrow at eight. Sober."

"What happens at eight?"

"You pay me my fee."

"For getting me a motel room?"

"For getting you out of Dodge. Remember? My services are not gratis."

"Well, how much is your fee, because I still don't have any money."

"You will tomorrow morning after we're done. Just be in the lobby at eight."

Filbert handed Adam a slip of paper with the reservation information on it. On it also was written a name: Arvid Winkle.

"Who's Arvid Winkle?"

"That's your new name, champ," said Filbert and opened the lavatory door.

"Wait," said Adam. "What about Cherry?"

"What about her?"

"Where's she staying?"

"How should I know?"

"I thought we were, I don't know, a team."

"Grow the fuck up," Filbert replied, and he returned to his seat at the front of the bus.

Adam plopped down next to Mrs. Cole. Fat tears streamed down her cheeks.

"Oh, Mrs. Cole, what's wrong?"

"I was … just thinking about my boy, Stephen … such a loser." Her shoulders bounced up and down with each sob. "He's twenty-two, lives at home, all he does is play video games on his Xbox. He's not like you, a real man."

"What video games does he play?" asked Adam, patting his neighbor on the back.

"He's obsessed with the baseball game."

"That's too bad, Mrs. Cole. Do you, um, know who Stephen plays as?"

"The New York Yankees."

"I see. On the highest difficulty setting?"

She looked at him, confused.

"Shh," he said, comforting her with a hug. "It's okay. It's going to be okay."

The bus merged onto Route 76, main artery to Philadelphia. It wouldn't be long now. Adam checked the time on Mrs. Cole's watch: 10:22. No stars shone in the black sky; this night was too cold for their torches. Once Mrs. Cole had dozed off again, muttering in her sleep about fried chicken, Adam quietly made his way down the aisle to check on Cherry.

She was perusing an issue of *People*, probably purchased in Harrisburg. He sat down next to her.

"Hi," he said.

"*¡Hola!*" Her grin lit up the bus cabin. "*¿Como estas?*"

"Yeah, I still don't understand a word of Spanish. Sorry. I just wanted to, you know, see how you were doing."

She showed him a picture. In it, several bottle-tanned movie stars posed in their designer tuxedoes and ball gowns in front of the banner for some charity event. Their bodies blocked the name of the charity.

"Very nice," Adam said. "Who's your favorite?"

"*¿Que?*"

"I said, who's your?—never mind. Listen, I was wondering what you were going to do after we got to Philadelphia. Do you even know we're going to Philadelphia? Anyway, I was just wondering. And you have no idea what I'm saying. Hold on."

Adam looked over at Filbert across the aisle and roused him from his rest.

"What?" growled the old man.

"I need you to translate something for me."

"I'm off the clock."

"Add it to my fee."

Filbert moved a seat over so he could be closer to the aisle.

"Okay," said Adam, "I'll tell you and you tell her. And whatever she says back, tell me in English."

"Oh, so that's how translation works? Thanks a lot, fuckface."

Adam glanced at Cherry and asked his first question: "What are you going to do once we get to Philadelphia?"

Filbert translated, listened to her response, then relayed it: "I don't know."

"Where are you going to stay?"

"I don't know."

"Where were you heading when you found me at the rest stop?"

"I don't know."

Adam sighed.

"She's not your responsibility, sport," said Filbert. "You got a shitheap of problems all your own."

"We can't just abandon her."

"She did fine before she met you and she'll do fine after you leave her behind."

Adam looked into Cherry's green eyes. He saw such innocence there. A little girl playing dress-up and lost in a foreign country.

"Ask her," said Adam, "if she wants to stay with me."

"What?"

"Ask her if she wants to spend the night in my hotel room. Make sure you tell her I have no ulterior motives or anything. It's cold outside and I just want to make sure she has a place to sleep. Tell her I'll sleep on the floor."

Filbert told her.

Adam searched for a response in her eyes.

She looked away.

"Did you tell her?" Adam asked Filbert.

The old man nodded.

"Then what is her answer?"

"You can see her answer for yourself, sport. Now I'm going to return to my seat and try to have a wet dream. Don't bother me."

Despite any further words Adam had to share, Cherry maintained focus on her shoes. Reluctantly, sadly, Adam slogged back to his place beside Mrs. Cole.

"Oh, what's wrong, precious?" she asked. "You look like your dog just ate your girlfriend. Would you like some toddy? I think I have some left."

"No, I'm fine, thanks. I'm just a little in over my head."

"Don't worry. We're almost in Philadelphia. Everything changes in Philadelphia."

Philadelphia. A city so nice they founded it twice, the Swedes in 1669 then William Pitt and the British in the early 1700s. Birthplace of American liberty and of course the cheesesteak. The bus pulled into a shopping district downtown and parked at the local Greyhound terminal. They had reached the end of the line.

The passengers filed out. Adam said goodbye to Mrs. Cole and quickly left the scene; he did not want to be around when the driver released Swastika Santa from his prison. But he also was avoiding Cherry and any awkward farewells. In lending him her costume, wig and makeup, she may have saved his life. All he had wanted to do in return was give her a warm room. He tried to purge these thoughts from his mind as he crossed the street to the SEPTA station.

He had been to Philadelphia twice before. The first time had been on vacation with his parents when he and Anna were nine. Mom and Dad had the idea of taking a road trip through history and so spent one summer in a station wagon trundling to Gettysburg, where Anna got stung on her eyelid by a bee; Philadelphia, where Dad lost ten dollars in ten seconds to a street hustler playing Three-card Monte; and Washington DC, where nothing terrible happened to them but nothing exciting either.

His parents didn't know about the second time Adam visited Philadelphia. The second time Adam visited Philadelphia had been to see a girl named Roxanne Banks. Growing up, Roxanne Banks had been Anna's best friend, sharing Barbie dolls, trading stickers, and doing all the safe little things that best friends in Newark did together. The summer after sixth grade, though, Roxanne's parents split up and her mother, a woman who could complain on a sunny day, received sole custody. She moved herself and her daughter back to her roots in Philadelphia. Roxanne promised to keep in touch with her best friend Anna, but Anna would be away that summer at a strict music camp which disallowed all communication with the outside world (and joy). So Roxanne did the next best thing; she wrote letters to Adam. Ostensibly the letters were all about Anna—how was she doing, had she made many friends at music camp, when was she coming home?— and Adam would then bring Roxanne's letters to Anna every weekend when he and his parents would drive down the shore and visit her. Anna would read these correspondences and entrust Adam to mail her responses.

One Sunday, on a whim, Adam included two letters in the envelope for Philadelphia. One, written in pink pen by Anna, detailed her latest adventures with the cello. The other, scribbled in black ink by Adam, was a brief update about life in the neighborhood. He assumed Roxanne might want to know the latest local gossip.

Truth be told, Adam wasn't completely sure why he had written that second letter. He dropped it in the post and nervously—nervously!— awaited her reply. As the days ticked into weeks, he was certain Roxanne had found his letter revolting and was spending all this time concocting the perfect retort for his sister to read and provide her with enough ammunition to riddle with misery her silly brother's silly life. Mercifully, his summer days were busy doing lawn work and pool cleaning for his neighbors and their friends at ten dollars an hour.

Then, on a sweltering weekday in the last week of June, Roxanne's responses arrived. Two separate letters in two separate envelopes. Adam threw his sister's on her bed, went into his room, shut his door, and sliced open his envelope with his Boy Scout Swiss Army knife. She had sent him three handwritten pages and a photograph of herself in shorts and a t-shirt waving hello beside the Liberty Bell.

Anna corresponded with Roxanne once a week; Adam wrote her a new letter every day. Sometimes he included photographs, but more often than not he just sent her words, his words, misspelled and sloppy and utterly heart-felt. And she wrote him back just as often. By the end of July, he had begun to form a plan. He had been frugal with his money, spending it only on movies and candy, and had almost four hundred dollars stashed away in his underwear drawer. Roxanne's birthday was August sixteenth. He knew exactly where she lived; he had her address memorized. He would take a bus down to Philadelphia and surprise her.

He did not mention his trip to his parents. His mother had been distracted lately with work and his father had, well, just been distracted, distant. He told them he was going to stay over his friend Keith's house, got dropped off at Keith's house, had a snack at Keith's house, and then called a cab to take him to the bus depot. He had made the important phone calls in advance; he knew departure times, arrival times, total expenses. He was ready and nervous and excited and scared. What if she opened her door, saw him on her stoop and laughed? What if he had read too much into their relationship? He had bought her the new book by an author she said she liked and scratched out a little black pen inscription on its title page. What if she had already read it? What if his inscription was childish?

He arrived in Philadelphia mid-afternoon. The humidity had reached toxic levels and during the cab ride to her house, Adam found the air difficult to breathe. He asked the driver twice to turn on the A/C. The driver twice turned up the radio. Cool jazz. They reached the house. Adam offered a 5 percent tip and got out. The cab screeched into the distance.

Roxanne lived twenty miles northwest of downtown in the suburban oasis of Chestnut Hill. Green lawns. Spacious backyards. Fences made of wood instead of chain link. Adam clutched his backpack to his chest and ambled up the cobblestone walkway to her front door. A few drops of warm rain tickled down the back of his green polo shirt.

He rang the bell.

Waited.

The drizzle rattled into a downpour. He tried to duck under the awning, but the protection it offered was barely adequate. His clothes and backpack quickly became supersaturated. He rang the bell again and again.

He ran around to the back of the house and peered inside the windows. One of Roxanne's cats, a stout calico named Maurice, hopped up on the sill inside the house and stared at him.

A neighbor, witnessing the drenched fiasco, finally came out to help him. She held out an umbrella, informed him that the Banks were away for the day. She asked him if he was a friend of Roxanne's, if he wanted to leave a message for her, if he needed a lift home.

"Yeah," replied Adam, wiping away rainfall and tears, "can you give me a ride to the bus depot?"

He never told Roxanne about his visit. He never told Anna, or his parents or anyone. When his friend Keith bugged him about it, Adam just played coy and said he would never kiss and tell. And July became August and August became September and sixth grade became seventh grade and the flow of letters became a trickle and then, as these things do, became nothing at all.

As Adam sat on the subway, zipping through the eclectic neighborhoods of Philadelphia on his way to his motel, he reflected on the foolishness of his youth. He saw Chestnut Hill on the SEPTA map and felt shame. He wondered, not for the first time, whatever happened to Roxanne Banks.

His destination lay far from the wooden fences and green lawns of Chestnut Hill. His motel, curiously named The Blue Canary, occupied the corner of a decidedly Puerto Rican block in northeast Philly. The night manager at the desk took one look at him in his clown garb and literally laughed himself off his stool.

"I'm sorry, brother," he gasped, "you're just not something I expected to see."

Adam waited until the man had climbed back onto his stool. "I was told you had a room reserved for me."

"Would that be under Barnum or Bailey?"

"Ha. No. Actually, I think it might be under the name Arvid Winkle?"

The night manager immediately ceased his revelry and handed Adam a crud-caked key. "We've been expecting you, Mr. Winkle. Room's on the top floor. Your room has a private bathroom and the sheets have just been washed. And you have a change of clothes on the chair. Don't worry, they provided it, not me. If there's a problem with the heat, or anything at all, just let me know. My name is Jesus. I'm here to serve. You'll receive your wake-up call promptly at 7:30, I promise."

Adam tripped his way up through dull overhead lighting and across rotting green carpet to The Blue Canary's fifth, final floor. His toddy buzz was quickly devolving into a headache, and he was eager to scrub the pretty colors off his face. He just hoped his bathroom had soap and running water.

One for two: his bathroom had running water. His bathroom also had its manila tiling fastened by mildew, its shower spigot covered with red lesions, and its metal towel rack dangling from the wall like a shorn limb. The bedroom was not much better, or larger, but the mattress was soft and the watercolor hanging above the bed, of a blue bird in flight over the sea at sunset, left Adam feeling almost serene. A black garment bag lay draped over a chair in the corner.

He slipped out of his clown shoes and prismatic regalia and spent the next twenty minutes in the bathroom wiping at greasepaint with one-ply toilet paper. He flushed the used paper down the toilet, lumbered to his bed, and tipped over like a chopped oak.

He awoke in the same position, akimbo on top of the sheets. A cold morning glow lit the motel room with oranges and yellows. The blue bird in the watercolor painting seemed especially alive today, and happy. Adam pushed himself off his bed, yawned for a minute and let his lips collapse into a sloppy smile. Somehow in these dregs he had had a good night's sleep.

Then he heard water cascading in his bathroom. His shower. He noticed the bathroom door, which he had left open, was now just ajar.

Someone was in his shower, and in this neighborhood, in his situation, that someone was not going to be a friend. He searched the room for a weapon and picked up the TV remote.

RING!!!

The phone on the nightstand rattled to life. Adam froze. That must be the wake-up call, he realized.

RING!!!

The shower stopped.

RING!!!

Clutching the remote control, which was barely larger than his hand, Adam slowly moved toward the bathroom door.

RING!!!

Adam reached out with his left hand.

RING!!!

Taking a deep breath, Adam raised his plastic weapon and pushed open the bathroom door.

Chapter Nine

In the center of the rancid bathroom stood a young mocha-skinned woman, sopping wet and buck naked. Water rained from her hair (brunette, natural) and shoulders (dark birthmark on the left, size of a dime) and breasts (twin birthmarks on the right, two o'clock from her areola) and belly button (an innie) and pelvis (unshaved) and legs (shaved) and pooled at her feet. Adam did not stare at the pool.

"Um," he said.

"¡Hola!" she replied and waved. If she was embarrassed, she hid it well. Where she possibly could hide it, Adam hadn't a clue. He forced his gaze to the left—the bathroom mirror, not a good choice, and then to the right—cockroach scaling the wallpaper, also not a good choice, and then, finally, to the craptastic floor.

"So, uh, Filbert told you where to find me? Good old Filbert. When I asked you on the bus, I thought, you know, that you didn't want to, I don't know, be here. With me. Here. But any port in a storm, right?"

From the movements of her shadow and the sounds of her body, she was using something to dry off. Maybe she brought her own towel. Adam let his guess stay a guess. In his short life his eyes had beheld seven naked women. The first three had been high school sweethearts. The second three had been college co-eds. Adam shied away in that ratty bathroom from peeking at the uniquely beautiful form in front of him and was mightily confused. He had seen seven other women. Why did even a glimpse at this one fill his cheeks with the hot blood of shame?

"I, um, I'm going to go into the other, you know, room," he said, head down, but as he turned to go, Cherry's hand gently grabbed him by the wrist and pulled him closer. She used her other hand to lift his chin up. They were now eye to eye.

"*Hola*," he whispered.

She smiled again, all teeth and glee. She then swiped a cotton swab of cold cream across his forehead. She had grabbed his wrist and pulled him closer and lifted his chin and stared into his eyes to better clean off his makeup. Adam spotted her pile of miscellanea collecting dust on the toilet seat. He felt like more of a fool than usual.

Cherry seemed very precise in her technique, furrowing her brow every now and then in concentration and concern. The process took ten minutes, and by the end Adam felt as if every iota of dirt his pores had ever carried had been scrubbed away. He looked at his reflection in the mirror, touched those familiar features. Had they ever been this clean?

Cherry stood behind him, admiring her work. Her arms rested on his shoulders. He reached up and cupped each of her hands in his.

"Thank you, Cherry. I—"

RING!!!

"Damn it." He rushed to the bedroom and picked up the receiver. "Yes?"

"Oh, good, you're awake." It was Jesus, the night manager. "I was worried for a second you hadn't heard the wake-up call. Which I did place on time. Anyway, Mr. Winkle, your car is here."

"My what?"

"They want me to tell you they know they're early," continued Jesus, "but they want you down here in five minutes. Goodbye, Mr. Winkle!"

End of call.

Adam zipped open the garment bag. Filbert had somehow procured for him a cardigan sweater, leather belt, pressed khakis, white socks, and a pair of polished brown loafers. And a car waiting downstairs? Suppositions and conjectures raced through his imagination as he changed from clown to preppie; the clothes fit, more or less. How exactly did Filbert expect Adam to repay him for these services?

As he finished fastening his belt, Cherry materialized from the bathroom, her face repainted, her body re-adorned.

"The car is here."

She stared at him.

"The – car – is – here."

She stared at him.

Adam made vroom-vroom noises and pointed down.

She cocked her head and eyed him as if he were batty.

"Let's go," he said and led her out of the room.

The car was a fat, black, shiny Saab SUV. As soon as Adam and Cherry emerged from The Blue Canary, after bidding farewell to Jesus the frazzled, the SUV's back seat door swung open and a gigantic Aryan in a pinstripe suit waved them entry. With little choice, Adam and Cherry joined him inside the vehicle.

"Yogurt?" asked the Aryan. He spooned the lumpy gel from a gallon container and downed it with a mug of coffee.

Both Adam and Cherry shook their heads.

The gigantic Aryan shrugged, fed himself another ounce of bacteria, and barked some Swedish to the driver, who also was a gigantic Aryan. The SUV squealed away from the curb.

"I apologize for your dwelling," said Yogurt in impeccable English. "Our mutual friend insisted you spend your evening in an armpit. He stayed at the Four Seasons."

Yogurt flashed a shark grin and Adam suddenly felt very, very uneasy.

"Our mutual friend also informed me about your predicament. He and I have a history. I like history. Now I know yours. I had a sister once. She gave me many headaches. She no longer does. Do you like Philadelphia?"

Adam nodded. Cherry, playing it safe, mimicked him.

"I have lived here for thirty-four years. When I was a boy in Stockholm, I never imagined I would be spending my adulthood in America. I was raised to be a fisherman, but I didn't want to be a fisherman. I read a lot of history. I wanted to be a Viking. My ancestors were Vikings. The Vikings found North America five hundred years before the Spanish. The Vikings found Philadelphia one hundred years before the British. They call us Scandinavians now, but we will always be Vikings. Isn't that correct, Rolf?"

The driver, apparently Rolf, did not reply.

"Please forgive Rolf. He used to be very talkative. He no longer has a tongue. He can still make noises, but he sounds very primitive. When I was seven years old I saw my father having sex with my mother and I thought he was killing her so I picked up his knife, the one he used to gut fish, and I punched the steel in between his sweaty shoulder blades. My mother sent me to live with our cousins in Philadelphia. Here, thousands of miles from home, I learned how to be a true Viking. I have always appreciated the irony therein. So now you know my history. We have all been educated."

The man stared so intently now that Adam had to look away. He tried to peer out the windows of the SUV, tried to get his bearings, but the windows were tinted and none of the sights looked at all familiar.

The man licked clean his spoon and chuckled like a little girl, and Adam suddenly, palpably, feared for his life.

"We are almost there," he said. "I was surprised to hear from our mutual friend. I didn't expect to hear from him. He has always made me sad. I hope you find your sister. In this life, we should always get what we want, don't you agree?"

The car came to a halt. Adam and Cherry climbed out onto the sidewalk. They had been deposited on Broad Street in the financial district of Center City, mere blocks from Independence Hall. The Saab peeled away; Adam had no idea what he was expected to do now, and really did not want to find out.

Then he spotted Filbert standing across the street, still in his hulking leather overcoat, nonchalantly reading the morning paper. Adam burned to turn heel and run, but he did feel indebted to the old fart. He just hoped that whatever mad task awaited him did not take too much time or break too many laws. As Adam crossed the street, he kept an eye out for churches, but saw only banks and coffeehouses.

"Did you have a good night?" asked Filbert, not looking up from his paper.

"Sure," replied Adam. "How was the Four Seasons?"

"You've stayed in one five-star hotel, you've stayed in them all. We're just waiting for one more and then we can go about our business of the day."

"And what exactly is that?"

Filbert glanced up. "It's how you're going to pay me back, sport. Everything else is just details."

"Yeah, well, I'd like to hear some of those details."

"Or you'll change your mind?" Filbert folded the newspaper under his arm. "You're under the false assumption that you have a choice. The man who brought you here, who paid for your hotel room and mine, the man who is sponsoring our adventure today does not allow his soldiers to make choices, and right now you and I are his soldiers."

"Is he, like, the don of the Swedish mafia?"

"The mafia is Sicilian, bucko. What our benefactor runs is ... different. But still quite dangerous. Which I informed Clownface here, and she was supposed to stay at the motel!"

This segued into a heated diatribe by Filbert, in Spanish of course, against Cherry Sundae. In the meantime, Adam scoped out the neighborhood, watching the clusters of men and women in business casual teeming up and down the sidewalks. Just another morning on the way to the office. These white-collar Philadelphians loved their media: cell phones, beepers, electronic attaché cases, global wristwatches, pagers, PDAs, laptops. It seemed the only people in Center City not sporting microchips were Adam, Cherry and Filbert.

"Okay," said Filbert finally, "it's time. Let's go. She is going to stay right here."

He brought Adam to a storefront on the corner of Broad and Fisher. Adam glanced up at the sign: Benjamin Franklin Bank and Financial Center. Twenty yards away, Cherry waved at him. She looked worried. He waved back and followed Filbert inside.

The Benjamin Franklin Bank and Financial Center, on the corner of Broad and Fisher, was beige. Beige carpeting, beige ceiling, and on its beige walls hung beige paintings about beige subjects. Adam wondered if the tellers wore bellbottoms. Given the time of day, not many people used this branch; including Adam and Filbert, there had to be a total of ten customers. Most were lined up beside the beige rope for the teller windows. Two sat in beige recliners in the waiting area skimming old copies of *LIFE* magazine. Filbert and Adam joined them.

"What are we doing in a bank?" asked Adam.

"What do people usually do in a bank?" replied Filbert.

Adam sighed and looked over at the street. So many people going about their merry way, none of them contending with madmen and vows.

The security guard, a portly Nigerian wearing the nametag FRIENDLY JOE, approached them.

"May I inquire as to your business?" he inquired.

Filbert offered the man a smile made of fool's gold. "Yes, hello, hi. I'd like to open an account for my grandson here. He just turned eighteen."

Friendly Joe smiled back. "It will just be a few moments and the next available bank representative will be with you." He then tapped on the shoulder of one of the gentlemen reading *LIFE* magazine. The customer and his life partner followed Friendly Joe to a glass-enclosed office, where the next available bank representative awaited them.

Adam picked up one of the old issues. Jimmy Carter was on the cover. He flipped through the pages and glanced over at Filbert. The old man was ogling the clock. It was 8:26.

"So, Grandfather, you're not going to tell me what we're waiting for?" asked Adam.

"You'll see soon enough. Grandson."

And ugly Swastika Santa from the bus strolled into the bank, still wearing his Claus costume and sporting a snarl of attitude.

The magazine fell from Adam's hands. "What the—?

But Filbert grabbed him by the arm and whispered in his ear,

"Whatever you do in the next five minutes, don't do a thing."

Swastika Santa nodded at them. Filbert nodded back.

What's about to happen, thought Adam, is not going to be good. Not at all. He glanced again at the clock: 8:30 on the dot.

Friendly Joe then appeared, directly impeding Adam's line of vision of the erstwhile hijacker. "Gentlemen," he said, "Mrs. Keller is ready to see you now."

Joe led them to the glass office.

Mrs. Keller, an attractive black woman with sparkling eyes, offered her hand.

Adam and Filbert sat down.

"So, I hear this young man wants to open a checking account."

Adam glanced back at the main area and found the jumpy Santa, just in time to watch him reach into his furry red coat and withdraw a sizable submachine gun.

"Everybody on the ground!" he growled. "This is a robbery!"

Friendly Joe reached for his sidearm, but Swastika Santa found him first and took aim.

"Everybody includes you nigger," demanded Santa.

Adam glared at Filbert and then looked to Mrs. Keller. She reached under her desk to the silent alarm; all across the bank, every other teller and associate did the same.

With his attention fixed on Friendly Joe, Swastika Santa did not notice two of the customers in line, a pair of middle-aged blondes, calmly reach into their pocketbooks and remove shiny Beretta automatics. The shorter woman shot the robber in his left knee, while the taller one fired a round into his right shoulder.

Fifteen seconds after ordering everybody to the ground, the only person actually on the ground was Mr. Santa, prone and screaming. Friendly Joe had easily snatched up the SMG.

"FBI," said the shorter woman, while her colleague took out the handcuffs.

Swastika Santa then shot a teary-eyed plea at Filbert. The old man did not make a move. He didn't even react. Moments later the police had stepped through the front door and efficiently controlled the scene.

"Don't worry," said Mrs. Keller to her two customers, "you were never in any danger. I promise. I'll be right back and then we can open up that checking account for you." She abandoned her desk to speak with the lead officer.

Filbert nonchalantly hopped into her seat.

"Filbert, what is going on here?"

"The kid was a patsy." He typed a series of commands onto her keyboard. "Your job is lookout. As soon as you see anyone coming this way, you say so or our benefactor will be none too fucking pleased. Meanwhile, I need to make a withdrawal."

"You're robbing the bank!"

"Know what the definition of moron is, sport? Someone who is shocked by the obvious. Now shush."

As Filbert pounded away, Adam watched the police interrogate witnesses. Mrs. Keller acted as liaison, introducing bank associates to the officer and encouraging them to offer testimony.

"The police will be here any second," said Adam, "wanting to ask us questions."

"I'm almost done. Oh, crap."

"Oh … crap?"

Filbert scowled at the computer. "Damn thing froze up. Hold on, let me reboot. Let's see … where's the damn power button …?"

Mrs. Keller looked their way.

"Filbert!" Adam flattened himself against the wall.

The old man glanced up, a complete lack of concern and/or compassion in his eyeballs. "Something wrong?"

Mrs. Keller strolled toward her office. Any minute now, she'd spot their intrusion and sic a whole battalion of inner city cops on their sorry asses. If they were lucky, the local law enforcement wouldn't know enough to hand them over to the state law enforcement; if they were lucky, they'd only end up sharing a cell with Swastika Santa.

Adam wasn't lucky.

Mrs. Keller arrived at the office door.

"Excuse me, sir," she said to Filbert, "what are you doing at my desk?"

The old man offered again that fool's gold grin. "Well, I saw you were busy and my grandson and I are on a very busy schedule—you know how it is— and well, I used to work at a branch of this very bank over in Roxborough. Worked there for thirty-five years."

"So why are you at my desk?"

"I told you. I'm opening an account for my grandson."

She crossed her office and glanced at her computer screen.

Adam's anxiety decided to manifest itself. He started speaking in tongues.

Both Mrs. Keller and Filbert stared at the boy.

Adam babbled back at them.

"You'll have to forgive my grandson," said Filbert. "He's a 'special' child and all this excitement … well …"

Adam, now indignant, babbled some more.

From her seat, Mrs. Keller sighed. "Yes, I can imagine. Poor child. I have a niece who's autistic. Anyway, Mr. Winkle, ordinarily I would have preferred you had waited for me to do this, but I suppose this has not been an ordinary morning. Everything here looks in order. Now how much would you like to deposit in your new account, young man?"

Shortly thereafter, their business in the bank concluded, Filbert and Adam strolled back up Broad Street. The marching crowds had thinned out, but Cherry remained where they had left her, shivering in front of a Starbucks.

"Our benefactor should be here any minute," said Filbert, "to pick us up."

"I want very much to slug you."

"Why would you want to do that? I just made you ten thousand dollars. Of course, the money's going straight to my pocket. Your debt, and all."

"You don't think they'll be able to track whatever account you transferred the funds into, put two and two together? They probably have us on videotape!"

"They stopped the videotape the moment the police arrived. Normal procedure after an attempted bank robbery. And the money's been transferred to an offshore account. Even if they figure out what happened, they'll never see us again. Unless you be a fuckhead and go back in there. But not even you are that dumb, are you?"

The hulking Saab pulled up to the curb. The three of them piled into the back seat and Rolf kicked down the gas pedal. Yogurt, apparently, had other business to attend.

"So what happens now?" asked Adam.

"We're going back to my room at the Four Seasons and we're going to order us some breakfast. Do you like pancakes? They've got some really wonderful pancakes."

The Four Seasons was situated not far from the bank, and soon Adam, Filbert and Cherry were back on the sidewalk. They passed through the hotel's gold-rimmed revolving door, made their way to the gold-rimmed elevator, sailed up seven gold-rimmed stories, and finally stopped at the gold-rimmed door to Filbert's undoubtedly gold-rimmed suite.

"The eggs are good too," said Filbert, sliding his key card into the door. "I promise you, today's breakfast will be much better than yesterday's."

The lock clicked open. Filbert coughed up a kilo of phlegm, swallowed it, smiled at his companions, and pushed into his room.

The giant ax swung out of nowhere and lopped his head clean off.

Chapter Ten

"Holy shit!" cried Adam, backing into the hallway.

Cherry snatched up a nearby vase full of chrysanthemums and held it as a shield.

Yogurt stepped over the body, stared at them and frowned. "Oh, don't break the vase. It looks expensive." Pints of blood dripped down from the double-bladed ax onto Filbert's overcoat. "And please, join me inside. I've ordered us pancakes. They've got some really wonderful pancakes."

Could they have made a run for it? Yes. Would Rolf be waiting for them on the ground floor with a similar medieval weapon? Most assuredly. Adam and Cherry delicately stepped over their dead pal and entered the suite. Yogurt pulled Filbert fully into the room, shut the door, and thumped the ax, handle-down, into the umbrella holder.

Sure enough, set up inside the suite was a table draped in white linen and covered with breakfast dishes. Bacon, cereal, waffles, biscuits, hash browns, eggs, and, yes, pancakes. Despite the carnage he had just witnessed, Adam felt his stomach rumble its delight. He had not fed it a proper meal in days.

"Sit, sit."

Adam and Cherry sat, sat. Yogurt also sat, and piled six pancakes onto his plate. He drenched them in maple syrup and ate.

"I eat two breakfasts a day," he said. "It helps keep me energized for whatever is needed of me. Breakfast is essential. Would you like some orange juice? It's freshly squeezed. They do things right at the Four Seasons. Whenever relatives come to visit, I always keep them here, and I always make sure they sample the pancakes."

He then filled two plates with pancakes and placed them in front of Adam and Cherry.

"Eat, eat."

Adam and Cherry ate, ate. The pancakes were really wonderful, soft and sweet and remarkably light, and as long as Adam kept his back to the corpse by the door, he was able to digest.

"Now I'm going to tell you why I decapitated your friend. I would like you to know the context of my actions. I do this not to avoid judgment. I assure you, I honestly couldn't care less what you or anyone thinks of me, but because you did a favor for me this morning and I would like to return it. In the meantime, have some orange juice. It's quite good."

He poured them some orange juice. It was quite good.

"Your friend has always made me sad. Our acquaintance goes back quite a while. When I first found him he was doping greyhounds on the track. There's a racetrack right outside the city. I enjoy making bets now and again. I took him under my wing, under my protection, and treated him well. He evoked sadness in me and I wanted to care for him, as one would a stray cat. Do you by any chance know the license plate of the truck your sister's kidnapper was driving?"

Adam blinked. The abrupt change in subject caught him off guard. Finally he nodded and scribbled down the information on a napkin.

"When your friend first worked for me, I offered him the lower priority assignments. I recognized his potential but I also recognized how broken he had become. He did a few jobs and he did them well and he made friends and I was pleased. Confirmation of a hypothesis satisfies the mind. So I gave your friend a courier job. The transport of goods from A to B. Simple but essential. Business needs to be kinetic."

Yogurt finished his OJ, dialed his cell phone, and read the license numbers to the person on the other line. He then added a few Swedish phrases and hung up.

"What goods was he transporting? The goods are the McGuffin. They mattered to me, they mattered to my associates, but they were of no consequence to your friend. What was of consequence to your friend was the transportation of the goods. What his responsibilities entailed was the secure passage of the goods from where they were to where they needed to be. In this case, the goods were in Cordoba, Spain and they needed to be here. You've never been to Cordoba. It is a glorious cultural nexus, rich in history both Roman and Moorish. It is in Cordoba that Columbus received his instructions to sail to the New World. In Cordoba, on Calle Cardenal Herrero, stands the Mezquita, a giant mosque that houses a Roman Catholic cathedral. A mosque cohabiting with a cathedral. It sings to the polytheist in me. Your friend's job was to pick up a small package at the Mezquita and bring it back to me. Was this complicated? No. Was he successful? No."

His cell phone emitted a concerto. He answered it, listened for a few moments to the voice on the other line, and then jotted down some notes on the back of Adam's slip of paper. That was all.

"Your friend arrived in Cordoba on a Tuesday morning. The package was to be picked up on a Wednesday afternoon. Tuesday night, your friend was caught picking the pocket of a woman standing on an ancient bridge. This woman was the mayor's wife. Your friend was locked up. They gave him one phone call. He called me."

Yogurt refilled his glass of OJ but did not sip.

"For his trip, I had given your friend an expense account. He did not need to steal anything, but then again, professional thieves do not steal out of material need. They steal because they are professional thieves. Your friend was imprisoned in Cordoba and he called me for help and I helped him. He was released the next day but arrived too late at the Mezquita to pick up the package. He returned home and he blamed the Spaniards for his predicament. He blamed them! This made me so sad that I wanted to weep. Some of my countrymen enjoy sadness. The literature of my people is rife with melancholy and suicide. I do not enjoy sadness. I told your friend to leave Philadelphia and never return."

With a sigh, Yogurt leaned back in his chair. In the artificial light of the hotel room, the spatters of blood on his pinstripe suit and white silk shirt appeared almost innocent, as if he were an overdressed child caught playing with his food. Several feet away, Filbert's brain had begun to ooze out the bottom of his skull.

Yogurt rose from his seat and trotted over to the scene of the crime.

"I've jotted down on that slip of paper the address and phone number of the car rental place that your license plate is registered to. It's in Las Vegas, Nevada. Now you have the first link in your chain. You can fly to Las Vegas and unearth history about your sister's kidnapper and use this information to track him down and rescue her."

Yogurt effortlessly hoisted Filbert's headless body over his shoulder and carried him into the bathroom. Chunky gore spilled down the Nordic's back like spilled soup. Yogurt returned moments later for the head.

"As luck would have it," he said, "there is a small parcel that I need picked up in Las Vegas. It will be in Room 512 at Caesars Palace for the next few days. Rolf will provide you with a cell phone, in case you need to contact me or I need to contact you; a new license, for identification purposes, airport security being what it is; and a credit card, which you can use as often as you like during your trip and on whatever you like. This will be your expense account. Try not to spend over $10,000. Tax Day is fast approaching and my accountants are harried enough as is. Regardless, Rolf will drive you to the airport. Use the credit card to purchase your round-trip ticket. Fly first class. Enjoy yourself. Use this weekend and this credit card to find your sister's kidnapper. Be back in Philadelphia, weather permitting, by Sunday evening."

Yogurt bowled Filbert's head into the bathtub.

"You may also say no. You may for whatever reason turn down my offer of assistance and find a way to Las Vegas on your own, and I will get someone else to go to Room 512 this weekend and pick up my parcel. Now, if you'll excuse me, I need to perform some old-fashioned surgery."

Yogurt picked up the ax, stepped into the bathroom and closed the door behind him. A few moments later, Cherry Sundae knelt beside the red shadow of their friend, moistening her knees with blood. She traced the amorphous shadow with her fingertips. Left alone at the table, Adam was forced to discuss his options with the only person available: himself.

ADAM

Hello.

ADAM

Hello.

ADAM

Fancy meeting you here.

ADAM

You're a barrel of laughs.

ADAM

Why are we even having this conversation? It's obvious what you should do.

ADAM

It's obvious I should agree to work for an ax-wielding mob boss?

ADAM

You want to find Anna, don't you?

ADAM

The ends don't justify the means.

ADAM

Like you even read Machiavelli.

ADAM

Maybe I'll read him someday. The Cliff's Notes make it sound real good.

ADAM

You blame yourself for this. You blame yourself for the kidnapping. Right now you're even blaming yourself somehow for Filbert's death.

ADAM

He came back to Philadelphia to help me.

ADAM

He came back to Philadelphia because he knew here he could make some money. You met him in the back of a police car. That cop was probably just giving him a lift. That's why the stationhouse wasn't informed.

ADAM

An hour ago I robbed a bank. Now I'm being asked to fly to Sin City to act as a courier for Thor.

ADAM

Thor was the God of Thunder. I think you mean Loki. He was the God of Mischief.

ADAM

So I haven't read a comic book in a while. Sue me.

ADAM

You dressed up as Thor one time for Halloween.

ADAM

Shut up.

ADAM

You even borrowed Dad's hammer.

ADAM

I said shut up.

ADAM

It's ironic, really, considering what happened to him. And I know you blame yourself for that too.

ADAM

La-la-la. I can't hear you.

ADAM

You're the one who was the disappointment. Maybe if you'd been a better son, he wouldn't have swallowed a bowlful of Xanax and died.

ADAM

This is not about him. This is about Anna.

ADAM

Yes. It is. And you have a responsibility as her brother to make sure she's okay. And an opportunity to make that happen has fallen into your lap. To turn your back on principle to this offer of help is foolish, and it will doom Anna and for once, you'll be right. It will be your fault.

❖   ❖   ❖

Adam walked past Cherry to the door. He glanced back at her and waved goodbye. She looked up from the stain on the carpet and stared at him. He had no idea what she was thinking. He never did, and never would, and decided to leave their brief, strange relationship at that.

"*Adios*," he told her, and left for the Saab down below and for the skies up above. On the way to the airport, in the backseat of the SUV, Adam reviewed his recent acquisitions. The flip phone fit neatly in the pocket of his khaki pants. He considered dialing his mother in Rhode Island, but upon realizing he had nothing rational to report, he just moved on to his next items: license (his photograph, Arvid Winkle's name and address) and credit card. His own credit card was in his wallet, in his car, in some part of the country he was determined to locate. Perhaps Ebbets had used his credit card? Adam promised himself to call American Express once he reached Las Vegas; if Ebbets had used his card, American Express would be able to track his location. Then there was his final item: the handmade cloth doll. A gift from David, the grieving ex-Mennonite. Adam held the doll close to his heart. It was a reminder of the only goodness to come, so far, from his misadventures.

"Oh shit," he muttered.

The State Police.

No doubt by now they had a warrant for his arrest. They would be looking in the airport for passengers fitting his description.

"Rolf," he said, "I need a disguise."

Rolf grunted, reached into the passenger seat and handed back to Adam a Philadelphia Eagles cap and a pair of wire-rim sunglasses. The sunglasses fit perfectly; the cap needed some adjusting. Rolf dropped Adam off at the airport and zipped away before any thanks could be offered.

Adam approached the closest airline ticket counter.

"Hi," he said. "Do you fly to Las Vegas?"

"Sir," the clerk did not look up from her computer, "we're British Airways. There is no Las Vegas in Britain."

Adam moved on to the next counter. This one had a five-person line, but it was for Continental, and Continental flew everywhere. Before long it was his turn at the desk.

"Hi," he said. "I'd like to buy a round-trip ticket to Las Vegas. First class. No baggage."

Two minutes later, he held a ticket and waited in line at the security checkpoint. Forty-five minutes after that, he was in the concourse and waiting for his flight.

To pass the time he bought a *Sports Illustrated* (and attempted to read it through the tinted lenses of his sunglasses). He ate an early dinner at a mini-TGI Friday's but only finished half his hamburger when his mind's eye flashed with images of Filbert's decapitation. He gave the rest of his food to a nearby family.

By 5:15 Friday evening, he was on board Continental Flight 251 for Las Vegas, Nevada. He had a window seat in first class and relaxed into its abundant cushioning. A maple syrup–hued woman in spectacles, with a dark pageboy haircut and a fat paperback, sat beside him. The plane taxied onto the runway, and then they were flying. Adam peered out the window and watched the city of Philadelphia fade into nothing but lights and lines. He missed his sister.

Then he felt the woman in glasses place something on his lap. Adam glanced down and saw a pepper shaker shaped like a chess piece, like a queen.

He looked over at the woman in specs, who smiled at him.

She removed the specs.

"So, Adam," said Cherry Sundae, with no hint of accent, "let's us have a real chat, huh?"

Chapter Eleven

Las Vegas, Nevada. Spanish for "the meadows." There has never been a hotel-casino on the Strip named The Meadows. There was, however, the Cosmos, a hotel-casino shaped like a NASA space shuttle. The Cosmos also boasted the Best Slots in the Galaxy. Adam and Cherry were on Floor J in Room 42 (J for Jupiter; 42 for the number, one would assume, between 41 and 43).

As Adam lay on his twin bed, flipping through hundreds of channels on Room 42's mammoth plasma TV, he glanced over at his companion, fast asleep on her twin and softly snoring. The pageboy wig she wore bounced up and down with each breath.

Who was this mystery woman, Adam wondered, and what was her real agenda here? He certainly had not expected to see her sitting beside him on the plane, and definitely had not expected the words out of her mouth to be English.

At twenty thousand feet, after several minutes of bewildered silence, he finally broke down. "So you're not Croatian?"

"I might be Croatian. My family tree's a little foggy around the roots." She picked back up the peppershaker from his lap and toyed with it and its salt cousin.

"You don't sound Croatian."

"Neither do you."

"I'm not Croatian. I'm from New Jersey."

"Vould you prefer I zveak my vords like thees and zound like Bela Lugosi?"

"No."

"Well, okay, then."

She slipped the shakers into her pockets and returned to her biography of Harry Houdini.

"But … I mean … you … and not to mention … I … but …who …"

His brain seemed to be short-circuiting. He took a breath, got a grip, sorted data, and posed the most important one of all.

"Cherry, what are you doing here?"

"Metaphysically?"

"No. Physically."

"I didn't want you to get lonely."

"You didn't want me to get lonely?"

"I'm very compassionate."

"Uh-huh."

The top-heavy stewardess popped her head in their row and took beverage requests. Cherry ordered a diet Coke. Adam ordered a shot of bourbon.

"Cheers!" smiled Cherry.

Adam downed his shot and clinked his empty glass against her half-filled cup.

"Cheers," frowned Adam.

Cherry shrugged and sipped at her drink.

Down below, twenty thousand feet below, Kansas and Nebraska went about their nightly business. Adam watched from the window. It all seemed so insignificant.

"I really do want to have a chat, Adam." Her hand brushed against his shoulder. "Filbert was my friend too."

"He didn't even know who you were." Adam stared at her reflection in the glass. "Neither do I."

Cherry tried a different tactic: "You know why I love clowns? They're always so damn happy. Some people are terrified of clowns, but not me. A clown's only purposes in this world are to be happy and to make others happy. What could be better than that?"

"It's unrealistic."

"That's the beauty of it!"

Finally, Adam faced her. "You want to have a chat? Let's have a chat. Filbert is dead. That cop back in Pennsylvania is dead. But all the time you're pretending not to understand a word of it."

"I'm sorry for that …"

"Oh, well, that fixes everything. Why didn't I think of that?"

"Adam …"

"You're sorry? Back at the rest stop, I told you what had just happened to my sister. Why didn't you say anything?!"

"I did drive the pickup," she muttered. "Look, believe me, I had my reasons. I have my reasons. It's just …" She retreated to her diet soda.

End of chat.

❖   ❖   ❖

The temperature in Las Vegas that evening, the Friday before Christmas, was a crisp sixty-eight degrees, but the cool desert winds, warned the captain over the loudspeaker, made it feel like sixty-three.

First class deplaned before everyone else; Adam waited in his seat for Cherry to get up and leave. Cherry waited in her seat for Adam.

Coach deplaned next; Adam waited in his seat for Cherry to get up and leave. Cherry waited in her seat for Adam.

The flight crew deplaned next. The top-heavy stewardess, eager to commence a night of naughtiness, stopped by Adam and Cherry's row and instructed them that this was, in fact, the airplane's final destination and they had to leave.

"She has the aisle seat," said Adam. "I'm waiting for her."

Cherry smiled, rose from her seat, removed her dainty grey suitcase from the overhead compartment and stepped back to allow Adam first passage off the plane.

The airport was stuffed with families, strangers, tourists and young adults hoping to win big. Friday nights in Las Vegas were long, open-mouthed moments of arrival, of promise, of opportunity. Adam followed the signs to Ground Transportation, and Cherry followed him.

"I think it's over there," piped Cherry. "Where Conan the Barbarian said Ebbets rented his truck."

To which Adam, who had been searching for that very location, grumbled, "I don't need your help."

"Consider it penance. For my earlier behavior. Besides, I know this town. Maybe you don't need my help. Maybe you don't want it. But this isn't about you or me. It's about your sister. Right?"

Adam sighed. Cherry was right. "Stay here," he said. "I'll be right back."

He approached the counter. The clerk, a boy named Dwight preoccupied with digging his index finger into his right nostril, waved at Adam with his free hand, finished his excavation with his other and then screamed, "HOW MAY I HELP YOU?"

"I ... why are you yelling?"

"IT'S LOUD IN HERE."

Adam looked around the airport. Busy, yes. Loud, no. "I need to inquire about a missing car."

"ARE YOU MISSING A CAR?" Dwight popped a wad of used gum he had been storing behind his ear into his mouth and handed Adam a form to fill out. "DO YOU NEED A PEN?"

"No, I'm—I'm not the one who's missing a car. You're missing a car. A pickup truck. The license plate is DJX512."

"DID YOU SAY DJX512?"

A few passersby glanced over to ogle at the ruckus. Adam sighed and nodded.

Dwight typed the plate information into his computer, inflated a gum bubble, sucked the bubble back into his mouth, and shook his head. "THAT'S NOT US."

"What?"

"I SAID ..." Dwight took a deep breath and bellowed, "THAT'S NOT US!"

"Are you sure? Because I think—"

"THAT VEHICLE'S OUT OF THE BRANCH ON CONTON. THEY'RE CLOSED NOW. DO YOU WANT THEIR PHONE NUMBER?"

"Yes, please."

Dwight scribbled the digits on his palm and then showed his palm to Adam, who copied the information on the back of the missing vehicles form.

"Thanks. Do you know when they open up tomorrow?"

"WHAT?"

"I said … never mind. Have a good night."

Adam wandered back to Cherry.

"Ebbets didn't rent the truck from this AutoMatic," he said.

"You know what you forgot to do, don't you?" she replied.

With a groan, Adam returned to the counter, where Dwight had resumed his nasal exploration.

"I need to rent a car," Adam said.

"WHAT?"

Twenty minutes later, "Arvid Winkle" and Cherry Sundae cruised down the electric streets of Las Vegas in a posh red BMW. Cherry clicked on the radio. Adam clicked it off.

"I want answers," he told her.

"How many would you like?"

"All of them."

They raced through a yellow light.

"Do you even know where you're going?" asked Cherry.

They raced through another yellow light. The neighborhood was quickly devolving from glitz to seed. No tourists roamed the sidewalks.

"Hang a left," said Cherry, "at the next intersection."

"Why?"

"Cause I know where we are and you don't."

At the next intersection, Adam took a right.

"Okay, fine." Cherry tugged on her seat belt, making sure it was secure. "Although I don't think you want to get pulled over by the LVPD, Arvid."

"Why would I get pulled over, Cherry?"

"You're driving a forty-thousand-dollar car in a twenty-thousand-dollar neighborhood."

Adam gripped the steering wheel. She was right.

"At the next intersection," she said, "hang a right. Please."

Adam complied. They sailed past a large pair of neon strip clubs.

"You need a guardian angel," suggested Cherry, smiling, "Desperately. Lucky for you I'm here. And yes, maybe I have something I need to take care of while I'm here, but I assure you, you won't be involved."

"Something you need to take care of?"

"I used to work here."

"As a clown?"

"Not exactly."

The light turned green. Adam punched down the accelerator and almost smashed into the Volvo in front of them.

"Want me to drive?" she asked.

"I'm fine."

"You're thousands of miles from fine, Adam, and you know it. And I know it. And I've got nothing better to do, so here I am."

"I don't even know who you are."

Soon they were back on Las Vegas Boulevard, surrounded by sparkle and glow. Traffic slowed to a crawl, braking for pedestrians, trolleys and sheer spectacle. The Sunset Strip turned everyone into a rubbernecker. They passed the three-faced skyscraper Mandalay Bay (and its own shark reef), the knights-and-damsels-themed Excalibur (and its jousting tournaments), New York, New York (and its mile-long outdoor roller coaster). Adam felt his jaw smack his lap.

"Not bad, huh?" teased Cherry.

Then he beheld it, a block away from the glitzy Mirage. The boy inside him wept for joy. The young man he had become got a little teary-eyed too. There, on the left, stood a NASA space shuttle. From aft to nose, the Cosmos Resort and Casino had to be thousands of feet tall. The landing pad on which it rested functioned as its parking garage. Adam swung a left and headed for space.

"Let me guess. When you were a kid, you wanted to be an astronaut."

Adam did not reply. He could not reply. He was in love.

The spacious lobby of the Cosmos was decked out in futuristic silicon, plastic and steel. Every few feet along the walls was a panel, its red buttons glowing in random sequence; every few feet along the ceiling, were tendrils of multicolor wiring, hanging down like vines. Mozart, via electronica, piped in from the speakers. If every bad science fiction film from the past twenty years had an orgy, the Cosmos Resort and Casino would be their progeny. Adam and Cherry approached the front desk. The concierge wore a bulky NASA spacesuit, *à la* Apollo 11, minus the bubble helmet.

"Greetings, earthlings," he said, "and welcome to the Cosmos."

Their hotel room, number 42 on Floor J, had Day-Glo wallpaper, and a label above each of the twin beds bragged that the mattresses were made of the same material used by NASA. What NASA actually used the material for apparently was irrelevant. Adam leapt onto his bed and giggled with glee.

"You did want to be an astronaut," said Cherry.

"Oh God, I so did. Like, ever since I was two. But I mean, every kid wants to be an astronaut, right? Either that or a fireman. I wonder why that is. Why do you think that is? What did you want to be when you were a kid?"

"I wanted to be a kid."

"Come on. You didn't have any aspirations? You didn't want to grow up some day and become, I don't know, a Spanish-speaking clown?"

Adam then remembered he was pissed at her and reached for the remote control.

He heard her plunk her suitcase on the floor and slink underneath her sheets.

Adam glanced over at his crazy companion. Her bare shoulder peeked from under her comforter, basked in green phosphorescence .

He clicked on the TV. Maybe there was a good ballgame on ESPN.

Something distracting. Right.

By one A.M. he was asleep.

He woke up around eight. The TV greeted him with an infomercial for BowFlex. He rubbed his eyes and looked over at Cherry but her bed was made and her suitcase was gone and so was she.

Chapter Twelve

After getting directions from the morning concierge, and buying a change of clothes from one of the many name-brand apparel shops inside the Cosmos, Adam was back behind the wheel, on the Strip, and heading toward the AutoMatic Rent-a-Car on Conton. The desert sun and relative warmth of the southwest provided an unnerving contrast to the white, icy December to which he had grown accustomed. He hadn't even needed to defrost his windows before departing the parking garage.

Adam's fraternity brother Ira Banner had been to Las Vegas a number of times. Ira Banner: he of the fridge-vomiting girlfriend, but also of the trust fund and fake ID, a toxic combination. While Adam, in his high school years, spent his winter vacation at home, reacquainting himself with eggnog and Xbox, Ira and his rich buddies from Lansing flew to Las Vegas and gambled.

"Time's not allowed in Sin City," Ira would regale between bong hits, "she just doesn't have the proper credentials. The casinos? No windows, no clocks. No holiday decorations or seasonal dishes. No Christmas ham in Sin City. But what do you expect, right? It's a fabricated world. It's like a pocket universe. Fuck, I love it."

Invariably one of the younger brothers would ask Ira how much money he had lost in Las. Ira would take another bong hit, for dramatic effect, and reply, "The most money I've lost in a single day? Well, I once lost eight thousand dollars in thirty seconds. Does that count?"

He would say it with pride, as if callowness were an achievement and foolishness an art form. Knowing he had their attention, he would then launch into the whole story.

"It was New Year's Eve and I was sixteen and I was there with two of my buddies, Sean and Ralph. Sean's dad owns a few factories out near

Flint and Ralph, well, Ralph was just Ralph. It's not important to the story. Although Ralph's the dude who procured the fake IDs. So we're staying at the Bellagio, real swank digs, man, and it's New Year's Eve and I'm so not wanting to watch some plastic ball drop down over Times Square. Been there, done that, so I head on down to the casino floor. *One* of the casino floors. Now what you got to understand is, everything exists on the casino floor to get you to spend your money. The slot machines are loud and simple and pretty, for those who like things loud and simple and pretty, and the roulette wheel spins round and round, for those who like things that spin, and the craps tables are always crowded, but craps are for loser tourists. I mean, the odds totally blow. The real gamblers play either poker or blackjack. Well, it's New Year's Eve and I don't feel like rubbing elbows with professionals, so I decide to test my luck with roulette. Big wheel spins, numbers 1 through 36 alternating red and black, you can bet a color, you can bet a set, or you can bet the big odds and put all your money on a single number. Well, I come up to the roulette wheel and wouldn't you know it, it's just landed on the number 16. My number. I'm 16. So I stand back and watch and people collect their winnings and more bets are placed and the wheel spins and—holy shit—16 again. I mean, come on. Naturally no one bet on it hitting the same number twice in a row. The dealer readies for a third spin and I take all my chips—eight thousand dollars—and put them all on 16. A hush. Everyone looks at me. What am I, stupid? No way it's going to land on 16 three times, they're thinking. Maybe. But that's not how roulette works. The odds are the same for every number every time the wheel gets spun. Fuck, it's middle school probability. And this wheel is fond of my number. I'd be stupid not to bet. So I sit my chips on my 16, red. No more bets. Around and around the wheel spins. White ball bounces around like a battered wife. Everyone's watching expectantly and everyone—everyone—is watching 16. There's an eight-thousand-dollar bet on the table."

"So what happened?" someone would ask, and the older frat brothers would chuckle and Ira would take another bong hit and sneer at the silly question and reply back:

"I started the story telling you I once lost eight thousand dollars in thirty seconds. What do you think happened, fool?"

As Adam navigated through downtown Las Vegas, he thought back to Ira Banner and his arrogant stories and his bitch of a girlfriend and the way he went out of his way to make everyone else feel just a little bit less. What a prick. But as Adam pulled into the AutoMatic parking lot, taking note of the silver tinsel and bulb strings, sure signs that time did, in fact, exist in this city, he also, strangely, felt his heart tug a bit. He missed that prick. He missed his brothers. He missed his life.

He walked into the Conton branch of AutoMatic Rent-a-Car determined to get it all back.

The shop was empty. Two desks for employees—no employees. Five vinyl seats lined up near the door for customers—no customers. A water cooler for thirst-quenching—no water. Then Adam heard the moans. Male. Intermittent. Not pain, exactly …

They came from behind the counter.

Adam approached the counter.

Another moan. Then a feminine squeal.

Adam peeked over the counter.

He found the two employees. He found their clothes too. The employees, a pair of young things, bounced off each other like paddleballs. Their clothes, scattered across the carpet, were at rest.

Adam pondered clearing his throat, changed his mind, sighed, spotted a bell on the countertop, picked up the bell, and threw it at them.

Their moaning and squealing abruptly ceased.

"I thought you locked the door," whispered the man to the woman.

"I thought you did," whispered the woman to the man.

"I'll just be over here," said Adam, and he plopped down in one of the vinyl seats. While the bunny rabbits dressed, he skimmed a brochure about air bags.

The workers popped back up, all clothed and tidied. His name was

Zed. Her name was Abilene.

"I'm really, really sorry," said Zed.

"Me too," said Abilene.

"So how may we help you?" they added.

Adam put down his brochure and re-approached the counter.

"A few weeks ago, or maybe a few days ago, this office rented a vehicle. A red pickup truck. License plate DJX512. The paint was flaking off of it."

Zed and Abilene nodded. Apparently they remembered the vehicle.

"Right, so, I'll put this as plainly as I can: I need to know everything you know about the person who rented that truck. This may sound ridiculous, but there are lives at stake. Really."

Zed and Abilene exchanged glances, and then frowns.

"Sorry, man."

"Can't do it, buddy."

"It's against the rules."

"We could lose our jobs."

Adam smiled at them, leaned in close. "Isn't it against the rules to have sex on the company floor during business hours? Couldn't you lose your jobs for that?"

Zed and Abilene took a moment to reflect on Adam's suggestions. Zed retreated to the restroom for a good long cry. Abilene sat down at her desk and typed information into her computer.

"Lock the door, would you?" begged Abilene.

Adam kindly complied with her request and sat down in the vinyl seat beside her desk.

"Okay, here we go: Ford F-150 rented last Thursday to a John Ebbets. Per rental agreement he was supposed to drop off the vehicle this past Thursday at our branch in Los Angeles ... let me see here ... nope, the vehicle has not yet been checked in at their lot. Your friend is going to owe us some money."

"He's not my friend. What else do you have?"

"What else do you want to know?"

"How did he pay? Cash? Check? Do you have a copy of his license on file?"

Abilene punched a key and her elderly dot-matrix printer spewed a page of pointillism. She ripped it off the roll of paper and handed it to Adam.

"There you go," she said.

"Thank you." He scanned the printout, pointed at the address on Ebbets' driver's license. "Can you tell me how to get there from here?"

Abilene scribbled out some directions on the back of the paper.

Adam thanked her and headed out to the front door to unlock it. "You can tell your boyfriend to come out now."

"He's not my boyfriend," replied Abilene. "He's my stepbrother."

"Okay then." Adam folded the printout, slipped it into his pants pocket, trotted out to his parked BMW, and did not look back, not even in the rearview mirror, as he merged with the traffic on Conton and followed Abilene's directions to 818 Brewster Lane, home of one John Ebbets, psychopath.

He flipped on the radio. Some Irish punk band was shredding "Let It Snow." When had Adam heard that song recently? He frowned, thinking. He knew it had been in the past few days. Not in the police station. Not on the bus or in any of the depots. Not in the bank. No, it had been in a car. His car, before he picked Anna up from Oberlin? No, he had rocked out to Zeppelin and The Who all through Michigan and Ohio. Anna hated hard rock. Anna really would have hated some Irish punk band shredding "Let It Snow." Anna. Anna.

The driving directions brought him from the gutted bowels of Conton Avenue onto the capped teeth of Brewster Lane, no more than three miles away. Every neighborhood in this city, it seemed, had two faces. Or more. Adam counted the numbers on the homes, easing off the accelerator as he reached the 800s.

At every inch, Brewster Lane breathed money. Lawns too green for December, they had to be bladed cash. Windows and shingles shone in the morning light like silver dollars. Houses standing two, three, four stories tall—what else could be stored inside such girth but rooms and rooms of money?

What, Adam ruminated, was a guy who can afford to live here doing with a beat-up rental from AutoMatic?

Then he remembered the bomb on the flatbed.

Then he remembered when he had last heard "Let It Snow." Wednesday night, during the blizzard. To cut the tension, he, Filbert and Officer Neal had sung "Let It Snow."

Now Officer Neal was dead.

So was Filbert.

"What have I gotten myself into?" whispered Adam. "Who's next?"

He wondered where Cherry was.

Spotting 818, he pulled the BMW to the curb in front of its spotless lawn. In front of the spotless lawn of Manor 820, an elderly woman in a bright yellow parka was painting her mailbox to match her canary outfit.

Adam felt insecure, ready to be found out for the fraud he was, but then remembered he had arrived here in a BMW. He waved at the old woman. She waved back.

He slowly moved up the paved walkway to the red front door—red like Ebbets' pick-up—of 818 Brewster Lane. His hand hovered before the doorbell. There were no cars in the driveway, but perhaps someone was parked inside the three-car garage. Perhaps someone with a gun.

The old woman made the decision for him. She called out from her mailbox: "Oh, are you a friend of Johnny's?"

And in two seconds, Adam had concocted a plan.

He casually strolled over to where she crouched and offered his hand in friendship.

"Arvid Winkle," he said. "And yes, I'm actually Johnny's cousin. From New York."

She put down her pail and brush and vigorously pumped his grip. "Oh! Pleasure to meet you, Mr. Winkle! I'm Sylvia Snow. I love your car. I just knew one of Johnny's relatives would show up here soon to take care of Bernard."

Bernard?

Adam nodded. "Well, here I am. Is Bernard home?"

"Oh no. Bernard's at the rink. Every Saturday and Sunday, eight A.M. to noon. Like clockwork that boy."

Boy?

"Well," said Adam, "I hear he does like his skating."

"Oh he loves it. Have you ever seen him? He's like a gazelle. Except wearing a scarf. He better be wearing a scarf. I knitted him a scarf. I even made it his favorite color. Red."

"Mrs. Snow ..."

"Oh please. Sylvia."

"Sylvia, I don't suppose you could tell me how to get to the rink?"

The rink lay within a mall and the mall lay several miles away, in the center of a rectangular parking lot roughly the size of Antarctica. On that Saturday before Christmas, the parking lot was stuffed with sedans, hatchbacks, compacts, towering SUVs, slender motorcycles and a fleet of family-friendly station wagons. Adam ended up finding a spot a good quarter-mile from the mall's front entrance.

Yes, thought Adam, time did exist in Las Vegas. Time and space and last-minute shopping at the mall. Away from the sparkle of Las Vegas Boulevard, this city was just like any other. Adam stuffed his hands into his pockets and trekked across the asphalt to the bright-eyed Benjamin Siegel Mall and Pavilion.

A thick glass wall, frosted for effect, marked the beginning of the rink on the third floor. On either side of the rink's double doors were long wooden benches, currently occupied by several sets of napping parents. As he entered the wide space, cold air smacked him like a barn door. Dozens of skaters, all ages, all sizes, raced across the massive white floor or sat in the bleachers in the cold, watching them race across the massive white floor. One of these dozens was Bernard. One of these dozens would lead him to Anna.

Adam scouted the stands for a young boy wearing a knitted red scarf, then stepped onto the ice.

"Yo!" beckoned a baritone from behind. Adam spun around and found himself face to face with a living tattoo. "No one on the ice without blades."

"No, I know, I'm just—"

"No exceptions, asshat."

So Adam rented a pair of figure skates (pink) and wobbled onto the rink. He gripped the four-foot wall for support. He hadn't been on ice skates in five years, when he'd briefly played hockey in a neighborhood league, and he felt as if he were walking on stilts. One-inch tall, razor-thin steel stilts.

As Adam meandered around the perimeter, colors whizzing past him, a Brahms waltz humming from subwoofers, he kept an eye out for Bernard. The boy had to be here. Sylvia Snow had promised.

"You need some help?"

A lanky black boy, maybe twelve years old, braked to a halt. His eyeballs were made enormous by a pair of bottle-thick glasses.

"Nah," replied Adam. "Thanks."

"Are you sure? You look like you're about to—"

Adam lost his grip on the wall and fell on his ass.

The boy helped Adam to his feet.

"Don't sweat it," he said. "Even the pros tumble every now and then."

"Is that what you want to be?" asked Adam. "A professional skater?"

"Among other things."

"Other things, huh?"

"Life's too short to limit yourself, right?" The boy winked at Adam and slowly skated away.

"Wait." Adam teetered after him. "Can I ask you a question? You come here a lot, right?"

"I do."

"Do you happen to know a kid named Bernard?"

The boy skated back to Adam and stared up defiantly into his eyes. "Who sent you? Child and Family Services?"

"You're Bernard, aren't you? I didn't recognize you without your scarf."

"I'll ask you one more time," Bernard growled, "who sent you?"

"I'm a friend of your father's."

"My father?"

"John Ebbets."

Bernard nodded, thought for a moment, and then sliced a steel-edged kick across Adam's chest. The skate ripped across Adam's shirt and several layers of flesh. Adam, stunned, tumbled back against the wall, slipped and fell flat on his back. The Brahms waltz continued.

Bernard placed the cold blade of his skate against Adam's soft throat.

"My father's dead," hissed Bernard. "Say hi to him for me."

The other skaters in the rink stared. Bernard noticed them, removed his blade from Adam's neck, bent down to Adam's right ear and whispered, "You still want to talk? Meet me outside by the first-floor loading dock in twenty minutes."

The boy then skated off the rink.

Adam remained on his back, still in shock. The gash across his pecs throbbed like a seismic wake. He dared not look. Slowly he sat up, reached for the wall and hoisted himself to his feet. Gravity pulled rivulets of blood down his chest and belly, staining his brand-new white shirt with fresh pinstripes.

The skaters gazed at him in hushed awe. No one offered assistance.

At the equipment kiosk, Adam traded his pink skates for his sneakers and asked the living tattoo where the first-floor loading dock was.

Once outside the unnatural chill of the rink, Adam's chest wound really began to sting and he knew he had to examine the damage. Bernard's skate had opened a foot-long crevasse across his pectoral muscles, splitting each nipple in half and exposing some very raw, very bloody sinew. Adam applied pressure to the wound, pressing his shirt against it, and felt light-headed. He ambled his way to the first floor, ignoring the passing looks from startled shoppers.

Back outside, Adam circumnavigated the mall to arrive at the loading dock, a large shadowy alcove in the back occupied by a rusted dumpster, a cement ramp, and, between the two, Bernard, awaiting Adam's arrival with arms crossed and lip curled. For a violent punk, the boy dressed well: plaid flannel top, khakis, hundred-and-fifty-dollar sneakers.

"I want an explanation," said Adam. "Then I want an apology. Then, maybe, I won't kick your ass."

"You had to ride the special bus to school every morning, didn't you?" Bernard brandished a small taser, pointed it at his guest, and zapped three hundred kilovolts into his nervous system until Adam collapsed to the pavement in a twitching semi-consciousness.

Chapter Thirteen

He awoke in a chair in a very hot room.

He smelled bubble gum.

His eyes were blindfolded. His wrists were bound with twine behind his back. He tried to scream, but his lips were sealed together with crazy-glue.

He panicked.

Time traveled forward. Adam couldn't budge at all. Bubbles of sweat skated down his cheeks, careened off his chin and landed with painful precision in the horizontal canyon across his upper chest. Each drop felt like a bullet, and he kept pulling the trigger.

He jerked his arms, but the twine handcuffs refused to give.

He heard his heart, flapping in his ears like hummingbirds. He tried to shout for help, but without the use of his mouth he sounded as coherent as a wounded dog. Behind the blindfold, his eyes welled with tears. More salty bullets for his gash to catch.

A door hinge squeaked.

Adam froze, listened.

A door closed.

Was someone there?

A sweat bead traveled down his left earlobe.

"Well," said a decidedly tea-and-crumpets voice, "this is quite a disgrace."

With a flourish, the blindfold was lifted and Adam saw, finally, the very hot room in which he was being held.

It was a kitchen. He was fastened to one of the four wooden chairs surrounding a nice pine table. The intense heat came from the oven behind him, before which the British gentleman, looking as dapper as he sounded, currently crouched, checking on a dessert.

"Oh, I don't think you would like this. Chocolate soufflé sprinkled with shavings of bubble gum. It's for Bernard. Tomorrow is his birthday. But you met Bernard, didn't you?" The gentleman sat across from him at the table. "I do apologize for his behavior. His first instinct has always been to treat strangers like enemies. My first instinct has always been to treat strangers like friends. Let me tend to that nasty wound on your chest."

He went to the counter and doused a purple dishrag with iodine. The reek of the chemical filled the room and Adam longed again for the scent of cooked bubblegum.

"This is going to sting like a son of a bitch, but it will kill any infection you may have." Once more the gentleman sat across from him at the table. "I'd ask you to hold still and not scream, but it appears our resident prankster has seen to that. Nevertheless, I will try to be gentle."

He dabbed the medicated rag against the cut.

For the next five minutes, Adam longed for death. His chest felt as if a swarm of tiny jaws from hell itself chewed away at each muscle and organ, licking and devouring in slow love. At times he felt his vision shimmer and dim. He wanted to scream—oh God he wanted to scream!—but all he could do was clench his teeth and flail against the inside of his mouth with his tongue.

Once finished with his dabbing, the British gentleman pulled a roll of tape out of one of the drawers and bound the iodine-coated purple dishrag to Adam's chest.

"Not quite the bandage you need, but it should suffice. Now let's take care of that mouth. Trust me, friend, you are not the first victim of Bernard's crazy-glue obsession nor will you be the last. It's not personal. By the way, they call me Fred."

British Fred perused the kitchen drawers for a remedy to Adam's sticky affliction. The gentleman moved with robotic precision, as if every gesture and glance were calculated and recalculated by a microchip hive in his brain. His features too were precise: careful angles along the cheeks and jaw, mustache brief and direct like a hyphen. He found an ointment in a drawer and spread a line of cold clear slime across Adam's lips.

"Give it a minute to work," said British Fred. "These things always take a bit of time. Meanwhile, I'm going to prepare myself some lunch. You must be starving. Care for a sandwich?"

Adam nodded.

British Fred meandered to the fridge and removed the necessary supplies: bread, corned beef, mustard.

"Thanks," Adam said, and then, realizing he could once again move his lips, smiled.

"My pleasure," replied British Fred, taking out a long butcher knife. He chopped the stuffed sandwiches into manageable halves.

"So I don't mean to be a pest, but, well, my hands are still tied behind my back. And I think my ankles are tied to the chair."

British Fred laughed. "You have a point there. I apologize. I can be so absent-minded sometimes. You know who absolutely never forgets anything? John Ebbets. He's got a mind like a sponge. But then, you know that. You're a friend of his. Want a pickle with your sandwich?"

"Yeah, about that," said Adam. "I'm not really a friend of his."

"No, I know. Otherwise you'd be aware he had no son, certainly not one like that rascal Bernard. Still, I am curious. How do you know John Ebbets? More to the point: how did you connect him with Bernard?"

British Fred set the two sandwich plates and the butcher knife on the pine table. He then filled two glasses with water.

"What happened was this," said Adam, taking a breath. "It's funny, really. Well, not funny. Not funny at all. I don't know why I said it was funny. John Ebbets held me up at gunpoint in a rest stop and ran off with my sister. All I want is to find them and save her. I came to Las Vegas because that's where he rented his truck."

British Fred sipped from his glass. "I see. And what truck would that be?"

At that moment, Bernard, hugging a laptop, rushed into the room, plunked the computer onto the table and pointed vigorously at the screen. Fred studied the screen for a minute, glanced up at Adam, back at the screen and then nodded. Bernard glared at Adam, picked up his laptop and stomped away.

"Big sale on ice skates?" asked Adam.

"I asked Bernard to run a check on the credit card and ID he found in your pocket. The information he ascertained has painted quite a picture. Tell me, Mr. Winkle: How did your boss find out about our project? Did Ebbets approach him? More to the point: What does your boss plan on doing with his recent thermonuclear acquisition?"

"Thermonuclear? Wait, you mean that thing in the back of the truck was a real bomb?"

"Don't toy with me, Mr. Winkle." British Fred leaned back in his chair. "The accomplishments of my small organization are just and humane. Each of us contributes unique skill sets and we are going to change the world for the better. In this country, states that have flexible gun laws have lower crime rates. We are applying a small-scale truth to the macrocosm. We are distributing our products, at a very reasonable fee, to small countries in desperate need of balance in a world that has become desperately unbalanced. For your employer to swoop in and take one of our products for his own taints the entire project."

"You keep using this word 'product.' What you really mean is 'bomb.'"

British Fred shrugged and nibbled on some corned beef.

"Twelve bombs. On the phone, Ebbets said twelve. And Ebbets stole one of them from you. Eleven atomic bombs. London, Paris, Moscow, Jerusalem—those aren't cities in small countries desperately in need of balance, Fred."

"I did my best to insure the products ended up in the right hands." His eyelids began to twitch. The rest of his body maintained its ice-cold composure but those eyelids started flapping about like bats. "Next time, I will not use unreliable middlemen."

"Next time?"

"We still have plenty of uranium," replied British Fred. "You don't need nearly as much as you would think to produce the desired effect.

And it's amazing what Bernard can obtain these days online."

"Okay. Fine. Live out your Dr. Strangelove fantasies. Whatever makes you happy. The world keeps turning. I just want to save my sister."

British Fred calmly finished his sandwich and wiped his mouth with a napkin. "Mr. Winkle, why did your employer send you here?"

"He's not my employer! I told you! I'm just here to find Ebbets and rescue Anna. My real name isn't Arvid Winkle. It's Adam Weiss. Look, have Bernard do a search on any outstanding warrants the Pennsylvania State Police currently have. He'll see my name."

"All that will prove, Mr. Winkle, is how dangerous you really are. I'm tired of having you in my kitchen. It will take me hours to disinfect it. It's time to transport you out of our lives. Please be unconscious again."

"What?"

"You can't expect us to take you there while you're awake."

"Sorry, Fred. I can't just will myself asleep."

British Fred sighed, nodded. "You're right. Bernard, could you please come in here again? Bring your stun gun."

Several hours later, close to dusk, Adam woke up face-down in a grease puddle near the dumpster behind the mall. He crawled to his feet. In the left pocket of his trousers he found a corned beef sandwich, sealed in a baggie, along with a note. Written on the note was one penciled word: LEAVE. In his right pocket he found his cell phone, credit card, fake ID, cloth doll, and car keys.

He tossed the sandwich into the dumpster, perambulated the mall to his parking spot a quarter-mile away, stopped, turned around, entered the mall, bought a new shirt at Abercrombie to replace his current one (which now displayed large stains both bloody and greasy), bought some actual Ace bandages at CVS to replace the purple dishrag currently taped to his chest, changed his bandages (and shirt) in the mall restroom, ate two hot dogs in the food court and then returned outside to his rented BMW and the plump, bedazzled darkness of Saturday night in Las Vegas.

He returned to his floor at the Cosmos.

His door was ajar.

Sounds of movement came from inside the room.

He wondered who the invaders could be. State troopers to arrest him? Swedish thugs to rough him up? More associates of British Fred to wallop him with stun guns and ice skates? So many enemies to choose from. Adam considered turning around, making a run for it. After all, he had nothing in the hotel room of value.

Except Cherry. If she was even there.

He pushed open the door.

The two dark-haired G-men scouring the room's sparse drawers immediately aimed their .45 pistols and FBI badges at Adam and, in duet, demanded that he freeze.

Adam froze.

The shorter of the two, Newton, rushed to the door and closed it. The taller of the two, Spate, kept his barrel fixed in direct line with Adam's forehead.

"On the ground," said Spate. "Face down."

Adam complied. Newton patted him down. It was not a pleasant experience. Newton removed the contents of Adam's pockets and set them on the nightstand.

"On the bed," said Spate.

"Face down?" asked Adam.

Spate did not reply.

Adam lay, face down, on his bed.

Then Spate asked him a question:

"Where is she?"

Adam turned his head on the comforter so that he could see the tall G-man. Spate, who now sat on Cherry's bed, aimed his .45 at Adam's forehead.

"Where is she?" he repeated.

"Who?"

"If I wanted to play games, I would've brought Monopoly instead of my gun. Where is she?"

"Who?"

"Just shoot him," inserted Agent Newton, from wherever in the room he was. "We'll write it up that he resisted a federal investigation."

Adam squeaked.

"We know that you booked this room last night," Spate continued. "We know that you booked this double room for you and a known felon. We know that this morning you left the hotel in your rented automobile. We know, based on the credit card you used to pay for your double room and your rented automobile, that you have ties to organized crime. We know you know where she is. Cooperate with us and we will cooperate with you."

"I honest to God don't know—"

Then Adam's cell phone buzzed.

"Who's that?" asked Spate.

"Is that her?" asked Newton.

"I don't know, guys," replied Adam. "I can't tell from where I'm lying."

The cell phone buzzed again.

"Answer it," said Spate. "But be smart."

Adam reached for the phone, flipped it open and held it to his ear. "Hello?"

"Hey Adam," chirped Cherry. "What's up?"

Spate's .45 glared at him.

"Oh, hi, Mom," said Adam. "How are you?"

A long pause. Then she spoke:

"Can you meet me on the gaming floor in thirty minutes?"

"Yes, Mom, of course. I'll remember to do that. Just because I'm on vacation doesn't mean I've forgotten my priorities. But you need to be a little more specific. Do you want a miniature slot machine or a miniature craps table or … I mean, they've got everything here."

"Just be on the floor. Doesn't matter where. Thirty minutes. I'll find you."

She hung up.

"Sure thing, Mom," Adam replied into dead air. "And don't worry about me. I won't spend too much money. I know that credit card is a loaner. Love you too."

Adam flipped shut the phone and set it back on the nightstand.

Spate glared at him.

"It was my mom," Adam said.

"Let me ask you something, kid. Do you think we're morons?"

"No."

Spate and Newton headed for the door.

"Where are you going?" asked Adam.

"By the slot machines."

"Or the craps table," added Newton.

"That's where we'll find her. Thanks, kid. And don't even think of trying to warn her. It's too late."

Spate and Newton left.

Adam sat up. His chest wound burned, his head throbbed, and the hot dogs from the mall swam a bit too rapidly in his belly.

He thought about Cherry. Or whoever she was. She certainly hadn't come to Vegas to be his "guardian angel." What she had been hiding from by hitchhiking cross-country in a clown suit had turned out to be the feds and they had found her. He had no doubt she was guilty of whatever crimes they had listed in her file.

He thought about Cherry. At the rest stop. Driving up in the pickup to offer him a ride. Coming up with the plan to rescue Officer Neal, albeit temporarily, from the teetering car. Lending him a silly hat in a blizzard. Cherry. In his seedy bathroom in Philadelphia, naked, vulnerable, wet. He thought about Cherry.

His cell phone rang again.

His heart leapt in hope.

"Hello." It wasn't Cherry. It was Yogurt. "I hope you're enjoying your sojourn in the American Southwest. My contacts have informed me that you still haven't picked up the parcel from Room 512 at Caesars

Palace. Please make sure you have it with you before you leave tomorrow night."

End of call.

Adam held his head in his hands. When would this madness end? Would it end in a thermonuclear inferno at midnight Christmas Eve?

Only four days away …

He dialed his cell phone. His real cell phone, which along with his real car and his real sister were in the clutches of a real madman named John Ebbets.

The phone rang and rang.

Then Adam heard his own voice mail message:

"Yo, what's up? Leave me a message. Don't leave me a message. Whatever. I got to pee."

Adam clicked off and sighed. He was out of options. He needed help and had no one to turn to. Anna would have known what to do. Had he been the one kidnapped, Anna would have figured it all out and had him rescued in hours.

And he knew he couldn't phone his frat brothers. Not on a Saturday night. Not during the annual Eggnog Chug-a-thon. Perhaps if he had been able to contact one of them on Thursday they might have been able to offer some assistance but now …

It was too late.

Adam launched himself off the bed, gathered his belongings, and headed for the elevator. Pouting in his hotel room accomplished nothing; the least he could do now was complete Yogurt's errand.

After Floor H (for Heinlein), an elderly black couple joined him on the elevator.

After Floor E (for Earth), the old man turned to Adam and said:

"This is our fiftieth anniversary."

Adam smiled back.

"We were married here fifty years ago today."

Adam nodded.

"There was a different casino here then."

Adam shrugged.

"There was a different country here then too."

Floor A (for Andromeda). The elevator doors parted. The old couple filed out.

"Best of luck to you," said the old man.

To reach the parking garage exit, Adam had to pass through the casino. Anything to create traffic on the gaming floor, mused Adam. Indeed, the place was jammed with howling lights and giddy tourists. The hotel's space-age theme revealed itself in the curved, silvery architecture of the tables and in the cocktail girls dolled up in skimpy, sequined lamé like characters out of a Flash Gordon serial. He wondered if Spate and Newton were here amongst the lambent rabble or if they had already captured their many-faced fugitive.

"Sir, would you like a drink?"

Adam shook his head and continued on his way. The waitress, with her tray, stepped in front of him, blocking his path.

"Follow me," Cherry said.

She led him to the busiest, most generic area of the gaming floor: the nickel slots.

"We don't have much time," she said. "I know they're here. Will you help me escape?"

"I don't even know who you are!"

"Sure you do. Both of my parents were born in a small village on—"

"The Adriatic Sea. I remember. I don't care. Who are you?"

A middle-aged man sitting by one of the machines poked Cherry in the arm, called her Babe, and asked for another Scotch.

"Sure thing, sir," replied Cherry.

Adam spotted Agent Spate no more than ten feet away, searching the room with federal eyes. Any minute now, he would find his quarry.

"Adam, please …" Cherry whispered. Her eyes dripped with tears, crocodile or otherwise. "I can't do it myself. I thought I could but I can't. I didn't want to get you involved. I swear. Will you help me escape?"

Chapter Fourteen

Cherry was a known felon on the run from the U.S. government. Given his circumstances, Adam really didn't have any choice at all. And he didn't like that one bit.

"Okay," he said, "how can I help you escape?"

Cherry smooched him flat on the lips for forty-five seconds. His toes curled. His arm hair curled. Even his chest wound curled a little, as their bodies pressed together in the center of the loud crowded arena of nickel slots. She smelled like sweet maraschinos.

Their lips and hips parted.

Adam's mouth curled into a big hug of a grin. "Okay, then. This is me helping you escape."

"Don't get cocky," drawled Cherry. "Pun intended. And don't fight with the security guard."

"The who?"

A meaty hand suddenly wrapped around his forearm. Adam traced the meaty hand to a beefy bicep to an absolutely bovine chest and head. The security guards at the Cosmos all wore white ceramic armor, appearing very much like George Lucas villains. This particular evildoer did not wear his helmet, but instead had his face and skull bleached white.

"Hands off the employees, sir," intoned the pale bull.

Adam backed away, glaring at Cherry. What had she gotten him into now?

"It's my fault," she answered. She drowned her syllables in Scarlett O'Hara. "I'm sorry. It's my first day. I guess I was too friendly. Please don't report it in." She then gave him a tight embrace, and planted a kiss on his chest plate.

The security guard, un-amused, returned to manning the Death Star.

Cherry leaned into Adam's ear and whispered, "Okay, let's go."

In her hands she flourished a purple card key, recently acquired from a faux albino storm-trooper. They scampered to a nondescript door that led to the closeted backrooms and serpentine hallways reserved for full-time employees. Cherry seemed to know her way and soon had navigated them out another door and into the concrete embrace of the parking garage.

They rushed to the third level, where Adam had parked the BMW.

"So on top of it all you're a pickpocket?" he asked, panting.

They reached the car, stuffed between a wide-bodied black convertible and a long-bodied tan station wagon.

"Give me the keys," Cherry said.

"What are you nuts?"

"You keep calling me names, Adam, and gosh, I'm going to have to start retaliating. The fact of the matter is I know the streets here a whole lot better than you do, and the casino's got cameras and they probably noticed our little trip through their forbidden alleyways so give me the keys, would you?"

Adam tossed her the keys.

They crawled into the vehicle.

Cherry shifted into reverse.

"You really should learn to drive a stick, Adam," she said. "Renting a Beemer with an automatic transmission is just plain sad!"

She stomped the gas pedal and they were off. The Sunset Strip sparkled at them with electric stars. They sailed west.

"So your reasons for coming to Las Vegas," mumbled Adam, "do they happen to include two assholes with guns?"

"I'm sorry. I really am. I thought you could do your thing and I could do my thing and … look, it will all make sense in a little while. I promise."

Soon enough, they had crossed the city limits and passed beyond the outskirts of neon civilization and entered the desert. Adam had never before been in a desert. He peered out the window and saw absolutely nothing. That was the desert: miles and miles of absolutely nothing under a canopy of vast, dotted blackness.

Adam felt impossibly small and curled up even smaller in his seat.

"You okay there, buckaroo?" She nudged him with her elbow. "Huh?"

"Did you just call me buckaroo?"

Cherry grinned and Adam felt a little less lost.

"My brother loved the desert," she said.

"Your brother?"

"His name was Erich. He was an illusionist."

"A what?"

"Sleight of hand. Hocus pocus. Abracadabra. He was one half of the Cockney performing duo Crowley and Moore."

Cherry opened her window. Cool air rushed into the car, turning her hair into a waving brown flag.

"What do you mean Cockney?" asked Adam. "I thought you said he was your brother."

"S'all in the presen'ation, briney-marlin."

"Excuse me?"

"Anyone can be anyone, darling," she answered, still grinning. "During the magic act, my brother Erich played the lead part of Crowley, the pompous know-it-all with the malapropisms and the unintentional gutter-mouth."

"Who was Moore?"

Her grin grew into a chuckle. She ran a slender finger across Adam's jaw. "I was Moore, of course. The wiser-than-her-years apprentice."

"So you were a magician."

"Actors go to LA to make it big. Magicians come to Vegas. We were raw and ambitious and willing to work long hours for little pay to get our foot in the door. More odds and ends. I took night classes in accounting. I was our business manager. We ended up with a regular gig at a small casino downtown called the Black Gold."

Her grin faded.

They traveled Highway 15 in silence. Even the wind had calmed to a whisper. Apart from the occasional cacti and sagebrush, and the infrequent appearances of cars heading in the opposite direction, Adam and Cherry were undeniably alone.

Adam once again felt uneasy.

"So where are we going now?"

"It doesn't have a name." She noticed his expression and added, "It's not far."

Somewhere not far, a coyote howled.

"Great," said Adam. "Mood music."

"Why don't I continue my story?"

"Please."

"Erich and I—Crowley and Moore—worked nights at the Black Gold. Our stage was about the size of this car. Maybe smaller. The rest of the room was round tables and round drinks and old alcoholics too drunk to applaud. But we had a regular gig. And we were good. Our stage patter worked. Our illusions worked. We always ended our act with our version of the bullet catch, even more impressive when, due to the size of our stage, the trick had to be performed at point blank range. We were invited into professional societies. We began to get a following. Young admirers began to join the old alcoholics at their tables, and fellow illusionists looking to copy the next new thing. To make ends meet, I worked days in the back office as one of the Black Gold's bookkeepers. Then the Black Gold got bought."

Cherry shut her window. Now not even the whispering wind provided a soundtrack. She continued:

"The Black Gold was bought by the Soak Entertainment Group."

"Soak? The porno company?"

Cherry stared at him.

"They make good films."

Cherry stared at him.

"I live in a frat house. What do you want from me?"

"So the Black Gold was bought by the Soak Entertainment Group."

Cherry sighed. "They weren't interested in a magic act, but they wanted to keep me on as a bookkeeper, at least during the transition, so they allowed me and my brother to continue performing. Every night we would appear at eight. At nine we were followed by a pair of top-heavy strippers named Barbie and Skipper. The Black Gold became seedy. The demographics of the audience changed. During our act they hooted and hollered for me to take my clothes off. Then the management pressured us to make the act sexier. We needed the money. We made the act sexier. One bit we came up with involved a few seconds of nudity. The management wanted sexier. We needed the money. Our reputation amongst our colleagues decayed. We started saving up. We were going to go to Atlantic City, make it there, and come back to Vegas in a few years revived and invigorated. We saved up, slowly but surely. Then Erich got sick."

"Sick?"

"The Black Gold had become a whorehouse. My brother took advantage. Since we were young, we'd been on the move. He never really had steady girlfriends. Now here he was, surrounded by beautiful women impressed by his charm. And he got sick. He didn't have health insurance. I had limited coverage through my job as a bookkeeper. I asked the owner of the casino for help. She asked why. I told her my brother was sick. She fired him."

"What a bitch."

"I got consumed with anger. It ate me up like a fire. I mean, I could actually feel it in my hands and feet, burning at my nerves. I couldn't think straight. My brother told me to calm down, but I couldn't. I wouldn't have known how or wanted to. Have you ever felt so much uncontrollable rage?"

"Yes," replied Adam.

Ebbets.

"Yes," repeated Adam, "I have."

"What I'm saying is, I wasn't in my right mind."

"What did you do?"

They came upon an abandoned filling station. Cherry pulled the shiny BMW up to an island of gutted gasoline pumps and shifted into park.

"We're here," she said and got out.

Adam joined her. The cool desert air traveled down the back of his neck like a team of spiders. He snuck his hands into his pockets and followed her to the rear of the rickety station.

"Far as I can tell," she said, "someone got the bright idea to build a gas station in the middle of nowhere, which is fine and almost smart except for one thing. No electricity. One night, I went through the casino's books and I fudged them. I falsified the numbers to make it look like they were laundering funds. Then I called the IRS."

"You didn't."

"I pretended to be a whistle-blower. I told them I knew the casino was improperly filing its taxes and I just couldn't have it on my conscience anymore and would they keep me anonymous and protect me and my brother and they said yes."

"So you found a way out."

"Yeah, I found a way out. And they found us. A few nights before I was to testify, Erich disappeared. I got a phone call to come out here if I ever wanted to see him again."

She led him behind the filling station, where someone had planted a knee-high cross of rotted timber into the ground.

"I snuck away from my protective service. Piece of cake for a Vegas illusionist. I came out here. They had already begun to bury his body. They were right. I got to see him again. One last time."

"I'm so sorry ..."

"I got back to town, gathered some supplies, and ran away like a coward. The clown bit came later, came from not being able to see my face in the mirror without ... and the thing of it is, it was the perfect disguise. Everything is hunky-dory to a clown, and even if it isn't, you never can tell because they're always smiling, always playing around. Hey, if you're going to escape, might as well go all the way, right?"

"What made you come back?"

"You did." The moonlight greasepainted her face. "The way you've … I mean, with your sister in jeopardy, taking the risks you have to rescue her … it reminded me of … gosh, would you look at that? Suddenly I can't talk. And when it turned out that you had to come here, to Las Vegas, well …"

"How did the FBI find you?"

"They haven't."

"But those two guys—"

"Spate and Newton? They're not FBI."

"They showed me their badges."

"And you can identify a genuine FBI badge?"

"Good point."

"They buried my brother. They work for Greta Luddell."

Cherry knelt down beside her brother's grave.

"Cherry, who's Greta Luddell?"

"She's the owner of the Black Gold. She's why I came back. To finish what I started. I got that crappy job at the Cosmos so I could find out what the word was on her—the back rooms of these places are hives of gossip. I thought I recognized one of the craps dealers, but I couldn't be sure. Turns out, he used to work for Greta too. The bastard must've remembered me."

Adam sat down beside Cherry and wrapped an arm around her shoulders. "Anyway, Adam, how did your search go?"

He lifted his shirt.

"Jesus! What happened to your chest?"

He told her.

"Well. Lady Luck has played cold with us today."

She lay down on the desert floor. Adam lay beside her. They eyeballed the cosmos.

"Do you believe in luck, fate?" she asked.

"I never gave it much thought."

Cherry slid her hand into his. "I think about it daily."

"Until the last few days, all I thought about at all was my frat, my friends, and my baseball game."

"You're a very shallow person, Adam," she replied sweetly.

"I am. I know I am. My sister is the deep one. She's the one with the ..."

"With the what?"

"I know who I am." Adam searched the stars for Filbert's Pole Star, their guide through the Pennsylvania woods, and found it twinkling right above them. They had come a long way since Pennsylvania. The Pole Star had not moved at all. "I know who I am."

Cherry kissed him on the cheek. She smelled like grenadine on ice.

They lay there for eons, fingers interlaced, faces aimed at the heavens. A young man. A young woman. The desert. A cool December night.

The young man rolled to his side, faced the young woman, and whispered in her ear:

"Let's have sex."

Cherry bid goodbye to tranquility, clocked Adam in the head with her elbow, sat up, and dusted the desert off her intergalactic uniform. "Way to ruin the moment, frat boy," she said.

They drove back to Las Vegas.

Adam leaned in to turn on the radio. Cherry slapped away his hand.

"Look," he said. "I'm sorry."

The city crested over the horizon like a bejeweled fist, forcefully glittering against a backdrop of blackness. Soon they would be within the city limits. Decisions needed to be made.

"So where are we heading?" asked Adam.

"At ten o'clock on a Saturday night?"

"Why not? They say it's the city that never sleeps."

Cherry smirked. "That's New York."

"They've got one of those here too. I saw it on the Strip. What do you say? You and me. With your tricks and my charm, we'll be unbeatable."

They entered the stream of city traffic.

"And how do you suppose we do this, Prince Charming? How are you and I going to bring down a casino boss and locate the global whereabouts of a crazy man from a group of people you've described as even crazier than he is? Do you have a plan?"

No, Adam didn't have a plan …

And then, suddenly, he did.

Chapter Fifteen

"Cherry, my absolute favorite Croatian-American clown-accountant," he said, his hands trembling with excitement, "do you know how to get to Brewster Lane?"

She shook her head. "Doesn't ring a bell."

He took out the driving directions Abilene from the Conton branch of AutoMatic had scrawled on the back of Ebbets' rental agreement. They sluiced the crowded streets of downtown Las Vegas, stopping at a laundromat for Cherry to pick up her stashed-away belongings, and rounded the incline leading up to chic Brewster Lane.

They passed an old lesbian couple walking their two Chihuahuas. The dogs' leashes and straps were diamond-encrusted. Adam had Cherry park the BMW several houses away from their destination: number 818, former residence of John Ebbets, current home to junior sadist Bernard.

"He probably has some kind of alarm system," said Adam. "He likes gadgets."

Cherry reached for her suitcase. "So do I."

They ambled across the street to the house with the red door.

"You try the front," Cherry suggested. "I'll go around back."

"I'm one thousand percent sure it's locked."

Cherry handed Adam a pair of thin metal rods.

"What's this?"

"Lock picks."

She bounded across the lawn and disappeared behind the house. Taking a deep breath, Adam climbed the walkway to 818's red door. The door indeed was locked. He glanced at the lock picks. Then back to the doorknob. Then back at the lock picks.

"What the hell am I supposed to do with this?" he muttered.

Shrugging his shoulders, Adam inserted the rods into the doorknob and jiggled them about. He turned the knob. It remained locked. He jiggled again. Knelt. Attempted to peer into the lock as he jiggled the rods.

"This is ridiculous. I'll never be able to—"

Click.

Adam stopped jiggling. Slid his hand over the knob.

It turned.

"Wow."

He pushed it open an inch. Then the door chain pulled taut.

"Damn."

Adam removed the lock picks from the knob, took a step back and assessed the situation. Was there any way he could use the rods to break the chain? Adam paced the stoop, weighing his options. He glanced back at the chain.

The chain had been removed.

The door was open.

Bernard, wearing Orioles pajamas and a little black pager, aimed his stun gun at Adam's sliced chest.

"You are a dumbass," observed Bernard.

"So are you," replied Cherry, appearing behind the boy. "Thanks for the diversion, Adam."

"Apparently it's what I do best."

Bernard caught a glimpse of the plastic orchid Cherry held in her hands and chuckled. "You're holding me up with a flower?"

"Oh, it's not just a flower."

It spat water over Bernard's hands.

"I wonder what will happen to someone," she said, "when they operate an electronic device while being hosed down with a highly conductive liquid. It sounds like a mighty interesting science experiment. Pull your trigger, kid. I'll pull mine. Let's see what happens."

Bernard lowered the stun gun. "A flower that squirts water. What are you, a clown?"

"Not currently." She winked at Adam and took the taser away from the boy. "Let's us have a chat inside like normal folk. Nice pajamas, by the way."

The living room was a ransacked convenience store. Paper bags and plastic wrappers formed a crunchy carpet. Pizza boxes and empty Coke cans served as wall sculptures. Most of the beige walls were spattered with various foodstuffs, although great care seemed to have been taken to spare the two red Christmas stockings, one labeled John and the other labeled Bernard, drooping below the mantel, and a king-sized poster, depicting an aerial shot of Camden Yards, hanging above the mantel.

"Orioles fan?" Adam asked Bernard.

"So? What's it to you?"

"I'm an Orioles fan too."

Bernard shrugged. "Whatever."

"You own an Xbox?"

"Of course."

"Played the latest baseball game?"

"Of course."

"On the hardest difficulty setting?"

Bernard stared at him. "No."

"I currently have my Orioles in the playoffs on the hardest difficulty setting."

"Bullshit."

"I bullshit you not."

Cherry loudly yawned. The boys ceased their yammering.

"So," she said, "let's talk."

"You here to kill me?" asked Bernard.

"No."

"Why should I believe you?"

"Which would you prefer?" asked Cherry, "That we're here to kill you or that we're here to talk?"

Bernard squirmed in his easy chair.

"Ebbets lived here with you," said Adam.

"So?"

"He took care of you."

"So?"

"You were close."

"So?"

"I think you know where he is."

Bernard replied with a glower.

"He has my sister," said Adam.

"So?"

"He stole a nuclear bomb."

"So?"

"He claims he has a device in his pocket that can detonate all the bombs. He claims that he's going to detonate all the bombs on Christmas Eve."

Bernard's glower lost some of its heat.

"Wait, wait, wait, wait," said Cherry, "so what Ebbets said is possible?"

Bernard turned away from them both. His hands had begun to shake.

And the light on his beeper had begun to blink.

"Adam, we got to get out of here."

"Not until I get my answers."

Cherry reached over to Bernard and snatched the beeper off his PJs.

"How long do we have?" she asked him.

The boy glanced up at her. His brown eyes were welling with tears.

"Ebbets is my friend," he whispered.

"Look, Bernard," said Cherry, "I'm sorry, I really am, but you sent out a 911 to your buddies, didn't you? They're on their way here right now to do some very nasty things to me and Adam, aren't they?"

Bernard nodded weakly.

"How long do we have?"

Four large tires squealed to a stop in number 818's driveway. Adam looked out the window. The tires were attached to a van. The van was piloted by a sumo wrestler. The sumo wrestler had an aluminum baseball bat.

Cherry slipped and slid her way across slippery streets of fast food refuse, slammed shut the front door, and refastened the slender gold chain.

"Call him off, Bernard!" Adam yelled. "We're not here to hurt you! Call him off!"

The doorknob rolled. The lock picks were still keyed into the lock. All that kept the door sealed was an emaciated link of chain.

Cherry took a step back and prepared the stun gun for fire. The sumo wrestler wedged the bat in the door crack and brought it down against the chain.

"Bernard! Call him off!"

But Bernard was off in his own sad world, tears flying down his cheeks and hands shaking like a pair of stuck engines. Every now and then his lips would mumble, "Ebbets is my friend ... Ebbets is my friend ..."

The sumo wrestler took another whack at the chain.

"Cherry, let's go. We can run out the back."

Cherry shook her head. "He's got a bat and he's got a van. You think you can outrun a lunatic in suburbia? Let him break down the door. I've got a couple thousand volts that just want to say hi."

"Cherry, you haven't seen the size of this guy. Zapping him will just make him angry."

The wrestler shoved his enormous bulk against the door, spitting splinters from the frame.

"Well, coming here was your plan, Adam. Do you have any ideas?"

Adam scanned the living room for something—anything—that could keep the beast at bay. They had maybe thirty seconds before bludgeoning commenced.

"Bernard?" called the wrestler. "You okay?"

Bernard was shriveled up in an easy chair. Bernard the street tough, Bernard the ice skater ...

Ice skater! Adam raced through the house. Where would this kid keep his treasured ice skates? Adam opened a door: a mauve guest room lay bare. Adam opened another door: mauve bathroom. Adam hopped up the staircase to the second floor and right there in front of him, door open, lights on, was Bernard's bedroom. Terabytes of gadgetry lay strewn across the floor. His precious laptop sat on his bed. His walls alternated NHL and MLB posters, except for a large framed photograph of Halle Berry.

The ice skates peeked out from underneath the bed.

Not far away, Adam heard the door crash in.

He grabbed the footwear and shuttled down the stairs. As he rounded the corner into the living room, the sumo wrestler was using his meaty forearm to pin Cherry by her neck against the wall. The other arm brandished the bat. The bat was raised to crash down on bone. Adam flashbacked to Filbert and the ax. He slipped his hands into the skates and charged at the sumo wrestler, yelping like Conan the Barbarian.

The wrestler swiveled his chunky skull in Adam's general direction; Cherry used the sudden opportunity to slam her left foot into his testicles.

The bat clanked to the floor.

Adam, still wearing his bladed mittens, stopped short and watched the mountain of a man topple onto the carpet and groan and groan and groan.

Adam glanced over at Cherry. "I provided another diversion?"

Cherry ran her hands over her bruised throat. "It's what you do best."

They both looked past the mountain at poor Bernard, still in shock.

"What do you want to do?" Cherry asked Adam.

"I don't know. I'm no psychologist, but that kid's majorly messed up."

"He thinks he's complicit," replied Cherry. "The weight of the world just came crashing down on his prepubescent shoulders. He can't help you, Adam. Not right now. We need to leave before the cops show up."

Cherry picked up the baseball bat and climbed over the fallen mountain and the fallen door and left number 818. But Adam had unfinished business. Amongst the garbage he found a green marker and used it to scrawl his cell phone number on the back of a Chinese takeout menu.

"Please," said Adam. "You can make this right."

Bernard didn't respond.

Thirty seconds later, Adam was back behind the wheel of the BMW; his mind, however, remained back in the house, and with the cold, glazed expression on the boy's face. It was the look of existential awareness, of recognizing just how in over your head you really were. He knew that glazed look. For the past few days, his face had held the same cold, glazed look.

"Where to now?" asked Cherry. Her voice seemed calm. None of the accusatory venom Adam expected to hear. Then again, nothing Cherry said or did was ever at all conventional.

Her unpredictability relaxed him. He could feel his grip on the steering wheel ease up. "I don't know," he said. "I guess since we struck out with my thing, we might as well take a crack at yours."

"How do you suppose we do that?"

Adam offered her a smile. "It'll come to me."

"Terrific," she replied. "Let me use this time to put on some body armor. Maybe rent a bazooka."

"We could always go back to the house and ask Bernard if we can borrow a nuclear bomb."

"Now that's a plan. Although we'd probably have to promise to give it back. He seems a bit possessive."

They entered the rumble and roar of downtown Las Vegas. The streets teemed with all manner of the nocturnal: punks, gamblers, prostitutes, policemen, indigents, tourists, gangs of would-be vampires, gangs of wannabe thugs. The real uglies didn't walk the streets at eleven P.M.; they walked the shadows.

"Are you hungry?" Cherry asked. "There's a parking lot right over there between that strip club and that greasy spoon. Let's get a bite to eat."

"What?"

Cherry pinched his right cheek. "You're so cute when you're retarded."

Adam parked the BMW between a Pinto and a Harley. Flickering bulbs on splintery wooden posts provided a lazy illumination.

"Are you sure it's safe here?" asked Adam. He tested all the doors to make sure they were fastened.

"Should be safe for another hour or so, and we'll be gone long before then." Cherry smiled at him. "What a worrier you are. Come on. Let's grab a burger. I'll buy."

They ambled into the tiny diner. A line of customers, mostly blue-collar men in their forties and fifties, occupied the counter stools. Adam and Cherry took a booth in the corner. A wave of *déjà vu* crested over him and he flashed back to a similar diner in the one-street town of Buchanan, Pennsylvania.

The waitress, a thirty-something blonde wearing a pink uniform and clunky boots, set their spots with utensils and napkins. "Know what you want?" A half-dressed Santa Claus was pinned to her lapel.

"Two burgers," Cherry said. "And fries. What do you want to drink, Adam?"

"Just a water."

"Just a water? Come on."

Adam couldn't shake that memory of Buchanan; it had become intermixed with that final glimpse of glassy-eyed Bernard. "Just a water," he repeated.

"Two waters," said Cherry.

"Two burgers, fries and waters coming up." The waitress thumped to the kitchen and placed their order.

Cherry picked up her fork and walked it across the tabletop. As it reached the edge, she let it drop.

"Suicidal cutlery," she said.

Adam shrugged.

She picked up the fork and wiped it clean with her napkin. "You're in a mood."

"I'm in a mood? Have you not been paying attention to my life? Every hour it gets stranger and more out of control. I'm supposed to be in New Jersey right now."

"Doing what?"

"I don't know."

"Hanging out with a friend? Having a late snack at a diner?"

"Maybe."

"Well, then, how's this so different?"

"It's different."

"Your life's just gone off the rails for a bit." She balanced her spoon on the tip of her nose. "Take advantage."

"Take advantage? My sister could be dead!"

"My brother is dead. I took you to his grave. It breaks my heart in ways you can't even begin to guess, but I'm here with you and I'm going to have a burger and fries and they're going to be greasy and I'm going to like it because that's all life is. A series of moments strung together without meaning or purpose, and in the end we all die. Your sister, my brother, you, me. So take advantage." The spoon bounced off her nose and tumbled into her lap. "Or don't."

Again, Adam shrugged. Around him, middle-income locals savored their hot meals. The only people who seemed out of place, other than Adam and Cherry, were a pair of business casual women, mid-30s, sitting across the diner in the other corner booth and chatting up the blonde-haired big-booted waitress. On the other side of the pane-glass window walked countless pedestrians heading toward their personal destinies. No, Adam did not believe life was meaningless. He refused to believe it. This—all this—was just life's way of kicking him in the ass for being such a lazy son of a bitch.

The waitress returned with their food.

"Looks great," said Cherry. "Smells even better."

"Enjoy," the waitress replied, and turned to go. Then she stopped, pivoted and added, "By the way, the ladies over in the other booth wanted to give you this. They said you'd know what it meant."

She placed two thin leather billfolds on the table and walked away.

Adam and Cherry stared at the billfolds, then at each other, then over at the pair of women (a short-haired Asian and a long-haired WASP) in the booth across the restaurant, who were each enjoying some pie, then back at the billfolds.

"What is it?" asked Adam.

"I don't know," answered Cherry. "Open them."

"Do you recognize those women?"

Cherry looked again. "No."

"I'm going to do it." Adam reached over to the soft black leather and flipped them open, revealing the badges and ID cards for one Kim Chang and one Elyse Epperson, Special Agents, Federal Bureau of Investigation.

Adam's mouth went dry. "Are these real?" he asked Cherry.

"Yeah," she replied, sinking in her seat. "They're real. And we're fucked."

Chapter Sixteen

"Should we make a run for it?" asked Adam.

Cherry and Adam glanced across the diner. Special Agent Chang and Special Agent Epperson raised their cups of coffee to them in salute (thus revealing shoulder holsters plump with handguns).

"No," Cherry replied to Adam, "I think running is not an option. The question is: are they here for you or are they here for me?"

"What do you mean?"

Then Adam realized what she meant. The Pennsylvania State Police had a warrant issued for his arrest. By now they must have suspected he had crossed state lines, which made his case the responsibility of the FBI. On the other hand, Cherry had been working with the federal government to bring down the Black Gold Casino when she skipped town, donned a clown suit and vanished. Undoubtedly, they wanted her back.

"Well," said Adam, "which one of us are they looking at?"

"I'm deliberately avoiding their gaze."

"You're the one who's facing them."

Cherry slinked down in her seat. "Now you're blocking their view."

"Cherry, a minute ago you told me how I need to 'take advantage.' Now you're six inches away from hiding under the table! We can't just sit here at our booth and wait them out."

"I have no problem with waiting. I'm a very patient girl. And I'm comfortable." She reached up, snatched a pile of fries from her plate, and shoveled them into her mouth. "Mmm. Fries."

Adam picked up the badges and rose.

"What are you doing?!"

"Resolving this."

He walked the tiled floor of the tiny diner. Every step brought him closer to the women's booth. He passed the door. Outside, a pair of young couples laughed over a joke. He approached the federal agents. They watched him. They took a break from their pie. It was peach pie. Special Agent Chang had eaten most of her slice. Special Agent Epperson had barely touched hers. They watched him not with their heads but with their eyes and with their hands. Their handguns slept nuzzled in front of their beating hearts. Adam now stood mere feet from where they sat. Special Agent Chang scooted to the window. Adam sat down next to her. He placed their badges on the table.

"Hi," he said. "What's up?"

They pocketed their badges.

Then Special Agent Chang replied:

"Want some pie?"

Adam shook his head.

"You like the pie here?" asked Epperson.

"It's delicious!" answered Chang.

"The filling is processed."

"I'm a product of my generation. I like processed food."

"I'm the same age as you."

"Yeah, but you're Episcopalian."

"True." Agent Epperson frowned. "True."

Special Agent Chang finished her plate, turned to Adam and said, "Finish your meal. Leave your waitress a nice tip. These women live off their tips. Then the four of us will go next door where we can talk in private."

"Want to finish my pie?" asked Special Agent Epperson.

Adam shook his head.

"Well, I offered."

He returned to Cherry and updated her on their situation.

"So which of us are they here to collar?" she asked.

"They didn't say."

"Sneaky bastards."

"You need to calm down."

Cherry slammed down her water glass. "Don't tell me to calm down!"

"I thought you came back to this town to set things right."

"Not with the Feds. With the casino. I don't want to have anything to do with the Feds. They let my brother die. We were supposed to be in protection. They let him die. I'm not afraid of the Feds, Adam. I hate them."

"Well, we're going to talk with them." Adam picked at his food. His stomach was in hiding. "We don't have a choice. I haven't had a choice in days."

Adam put their meal on his credit card and they followed the FBI agents next door to a male strip club. Red and green spotlights danced across the spacious room to the loud thumping beat of Euro-pop. Bodybuilders in Speedos boogied on white platforms surrounded by middle-aged women waving five-dollar bills. The agents led Adam and Cherry to a leather booth not unlike the ones in the neighboring diner. Their waiter, Jorge, wore a purple jock strap. Special Agent Chang ordered a round of Shirley Temples for the group.

"So," she said, "what is your connection to the Engles Group?"

Adam frowned. "The who what?"

Jorge returned with their drinks. For Special Agent Epperson, he added a toothy grin. When he walked away, his bare ass cheeks swished back and forth like window washers.

"Why do they always flirt with you?" asked Chang. "Is it the blonde hair?" She turned to Adam. "Is it the blonde hair?"

Adam shrugged.

"No. Honestly. What is it? This one hates sex and men are always throwing themselves at her. I'm a nymphomaniac and no guy even looks at me twice."

Adam blinked. "You're a nymphomaniac?"

Cherry kicked him under the table.

Special Agent Epperson whipped her long blonde hair around, reached into her side bag, and removed four glossy photographs. She spread them out on the table. They depicted Adam chatting with Sylvia Snow while she painted her mailbox; Adam and Cherry skulking around number 818's yard; Adam applying lock picks to the red door; and the sumo wrestler attacking the door several minutes later with his baseball bat.

"They say every picture tells a story," said Special Agent Chang. "Why don't you tell us this story?"

Suddenly the music from the speakers cut off. A spotlight blazed across the room and focused its beam on the club's main runway.

"Ladies, it is time," boasted a female announcer, "time to see what you came to see and enjoy what you came to enjoy. It is time to feast your imaginations on the abs made of granite, an ass carved from marble, and, ladies, these are not the only rock-hard attributes our main attraction sports. I present to you, the star of our show, Rocky Roman!"

The crowd screamed. A microphone rose up from the stage. Rocky Roman emerged from behind the curtain. Top hat, tuxedo with tails, polished black shoes—he looked like he had just fallen out of a thirties musical. He swaggered up to the microphone and did a baritone rendition of "Santa Baby." Twenty seconds into the tune, he peeled off his gloves and tossed off his hat. The crowd screamed some more. The stripping had begun.

Adam felt homophobically nauseous. "Why are we here?" he asked.

"Anonymity," replied Special Agent Chang. Her gaze followed Rocky Roman up and down the runway. "Everyone's paying attention to the show. Nobody's paying attention to us. So feel free to say anything you want."

"Why don't you start with explaining these photos?" added Special Agent Epperson.

Adam glanced to Cherry for help. She pretended to enjoy the performance, but he could tell her mind was elsewhere. He reached under the table and squeezed her hand. She looked over at him and offered a small grin.

"You are aware that it is illegal in the United States to traffic nuclear materials without a special permit," said Special Agent Epperson. "You are aware it is especially illegal to traffic nuclear weapons. This evidence proves a relationship between you and the Engles Group. You should tell us what this relationship is. Tell us and we'll go easy on you. Refuse to cooperate and, well, plan on spending the remainder of your days in a federal penitentiary."

On stage, Rocky Roman had segued into a bluesy "Jingle Bells." He flung his necktie into the estrogen-laden throng. The woman who caught it leaped up and down with frenetic glee, as if she were the next contestant on *The Price is Right*.

"This is a one-time offer," said Special Agent Epperson. "Work with us now or go down with the ship. You need to make a choice. Make the right one." Then Adam's cell phone chirped. He hadn't heard it above the hooting and the music but Cherry had and she picked it up on the second ring.

"Hello? Yes, he's right here." She handed Adam the phone. "You need to take this. It's your little brother."

Adam looked to the Feds for permission. Special Agent Chang remained preoccupied by the strip show, but Special Agent Epperson frowned and nodded.

"Why don't you go over by the restroom?" suggested Cherry. "You can probably hear better there."

Adam looked to the Feds for permission. Special Agent Chang remained preoccupied by the strip show, but Special Agent Epperson frowned and nodded.

"Don't try anything," she warned. "We're not the only agents in the vicinity."

Adam wandered over to the relatively quiet alcove by the restrooms and placed his phone to his ear. "Hello?"

"You got to promise me you won't hurt Ebbets," Bernard said.

"I promise," said Adam. "I just want my sister back. I swear."

Bernard sighed. "Because I've got your personal information right here on my laptop. You hurt my friend and I will bring the pain twenty-first century style."

"Understood," Adam replied.

A pair of hot-faced women rushed past him and pounced into the ladies' lavatory.

"By the way," said Bernard, "I thought it was cool what your lady friend did to Jimmy Ha. Like out of a movie. So what's the game plan, chief?"

Adam stepped aside as Filbert passed him, heading for the men's room.

Filbert?

"Filbert?" Adam reached out to him before he disappeared into the bathroom. Same big coat, same Neanderthal posture, same hair …

The man spun around. This was not Filbert. This man had green eyes, close together like a pair of dice. A curlicue scar snarled across both cheeks. This was not Filbert.

"Sorry," said Adam. "Sorry."

The man grunted and went about his business in the strip club's lavatory. Adam sighed. Filbert.

"Hey," Bernard shouted, "you still there?"

"Yes. Sorry. I thought I saw someone I knew."

Filbert.

"Whatever. So what's next? What's the call?"

On stage, Rocky Roman popped the black buttons off his ruffled white shirt. Adam sat down on the floor. What was the call? What was the game plan? He now had Bernard in his corner, but ten feet away sat the FBI.

Adam thought again about Filbert. Poor Filbert. Poor headless Filbert. Leading them through the woods. Getting them out of Buchanan. Filbert the Decisive. Connecting them with—

Adam's pupils dilated. His limbs tingled.

He had a plan. A very Filbert-esque plan.

"Well?" said Bernard. "I'm waiting."

So Adam told him his plan.

It took two minutes. In the meantime, on stage, Rocky Roman whipped off his Velcro-sealed pants and rotated his Speedo-encased hips to a curiously come-hither version of "Santa Claus is Coming to Town." The crowd ate it up. Everyone except Cherry, who ogled her drink, and Special Agent Epperson, who ogled Adam.

"So, Bernard," Adam inquired, "is that doable?"

On the other end, the boy sighed. "It'll be complicated. But I can totally make it happen. I'm a genius. You're the one who has the tough part. You're a moron."

"Okay, okay. I'll call you tomorrow morning."

"Hey, listen, Arvid."

"Yeah, Bernard?"

"Never mind. I'll talk to you tomorrow."

Click. End of conversation.

Adam wandered back to the booth.

"How is he?" asked Special Agent Epperson.

"Hm? Oh, he's fine."

"Your younger brother?"

"Mm-hm."

"What's his name?"

"Filbert."

Cherry glanced up from her glass.

"How old is Filbert?" asked Special Agent Epperson.

"Twelve."

"Isn't it a little late for him to be up?"

"It's Saturday."

To a symphony of cheers, Rocky Roman finished his act and strutted offstage. The Euro-pop returned to the speakers, the male go-go dancers returned to their platforms, and Special Agent Chang returned her attention to Adam and Cherry.

"Well?" she asked. "What's it going to be? Are you ready to talk?"

Adam nonchalantly squeezed Cherry on the knee and replied, "Yes. Yes, we are."

She squeezed him back. Not on the knee. His future grandchildren wept.

Special Agent Epperson collected the photographs off the table, slid them into her valise, and took out her tiny tape recorder.

"Will that work in here?" asked Adam. "I mean, with all this noise?"

Epperson poised the recorder by her lips, introduced herself, the date, the time, and then positioned it near Adam's lips.

"State your name," she said.

Adam picked up the recorder. He watched the tape wheels slowly whirl.

"And remember," added Chang, "you really don't want to offer false testimony to the FBI."

Adam nodded.

Cherry frowned.

He began:

"My name is Arvid Winkle. My employers discovered that a secret group of communists known as the Engles Group was quietly manufacturing and selling nuclear bombs on the black market. My employers decided to acquire one of these nuclear bombs for their own personal use and commissioned myself, and my associate Fiona, to arrange this transaction. We ran into a few snags in the negotiations and were briefly accosted tonight by one of the Engles Group's enforcers, but we are confident that the sale will continue as planned tomorrow afternoon."

"Who is your employer?" Special Agent Chang leaned forward. "Where is this sale going down?"

"Our employer is Greta Luddell," answered Adam, keeping one eye on Cherry, "owner and operator of the Black Gold Casino in beautiful downtown Las Vegas."

Chapter Seventeen

Adam missed his two beds. His bed at school was a cushy queen-size he and his brothers had "acquired" last summer from rival fraternity Lamda Epsilon Epsilon. He loved his bed at school. He loved how the mattress contoured to his body (and left an impression of every female guest he entertained). Most nights, he just loved lying diagonal on his bed at school, confident that his feet were in no danger of dangling over the edge, safe from the monster under his bed. His bed at home, back in New Jersey, was much smaller, older, harder and meaner, but it was his bed at home, and he missed it desperately.

He reflected on his two beds as he lay down on a third, a well-groomed twin whose forest-patterned sheets smelled of Lysol and latex. He and Cherry had taken a second-story room at a two-floor, all-stucco motel near UNLV. He was beginning to loathe motels and their indifferent, interchangeable beds.

He turned on his side and peered out at the slender back of the woman perched on the balcony. Right now she was none too pleased with him. He wanted to roll out of bed, amble to the balcony and plop himself next to her on its raised stucco wall but no, he remained idle on his indifferent, interchangeable bed.

Given that his plan contained the distinct possibility of their painful deaths, she had not taken news of it very well.

After making arrangements for tomorrow's sting operation with Special Agents Chang and Epperson, Adam and Cherry left the strip club and motored around Las Vegas for a discreet motel in which to spend the night.

"We can put you up in a safe house if you want," Special Agent Chang had offered, to which Cherry had emphatically replied, "No."

This was her only contribution to the conversation.

Adam sat up in his motel bed. The digital clock on the nightstand read 2:38 A.M.

"Cherry," he said.

She must have heard him. The balcony was only ten feet away. She must have heard him. But she did not even turn her head.

"Cherry," he said, "please. I don't know what I did, but I'm sorry."

Her dark hair curled a bit in the evening breeze, but the rest of her remained immobile.

"Cherry," he said again and then gave up. He pulled himself out of the bed and strolled into the bathroom. The bandage over his chest appeared clean; his wound must have scabbed over. Soon it would itch.

He slipped into his clothes and headed for the door.

"I'm going to get a snack from the vending machine." He did not turn around. "Do you want anything?"

Silence.

As he headed for the soda machine by the stucco stairwell, Adam found himself consumed by a thirst to know what Cherry was thinking. Was she contemplating another fast escape? Surely their re-acquaintance with the FBI tonight had stirred memories already cooking in her mind at a rapid boil. Still, she claimed that this was why she had returned to Las Vegas: to avenge her brother's death and bury the Black Gold Casino. Hadn't he concocted tomorrow's wildly improbable plan for her?

Maybe she was so overcome with gratitude that she couldn't handle it. Maybe that's why she refused to speak with him.

Yeah, right.

Arriving at the soda machine, Adam searched his pockets for coins but then recalled that his wallet was in his car and his car had been hijacked by a nuclear lunatic. Silly me, he thought. He stared at the machine and sighed. Silly me. Standing there foolishly helpless in front of the simple machine, Adam suddenly felt six years old. Ah, six. Not a care in the world at six. Although that wasn't quite true. Even at six, Adam had cared—had cared a lot—what his father thought of him. Fetus Adam had probably made sure to emerge from the birth canal before his twin sister just to please the old man.

His father.

And one summer, when he was six years old, one weekend, his father had asked him if he wanted to join him for some food shopping, and that day he had battled a soda machine, a cousin to this one here in Nevada.

Two years had passed since the morning his mother had temporarily "abandoned" him in the cereal aisle; his fear of grocery stores had subsided. Also, he knew that if he accompanied his father, he stood a better chance of choosing one or two items he liked. Maybe, while waiting in the checkout line, Dad would even get him a Snickers or a Three Musketeers. It was a leafy Jersey autumn, and the Weiss men were going to the local A&P to buy groceries.

His father asked him if he wanted to ride in the cart. Adam did, he really did, but he also wanted to impress his father and act like a big boy so he said no. They walked side by side, hand in hand, down the aisles. His father's hand smelled of motor oil. The smell made Adam feel … comforted. They filled up the cart with the varied staples on their list— bread, butter, apples, bananas, cereal, milk, eggs, frozen dinners—and paid for it all by check at the cash wrap. Adam was too shy to ask for a candy bar. On the way out, Adam's father angled the cart toward the row of vending machines lining the front of the store.

"Pick one thing," he said.

"Really?" Adam beamed. "Anything?"

"Sure. You're my big helper today."

Little Adam surveyed the four vending machines. One for Coke products, one for Pepsi, one for juice and one for candy. So much variety! So many delicious items to choose! This was his reward—he had to choose wisely. If he picked something childish, his father would think he was immature and wouldn't want him to be his big helper ever again.

Standing on the second-floor of the cheap motel, lost in his thoughts, Adam could not remember what item he chose. Had it been a candy bar to sate his cravings or a root beer to please his father? His father loved root beer. Frothy, syrupy root beer. He drank root beer with his morning eggs. His father. Adam missed him and hated him and wished he were there beside him so they could hug and wished he were there beside him so they could argue. They had much to hug and argue about. So many questions needed answering. Adam realized then and there that Cherry was not the most inscrutable person he had ever met.

Sitting there on that balcony edge, was she contemplating suicide?

On that leafy autumn day, Adam probably had selected a root beer. A&W. These two machines here in Las Vegas didn't offer any brand of root beer. One provided a paltry selection of flavored iced tea, priced from ten years ago, while the other displayed empty rows and chewing gum. A pauper's pickings, and Adam unable to scrape up a dime to save his—

A hand clawed the back of his collar and yanked him off balance. He tumbled, tumbled. The hand retained its grip on his shirt and dragged him down the stucco stairs—thump, thump, thump, thump. He felt the flesh along his shoulders shred into ribbons. Adam struggled to regain control, but his assailant was too strong and moved too quickly. They reached the parking lot and he was tugged along like a little boy's wagon. Pavement scraped across Adam's back and legs. His shirt became untucked. The cold concrete chewed at his exposed skin. Blood seeped out and dirt caked in.

In the moonless darkness, Adam could barely make out the features of the tall man. He flailed his arms about, but his efforts accomplished nothing. The tall man was the crazed captain, Adam the helpless wrecked vessel. Finally they reached their destination: a black Buick sedan. The tall man let go of Adam's collar.

It was Spate, one of the faux FBI agents who had accosted him back at his hotel room at the Cosmos. Spate raised his booted foot and gently pressed it down against Adam's bandaged diaphragm.

"You're a dim bulb," he said. "You know that?"

Adam coughed up some dirt. "I've been told."

"Using that credit card to book this room. Could you have made tracking you any easier? Me, I like a challenge, but our boss don't, and so here we are. My partner's taking care of your lady friend. Boss wants her taken in alive. About you, we have discretion. That's why my partner's the one up there and I'm the one down here. I like discretion."

"Fuck you," replied Adam.

Spate crawled his booted foot up Adam's chest to his chin, lips, nose. He pressed down on Adam's nose. Adam howled into leather. The boot lifted from his face, drawing with it a drool of red from both nostrils.

"Are you left-handed," asked Spate, "or right?"

Adam, moaning, wiped at his bruised, soiled face.

"Are you left-handed," repeated Spate, angling his heavy boot over Adam's genitals, "or right?"

"Left! Left!"

Spate nodded and grabbed Adam's left wrist.

"Sadism's not unnatural," he calmly explained, opening the Buick's front passenger door. "Mercy's unnatural."

He placed Adam's limp left hand at the edge of the door opening and held it steady with his own firm grip. His right hand held the door itself. He gently touched the car door's steely edge against the bones of Adam's left hand, and then pulled the car door back.

"You may want to close your eyes," said Spate.

Adam struggled, shrieked. His gaze stayed fixed on his trapped left hand.

"Oh well," said Spate, and he shoved the car door shut.

Adam was pre-med. He knew anatomy. The cluster of bones located between the fingers and the forearm were known as the metacarpus, as in carpal tunnel syndrome. These five bones were oblong in shape and quite thin. They really were nothing more than five slender strips. When the car door slammed shut on his left hand, Adam's rational mind was able to identify and diagnose the cracking sound, which sounded very much like a stack of potato chips being chomped. Adam's rational mind, however, currently was being overwhelmed by the irrationality of his situation, and all he could really think was this:

FUUUUUUUUUUUUUUCK!

Spate opened the car door. Adam's hand was barely in one piece.

Dozens of slender, bloody bone shards jutted out like wet pins through the purple-black soup which used to be his palm. Adam cupped his left wrist in his right hand and clenched his teeth so hard that he popped his eardrums. He could not scream. He could not cry. He could only breathe and stare and breathe and stare and rock back and forth, back and forth.

"Now, my friend," Spate muttered, "you're right-handed."

Adam rocked back and forth, back and forth. His breathing sputtered. His arms—both of them—shook and his senses began shutting off. First his taste. His tongue swam without a mission around the inside of his mouth. Then his hearing, but his eardrums already had ruptured over thirty seconds earlier.

Then Spate crumpled to the ground. The left side of his skull lay open like a freshly-unsealed can of tomato paste. Cherry stood beside him, holding Jimmy Ha's aluminum bat. The bat dribbled Spate-gore onto the parking lot pavement.

Cherry said something to Adam, but he couldn't hear her.

Cherry touched his shoulder, but Adam couldn't feel her.

It was her scent that awoke him. Cooled maraschinos.

"Cherry?" he muttered. His eyes found hers. "Cherry?"

She helped him stand.

"Everything's going to be okay," she said. And he believed her.

They made their way to their BMW. Cherry gently laid him in the back seat.

"My keys ..." he blurted. "My phone ..."

"Shhh. Everything's been taken care of. Just lie here. I'll be right back."

The car door shut with a bang and Adam felt nauseous. He didn't know why. His vision became soggy. He tried to sit up but couldn't. He tried to think clearly.

"Oh, Adam," said his sister, "what have you gotten yourself into now?"

She was in the passenger seat. She was six years old and wore a dark pleated dress with shiny black shoes.

"What time is your recital?" he asked.

"Silly Adam. There is no recital. I'm a hallucination induced by your subconscious mind. You're in shock."

He nodded. What a precocious six-year-old she was. "I like your shoes," he said.

"Thank you." She kicked her feet playfully back and forth.

Their conversation continued:

HER: "Listen to me, Adam. I need to give you some bad news."

HIM: "I don't like bad news."

HER: "Nobody does. That's why it's so popular. Are you listening?"

HIM: "Yes, I'm listening."

HER: "Good."

HIM: "I'm not stupid."

HER: "No, you're not."

HIM: "Just because I'm not as smart as you. I have other qualities."

HER: "Yes, you do."

HIM: "I'm athletic. Reasonably athletic. I'm resourceful."

HER: "You got the Orioles to the playoffs on the highest difficulty setting."

HIM: "That's right. Not many people could do that."

HER: "Not many."

HIM: "My hand hurts."

HER: "Yeah. You hurt your hand."

HIM: "Oh."

HER: "That's part of the bad news."

HIM: "What's the other part?"

HER: "I'm not sure, but I think I may be dead."

The driver's door opened. Cherry climbed inside and started the ignition. Adam tried again to sit up. This time he succeeded. The passenger seat was empty. Adam leaned his cheek against the car window and peered through glass at the two-story stucco motel and watched it shimmer away, like a desert mirage, into a colorless, shapeless, lifeless heaven.

Chapter Eighteen

He awoke. Single-occupancy room. Hospital. Sunlight lolled through the large window to his right. He had missed the breaking of the dawn by minutes.

His mouth tasted like cotton. His left hand, from fingertip to wrist, was swathed in a stiff fiber cast. He tried to lift it and felt a wave of dizziness wash over his brain.

He shifted his gaze around the room. He was alone. An old leather chair, presumably for visitors, lay empty a few feet from his bed.

Cherry had left him.

It made sense. She didn't need him anymore. She hadn't really needed him ever. She had come to Las Vegas to avenge her brother, apparently had changed her mind, and now probably was on her way toward the Nevada-California border, dolled up as a clown and not looking back. Had she taken the cell phone and credit card with her? Adam would not have been surprised.

He longed again to hallucinate. Being lectured by his sister had felt so natural. So comforting. His stomach wound itself tight. He missed that brat so much!

"I'm not sure," she had said, "but I think I may be dead." What had that been all about? Had that just been a byproduct of his subconscious mind or did he somehow share a link with his twin sister? They had always considered that notion as supernatural hooey. When they were growing up, that was the one question most often asked them by cousins and uncles. No, he didn't feel pain when she did. No, she couldn't automatically find him when they played hide and seek. Where did people get these silly ideas? And yet ...

No. Adam closed his eyes. He would not even consider the option. His sister was not dead. Ebbets had promised him. Ebbets. Trustworthy car thief/nuclear terrorist.

The sunlight licked at Adam's right shoulder. Today was Sunday. In a few hours he was supposed to be coordinating a sting operation with the FBI against a cartel of communists and a two-bit casino owned by greedy pornographers. By tonight he needed to be back in Philadelphia or a Swedish mobster would slice off his head with a battle ax.

Or he could just remain in bed.

He pulled his meager bed sheets up to his chin. He didn't know what time it was and he didn't care.

Nearby, a toilet flushed. A narrow door in the corner of the room opened, and out stepped Cherry. Seeing Adam was awake, she rushed to his side and delicately hugged him.

"How are you feeling?" she asked.

"Ah'm nah feewin anyfing," he replied.

"Yeah, I made sure they pumped you full of Grade A elephant tranquilizers. Nothing but the best."

"Nofin buh da bess," he echoed. His voice had become a rasp. He closed his eyes.

"Nope, sorry, nice try, but I need you to stay awake." She wrapped her fingers around his shoulders and tenderly shook him. "We have a big day ahead of us."

"You go," he said. "Ah'w stay heh."

"No can do. Soon as I step through the doors of the Black Gold, I'll be escorted into a back room and shot twice in the head. And that's if I'm lucky. I hate to break it to you, champ, but your plan depends on you."

Adam opened his eyes. Cherry sat in the shadows but still her beauty shone. He smiled up at her. "Ah fought you hated my pwan."

"I hate the FBI." She clasped her hand in his. "I can't trust them. They may not have killed my brother but they sure as hell made it possible. We were supposed to be safe. We were supposed to be protected and they ... but that's water under the bridge, right? Now we need their help to do this thing. This impossible thing you're doing for me. For me. So let's go. I got you some painkillers for the road."

She carefully unplugged his IV from his right arm and helped him to his feet. The first ten minutes were wobbly, but soon they had managed their way to the narrow locker by the room's small lavatory and had retrieved his clothes and accessories.

"I … think my phone needs … to be charged," slurred Adam.

"I already charged it. Let's go."

"My legs feel like licorice."

"You're sounding better. Lean on my shoulder."

He leaned on her shoulder, slipped down her arm and fell to the floor with a loud slap.

"The floor is comfy."

"I'm sure it is, Adam. When we're done with all we need to do, we'll come back here and you can sleep all you want on the floor."

"Promise?"

Adam smiled against the cold hard floor. "Oh goody."

She took out a flask of whiskey, emptied some of it on his dressing gown, which he had left in the lavatory, and proceeded to apply the doused fabric in splotches to Adam's cheeks and neck. In minutes, he smelled like a recovering alcoholic's wet dream.

"Now you're just another stumbling boozer. Highest patient population at any given hospital. Let's go, you wild drunkard you."

Although the dizziness was subsiding, Adam leaned on Cherry for support. She guided him through the hallways. Nurses waved their hands in front of their noses. Orderlies whispered jokes to one another. Nobody stopped them. They emerged into a crisp Vegas morning and approached the BMW, judiciously parked twenty-five feet away.

They peeled away, Cherry behind the wheel.

"Where to, Jeeves?" asked Adam.

"Only one place to go," she replied.

They headed north.

"By the way, I don't remember giving the doctor my insurance information."

Cherry handed him back his credit card. "Accepted by health care providers nationwide."

"Jeez. How much have I spent on this thing?"

They passed the airport, heading up Highway 15. A jet liner roared overhead. Soon they would be approaching downtown Las Vegas.

"What about those guys back at the motel?"

"What about them, Adam?"

"Won't they be coming after us?"

"No. They won't be coming after us."

Cherry took the downtown exit. They stopped at a light. Sunday mornings left the streets of Las Vegas eerily unpopulated, as if every gambler, tourist and local had been temporarily laid to rest for the Sabbath. Cherry followed the streets until they approached the now-familiar neighborhood. She parked in the driveway at 818 Brewster Lane.

"Cherry, my hand's beginning to hurt."

"Maybe Bernard has an aspirin."

"I thought you said you stole some pain pills."

"Everything in moderation, dumpling." She hopped out of the BMW and opened his door for him. He shooed her away and pulled himself to his feet.

"He can walk. It's a Sunday miracle. Hallelujah. Let's go wake up Tonya Harding."

The house's red door had been reattached to its frame with duct tape and screws. It did not take much effort for Cherry to open it; it took considerably more effort for her to keep the door from falling to the floor. The den appeared pretty much the same carefree mess as last night. Adam ascended the stairs to the bedroom. Cherry, after securing the front door, followed.

Bernard was asleep in his bed. His laptop lay beside his pillow like a teddy bear. Eyes closed, breathing shallow, a mild smile on his lips, Bernard seemed almost the antithesis of the violent, foul-mouthed, angry young man Adam and Cherry had come to know.

Cherry opened the Venetian blinds, zapping the room with morning rays.

"Bernard," said Adam.

The boy slept.

"Bernard," repeated Adam.

The boy slept.

Adam reached down with his good hand to Bernard's shoulder and gently shook him.

The boy awoke. And lunged at Adam with a steak knife he must have had hidden under his pillow. They both ended up on the floor, knife poised in a direct arc over Adam's right eye.

"What do you think you're doing?" growled Bernard.

"What do you think you're doing?!" replied Adam.

Bernard sighed in disgust and sat down on his bed. Cherry helped Adam to his feet.

"Paranoid much?" she asked.

Bernard snuck the knife back under his pillow. "I have reason to be, don't you think?"

"Everyone's got a reason, Bernard." She leaned against the wall and stared at him. "That doesn't make it right."

"Yeah, well, whatever." The boy unlocked his laptop. While waiting for it to reboot, he noticed Adam's cast. "What happened to you? Bear attack?"

"Yeah. It was a bear attack. Did you contact Fred?"

Bernard tossed him the phone. Adam instinctively tried to catch it with his left hand; it bounced off his cast and landed on the floor. He picked it back up.

"What's the number?" asked Adam.

Bernard told him.

"And you're sure he'll be up?"

The boy, checking his email, answered, "The man never sleeps."

"And you're sure you're on board for my plan?"

Bernard glanced over at Cherry. "You think it's going to work?"

Cherry shrugged her shoulders.

"Yeah," replied the boy. "Me too. But what else have we got, right? We all need something. I need out. I need to find Ebbets before he does something ... regrettable."

"How exactly can he just detonate an atomic bomb from around the world by remote control?"

Bernard propped up his pillow and leaned back. "It's not one atomic bomb. It's twelve. And it's not really a remote control. It's a remote trigger. It sends out a satellite signal to the nearest receiver on the nearest bomb and then that receiver piggybacks the signal to the next nearest bomb. As soon as it's done its job in the circuit, the receiver activates its warhead. Boom. Big boom. Twelve big booms, really, in a matter of about thirty seconds."

"But why would Fred build a remote trigger in the first place? Is he that psychotic?"

"Fred didn't build it. Fred couldn't build a table if he had a list of instructions and a box of nails. I built the trigger."

"Why?" asked Adam.

Bernard stared out through the blinds at the Sunday gleam. "Ebbets ... thought it would be funny."

A toxic silence filled the room. All parties looked to the floor for words. Outside, some bright-eyed bird, immune to this fog of quietude, chirped its own tuneless melody. Maybe, like Adam and Cherry, it had just arrived from the North. Maybe it was indigenous. Some birds didn't distinguish. They ate, chirped and traveled. No complaints from them of social injustice or nuclear terrorism. No kidnapping. No guilt. Birds ate, chirped and traveled.

"Make the call, Adam," said Cherry.

Adam made the call.

"Hello?" answered British Fred. The man did, indeed, sound wide awake.

"Hello, Fred. Remember me?"

"Mr. Winkle. I had a feeling I'd hear from you. How's your chest wound? I hope you had my bandage replaced."

Adam sat down at the window sill. "You were right, Fred. I am here for business."

"I know you are. I told you that you were. You denied it with that silly story about your sister but we both knew the truth. You were feeling out my organization. I assume by this phone call that you have come to a conclusion?"

"I've been instructed by my boss to make you an offer for some merchandise."

Cherry rolled her eyes. Bernard seemed to ignore them both, busily typing away at his keyboard.

"As I told you, Mr. Winkle, my objective is not to make trades with private individuals. I am trying to harmonize the world, not give a local mobster extra ammunition for his gun." British Fred hummed a brief sigh. "That said, for the time being, I am still a prisoner of capitalism. I would be remiss if I didn't at least listen to your offer."

"Good to hear. Name your price, Fred."

British Fred named his price.

Adam covered the phone with his good hand, mouthed "holy shit!" to Cherry, placed the phone back to his cheek, and replied, "I think we can do better than that."

British Fred tossed out figures. Adam retaliated with whatever his imagination could conjure. They haggled for a few minutes before settling on a price.

"So here's what we're going to do, Fred." Here it was: the lynchpin of the plan. Adam glanced out the window at the bird. The bird stared back. Blinked at him. "I need to fly out tonight but I think we have time for papers to be signed, etc. Can you meet at, say, noon?"

"Where would you like to meet?"

"Do you know the Black Gold Casino?"

Chapter Nineteen

In renovating the Black Gold Casino, Greta Luddell had replaced all of the old upholstery and decorations, most of which dated back to the building's birth in 1964, with female erotica. Chairs were shaped like long-fingered hands. Doorknobs resembled breasts. The three conference rooms, located on the ground floor, were renamed The Box, The Snatch, and The Minge. Not many companies booked rooms at the Black Gold; not many business conferences took place in The Box, The Snatch, or The Minge. Nevertheless, the Black Gold never seemed short of clientele willing to pay high fees for cheap rooms; fantasy, coupled with discretion, was what whirled much of Las Vegas into its dizzying spin.

Stepping through the casino's front doors, which were manned by two bodyguards who carefully checked ID, Adam knew immediately that several of his frat brothers would absolutely have loved this place. The establishment's decadent lobby included suggestive four-color painted pillars depicting two, three, four women engaged in various acts of flexibility. Embedded in the walls were twelve television screens, all showing pornographic films and all just small enough that the interested party had to stand very close to view and enjoy.

The lobby's singular achievement, though, was its centerpiece: a twenty-five-foot-tall marble rendition of the idealized naked feminine form, posed forcefully akimbo and gazing down with implacable dominance at all mere mortals daring to frequent her space. After staring up her long, long, long legs for a good five minutes, Adam located the nearby plaque depicting the grande dame's name.

The statue was named Greta. Greta Luddell, owner of the Black Gold and bane of Cherry's existence, had entitled this anatomically-impossible carving after herself.

A pig-tailed bellhop wearing lederhosen (and little else) approached Adam and asked him if he needed assistance. Adam told her he had a reservation in The Box. She directed him to the left, past the museum of Soak Entertainment memorabilia, and bid him goodbye with a long kiss on his cheek.

"I don't know if I'm in heaven," muttered Adam, "or hell."

"Keep the chatter to a minimum," Special Agent Chang replied, her voice emanating from the earpiece craftily hidden inside his left aural canal. "Do the job."

The job. Adam smirked. The plan. His plan. Kill two birds with one stone: British Fred the Atomic Communist and Greta the Egomaniacal Pornographer. His plan. Risky, foolhardy and very easy to botch. A gigantic gamble in the house of gambling, and the house always won in Vegas. He yearned for Cherry's comforting presence by his side. He even longed for Filbert. Filbert would have loved this plan. After all, Filbert's bank job in Philadelphia had in many ways inspired Adam's crazy careless plan.

The plan was this:

Adam knew he had to shut down British Fred's operation, if only because it would allow Bernard the freedom to assist in finding Ebbets. Upon hearing and recording, via Adam's wire, the sale of nuclear weapons, the FBI would have the final piece of evidence necessary to move in for the kill. But in order to purchase the weapons, Adam needed massive funds. Herein lay the kicker. No one expected Adam to carry the cash on him. Overstuffed briefcases were so twentieth century. The transaction would be processed in the room by Bernard. He would use his laptop to tap into the local network and transfer funds into Fred's bank from an offshore account ... belonging to Greta Luddell in the name of the Black Gold Casino. Cherry still had the dirt on Greta from her days as an accountant and she had confirmed its validity earlier that morning on Bernard's computer. Greta Luddell would be complicit in the purchasing of nuclear weapons and would be spending the rest of her life in the same FBI detention center as British Fred and Jimmy Ha.

Given Adam's luck over the past few days, he wondered just how badly this plan was going to blow up in his face.

The Box was easy to locate. In a sea of black sin, the small conference room was a white gull. Even the door was white. Adam offered the white door a desultory knock and then entered.

Fred, Jimmy and Bernard were already assembled at the tail end of a long obsidian table. Ample lighting bounced off the white walls and made the table shine like a strip of black glass. Bernard had his laptop out and ready.

A pale cardboard box sat in the center of the table and beside it a triangular steel knife.

"Good afternoon, Mr. Winkle," said British Fred.

"What's in the box?" asked Adam.

Bernard refused to meet his stare.

Jimmy Ha leaned over the table and with a meaty hand picked up the knife by its weighted hilt.

"We're in The Box," replied British Fred. "That is the quaint little name given to this room. We're in The Box. You and I."

While taping the wire underneath the bandage on Adam's chest, Special Agent Chang and Adam had agreed on a safety phrase, in case the situation in The Box became dangerous. If he found himself in "mortal danger"—her choice of words—then he was to say the safety phrase and the FBI task force would come to his rescue.

The safety phrase, incidentally, was "mortal danger."

As Adam watched Jimmy Ha hop that nasty blade from hand to hand, his lips reflexively mouthed "mortal danger, mortal danger, mortal danger ..."

No. He had to work this out. He had to close the trap.

"Mr. Winkle, I am curious. What happened to your hand?"

"Cooking accident." Adam kept his eyes on the shiny blade. "Scrambling eggs. What's with the knife?"

British Fred smiled at his two compatriots and then back at Adam. "Well, we've been waiting for someone to return with plates and utensils but we might as well commence our cutting now. Jimmy, if you would? Mr. Winkle, you remember Jimmy, don't you? From last night's unfortunate miscommunication."

Jimmy Ha reached over the table and lifted the top off the box, revealing a round chocolate soufflé sprinkled with pink shavings and punched with thirteen thin blue candles. Today was Bernard's birthday. British Fred had been cooking this soufflé yesterday afternoon, when he had Adam tied up in his kitchen. Today was Bernard's birthday. Adam had completely forgotten.

"Happy birthday," said Adam to Bernard.

"Thanks," Bernard replied, still avoiding Adam's gaze.

British Fred used a pocket lighter to ignite the candle wicks.

"Can you get the lights, Mr. Winkle?"

Adam found the switch near the door and flicked it.

"Make a wish, Bernard." British Fred's toothy smile glowed in the basking candlelight. "Anything your heart desires."

Bernard briefly glanced up. In the smoky silence, his eyes found Adam. This time it was Adam who looked away.

The thirteen-year-old boy blew out his candles.

As British Fred and Jimmy Ha regaled their young associate with applause, Adam flicked on the light. He suddenly felt very, very nervous.

Jimmy Ha, employing his eager blade, sectioned the soufflé into eight equilateral triangles. British Fred patted Bernard on his scalp. "If only John Ebbets were here," whispered the Brit, "this party would be complete."

"Yeah," said Bernard.

Adam sat down at the other end of the table.

"You don't know where he is, do you, Mr. Winkle? Or the item he stole from us?"

"We've been through this."

"I like to be thorough."

"I don't know where he is. Or your 'item.'"

"John Ebbets was a very stubborn man. I remember when I found him." British Fred sighed. "I remember when he found you, Bernard! I remember the phone call. I was reading some futurist poetry and my telephone rang and it was John Ebbets calling from, of all places, Canada. Just outside Toronto. A little town called …"

"Crocker," said Bernard. "A little town called Crocker."

"That's right! Crocker, Ontario. What the bloody hell was he doing in Crocker, Ontario, I wondered. His job was to recruit us a replacement for IT. Our former IT specialist, a dour gentleman named Ike … that didn't quite work out."

Jimmy Ha snorted.

"Behave yourself, Jimmy. So John Ebbets called me up and told me he found the perfect guy. Bright and creative and, most importantly, anti-establishment. So many hackers think they are anti-establishment but they're really just pests with power. To truly be a rebel requires the kind of bravery and fortitude lacking in, frankly, most men. But no child growing up in any country wants to be an anarchist. I wanted to be a fireman. I'm sure you, Mr. Winkle, didn't long to be a stooge for the mob. Then how does this happen? How do boys like that become men like me? Do you know the answer, Mr. Winkle? But it doesn't matter. Today is Bernard's thirteenth birthday. Thirteen is a remarkable religious number. At age thirteen, a Jewish boy becomes a Jewish man. There were thirteen Jewish men present at the Last Supper. It takes a real atheist to appreciate this. But I'm off topic. We were discussing the moment that John Ebbets found our boy Bernard in Crocker, Ontario."

The door to The Box opened. Adam spun around in his seat but saw only an ancient Egyptian harem girl carrying plates and forks. She placed the goods in front of Bernard, wished him happy birthday in a breathy voice, and exited the vicinity chest-first, ass-last.

As Jimmy Ha divvied up the chocolate soufflé, British Fred recommenced his tale:

"When I showed up at the airport to meet John Ebbets and his new protégé, I expected to find, I suppose, a gangly, bookish sort. Our nature is to stereotype. Instead I see this brash youth with a face full of attitude and the first thing he says to me, the very first thing, is: 'Don't even try to be my father, because the real bastard's dead. They sent him to jail for molesting me and he's dead now and I couldn't be happier.' Bernard, my darling boy."

British Fred then leaned over Bernard's skull and planted a paternal kiss on the lad's dark scalp; Adam stared absently at his own soufflé portion. He was not hungry. Had he misjudged the situation? Was British Fred merely an eccentric? No. He was a dealer in atomic weapons. He needed to be stopped. But why? Was any of this really Adam's business? His only goal had to be the safe liberation of his sister; everything else was distraction. What was he even doing here in this room? Greta Luddell was Cherry's problem, not his. One of Cherry's problems. The woman seemed to be a long buffet of oddities and secrets and problems. How could he trust her? Maybe the grave behind the gas station wasn't even her brother's. What if she was no less a con artist than Filbert? No wonder the two had palled around so well …

Oh God, thought Adam, sinking in his seat in the conference room of a wing of a casino-whorehouse in Las Vegas, Nevada, four days before Christmas—oh God, what have I gotten myself into?

"So," said British Fred, "I have babbled enough. It's a trait I fear I acquired from the absent Mr. Ebbets. That man liked to talk."

"Yes," replied Bernard faintly, "he did."

British Fred passed a sheaf of papers and a ballpoint pen across the smooth obsidian to Adam's side of the table. The ballpoint pen bore the insignia of a leopard. The sheaf of papers detailed the (fraudulent) deal they were about to strike.

"Read them over, Mr. Winkle. Take your time. I insist. Nobody likes surprises."

Adam stared and stared at the words on the page but didn't read them.

"While you're perusing the document, I'd like to inform you how the money your organization is providing us is going to be spent. Mr. Winkle? Are you well? Mr. Winkle?"

Special Agent Chang's voice crackled in Adam's ear, "Answer him, damn it! The more damning information we record, the better our case will be!"

Adam leaned back in his chair and sighed. "You're going to build another bomb." His tone rang hollow and empty.

"Yes. Yes, we are. But that is not the ultimate destination for these funds. No, sir. In the past few months, my associates and I have become very economical at building bombs. The ultimate destination for these funds is on the East Coast of your United States. You see, Mr. Winkle, I am impatient with the progress of reform. Equalizing the global balance of power does not occur only by enlarging the small. One must also shrink the enormous. I imagine some will label our actions terrorism but our aim is not to terrorize but to humble. I'm sure everyone in this room will agree that humility is a trait in short supply in your United States."

Adam frowned, leaned forward in his chair. "What are you going to do?"

"I'd like to detonate the bomb in New York, of course, but Mr. Ebbets, before he left, talked me out of that. He has family in New York. Another obvious target would be Washington DC, but that would be deemed too political. But there is a perfect site close enough to Washington to make the desired impact. I got the idea, actually, from a photograph on the wall of Bernard's house."

Adam glanced at Bernard, then back at British Fred. British Fred was smiling.

"You're going to blow up Camden Yards," said Adam.

"We are, yes. The loss of life will be tragic but the end result will be staggering. Oppressed nations will question American autonomy and we will be on the road, finally, to a true global utopia. This isn't the World Trade Center. This is a ballpark. A symbol of Americana. You might want to be elsewhere on Opening Day.

Adam picked up the ballpoint pen and autographed the papers. He wanted to take the pen tip and drive it into the anarchic Brit's bobbing pink throat.

"Excellent! So we're settled. Now all we need, Mr. Winkle, is for you to give your account information to Bernard so he can make the transfer on his magical toy and you can be on your way back to your employer in sunny Philadelphia."

As Adam recited the numerical sequence and password Cherry had had him memorize, Bernard keyed it into his laptop. Once the transaction was complete, Adam would leave the room and say these words into his wire: "The transaction is complete." Then the FBI would swarm the casino and the Las Vegas chapter of Adam's misadventures would be—

"It's not working," said Bernard.

British Fred peeped over Bernard's shoulder.

"It's not working," repeated Bernard, this time directly to Adam. "It says the password is invalid."

"That's ... not possible ..."

"Uh, Mr. Winkle, perhaps now would be an opportune moment to phone up your employer and verify the password."

Adam rose to his feet. He had absolutely no idea what to do, but standing at least helped morph his sudden anxiety and panic into slightly less disconcerting sensations of terror and dread. He could not, of course, call Yogurt; the account did not belong to him. The account belonged to Greta Luddell. And he couldn't very well call her ... which didn't matter, because at that moment the door to The Box swung open, and in walked itty-bitty entrepreneur Greta Luddell. And her bare-chested Brazilian bodyguard. Who held a whip. Everyone in the room instantly identified Greta Luddell because Greta Luddell wore a sticker on her pint-sized navy pantsuit that read in crimson marker: "Hello, my name is Greta Luddell." Either she had just come from a conference or she really wanted everybody she met to know who she was.

"Hello, trolls," she squeaked. "You've all been behaving very badly."

British Fred casually walked over, hand extended, to where she stood.

"It's a pleasure to make your acquaintance, Ms. Luddell," he said. "My name is Fred Hamsford-Bucking."

She sneezed on his outstretched hand. "I usually would send my flunkies to clean up a mess in my casino, but for this I wanted to watch."

"What's going on?" buzzed Special Agent Chang. "If the situation has been compromised, just say the safety phrase. 'Mortal danger.' Say 'mortal danger.'"

"Might I ask to what mess you're referring, Ms. Luddell?"

"Earlier today someone tried to hack into our server. They tried to access classified files." Greta Luddell again sneezed. "Damn it! Did someone in here use shampoo that contains coal tar?"

Jimmy Ha, bald sumo wrestler, slowly raised his hand.

"Jimmy, you use shampoo?" asked British Fred.

Jimmy Ha nodded.

"Why?"

Jimmy Ha sheepishly stared down at his shoes and muttered, "I have dandruff on my pubes."

"Wow," replied British Fred, turning back to Greta, "that's one sensitive allergy you've got."

Greta nodded at her bodyguard, who then cracked his whip several centimeters from British Fred's right eyeball. British Fred flinched all the way to the floor, where he remained, appalled.

"We ran a security check," continued Greta, "and easily tracked the hacker. We also planted a small tracing program on his computer. On that computer. On my table."

All eyes looked to Bernard. Bernard's eyes looked to Adam.

Save me, they said.

I can't, Adam's gaze answered, not yet.

He took a deep breath, exhaled slowly and turned around to face Greta Luddell. It was time to end her.

"Looks like you're having yourself a very bad day, Greta. Not only does it appear someone is trying to hack into your accounts, but didn't you also misplace a pair of bodyguards recently?"

Both of her eyebrows lifted. "What did you say?"

"Well, I see you came here with this guy. By the way, Indiana Jones called, and he wants his whip back. Anyway, I could have sworn you had two other bruisers who did your dirty work. Nice fellows. Snazzy dressers. What were their names again? Oh right. Spate and Newton. Whatever happened to them?"

"Mr. Winkle ..." mumbled British Fred from the floor, "what is going on here?"

Her lips rippled into a snarl. "You're working with her. This is all about her. She's behind this."

"Now why would someone want to do something as mean as this to someone as nice as you?" replied Adam. "And no, this isn't totally for her. This is for her brother too. You remember her brother, don't you?"

"If you remember him, Mr. Winkle, you'll remember what I did to him. You'll remember how nothing could protect him from what he had coming, not even the FBI. And, knowing the lengths I'll go to, you come in here in my casino and try to hoodwink me? You are either preposterously suicidal or the dumbest human being on the planet."

"So you admit it. You had him killed."

"Of course I admit it!" she answered. "That's what you do to rats." She sneezed. "You squash them." She sneezed. "I'll make sure your grave is near his." She sneezed. "Up against the wall." She sneezed. "All of you."

"Well," Adam said, complying, "looks like we're in mortal danger."

British Fred crawled toward the mighty midget. "Ms. Luddell, I assure you, my associates and I had nothing to do with—"

The bodyguard cracked his whip. This time it wasn't a warning. British Fred's chin split open like an old seam. Jimmy Ha rushed to help his boss but a whip-crack sent him, too, to the floor. A piece of the sumo wrestler's left ear landed nearby. Both men, master and servant, lay on the carpet, moaning in blind wet pain.

Bernard joined Adam at the wall and grumbled, "Some plan."

"Yes, it looks like we're in mortal danger."

"You already said that."

The door did not burst open with FBI agents.

The Brazilian bodyguard, grinning like a lion, advanced toward them.

"Mortal danger!" cried Adam. "Mortal danger! Mortal danger!"

The bodyguard brought back his whip, and prepared to strike.

"You are the dumbest human being on the planet," muttered Bernard to Adam.

Now the door burst open with FBI agents.

Chapter Twenty

"And don't leave town," warned Special Agent Chang. "As soon as we're finished processing these nimrods, we're going to need to debrief you. An immunity agreement only goes so far."

Adam, Cherry and Bernard smiled and nodded. Leave town? Them? Never!

Right.

They emerged into the cool afternoon air and climbed into their BMW. Adam wanted to take the wheel, but the combination of painkillers in his bloodstream and giant fiber cast on his left hand made driving not an option. So he rode shotgun. Bernard took the back seat, where his luggage was already stashed. Cherry piloted them toward Caesars Palace. They still had one more errand to run before catching a flight to Philadelphia and from there … Providence, Rhode Island (where the funeral for Adam's wacko uncle Dexter, who had envisioned himself the exiled king of Mars, had recently gone unattended by either Weiss twin due to a bad bowl of chili and an errant kidnapping).

"If anyone would know where Ebbets is," Bernard said, "it's his mother."

"I thought she was in New York."

"She's in a nursing home outside Providence. He phones her every few days. I even spoke with her once. He called me his best friend."

Adam glanced in the rearview. "We'll find him."

They pulled into the old parking garage for that gem of the Strip: Caesars Palace. Where Evel Knievel and his motorcycle once tried to hop a water fountain. Where Mike Tyson k.o.'d Trevor Berbick to become the heavyweight champion of the world. To many, Caesars Palace remains the classiest joint in all LV. Adam was there to pick up a mysterious parcel for an ax-friendly mob don.

Cherry followed him inside the casino. Bernard and his laptop remained in the BMW. The boy seemed quite involved in an online chat room. Somewhere downtown, British Fred and Jimmy Ha were being read their rights by the Federal Bureau of Investigation. The FBI had them for the possession and trafficking of illegal weapons. In another room sat Greta Luddell. The FBI had her for murder. Special Agents Chang and Epperson would be too busy to notice three of their primary witnesses vanish on the eight P.M. flight to Philadelphia.

Adam felt a little miserable about ditching the FBI, but in truth, they didn't really need him around to prosecute their case. They had the taped confessions. Bernard had given them the location of British Fred's storage unit. Still, this was the FBI. Did Adam really need more enemies? He entered the lobby of Caesars Palace with an anchor on his conscience and a frown in his heart. Cherry bought a bottle of water from a Roman-themed kiosk and followed him to the bank of elevators.

As soon as they found one to themselves, she pressed the STOP button.

"What are you doing?" asked Adam.

She locked her eyes on his.

"Something on your mind?" asked Adam.

She whispered what was on her mind into his right ear.

"No," he replied, "I can't say that I have. Although I once received one in my high school lavatory with a girl named—"

Cherry placed a long finger against his soft, thin lips.

She smiled.

He smiled.

He licked at her fingertip with the edge of his tongue.

She teased her moist fingertip down his chin, collar, shirt front, waist, thighs … back up to waist. Her lips locked on his neck while her index finger probed his clothed groin. Other fingers joined the index in its exploration. Adam gasped; the fingers had found the object of their search and seized it with gentle determination. A four-part concerto filled the elevator: exhalations, groans moans and unzipping.

Cherry's fingers unearthed Adam's bestest friend in the whole wide world. My, how he swelled with pride. He so loved to be touched. Just as he had puffed himself in full salute, her fingers suddenly drifted away. Not to worry, though, her lips had whispered their farewells to Adam's neck and were now on a steady voyage south. What her fingers had started, her lips would complete.

Adam closed his eyes and saw God. She winked at him. God was an amalgam of every woman with whom Adam had gone past first base. "I love you," God said, and Cherry's mouth closed around his veiny cock. Adam's good hand gripped the elevator's steel railing; without its support he probably would have collapsed onto his weak, wobbly knees. Cherry deepened her dipping and quickened her pace. Inside his shoes, Adam's toes curled against leather encasing. Deeper, quicker, more. Adam's mind ceased conceiving cogent thoughts; it lacked the necessary blood flow. In the span of two minutes he had regressed into a well-dressed beast and beasts not only lacked all self-control but lacked the desire to obtain it. Adam blasted ten cubic centimeters of hot white fluid against the back of Cherry's throat.

"Thawaawsum," he mumbled.

Cherry popped open her bottle of water and chugged down a quarter liter.

"You did a good thing for me today," she replied. Her thumb punched the STOP button and the elevator's motor rumbled back to life. "Thank you."

They wandered out into the swanky corridor. Caesars Palace made every effort to make its guests feel like emperors. Adam and Cherry followed the room doors until they found 512.

"Zip up your fly," suggested Cherry.

Adam zipped up his fly. "So, I mean, what does this mean?"

"What does what mean?"

"What just happened. In the elevator."

"It means I gave you a blowjob."

"Right. I know. I was there. But what does it mean?"

"It means I was grateful." She looked away. "I don't expect anything."

"Just because you don't expect anything doesn't mean you won't get what you want."

She looked back at him. Her gaze traced his smirk. She couldn't help but match him, grin for grin.

"Since when did you become so charming?" she asked.

"It's a phase," he replied.

She nodded, and then knocked on the door of Room 512.

"By the way," inquired Cherry, "do you have any idea what we're picking up?"

"I don't know and I don't care."

"You don't know and you don't care?"

"We go in, we pick it up, we take it back to Philadelphia and we continue on our way. Whatever's in this parcel is no business of ours. The less we know, the better."

"Well. Listen to you. Charming and pragmatic."

Adam shrugged. "I've had a bit of an interesting week."

Something thumped against the other side of the door. From inside the room emitted a deep feminine voice:

"Who is it?"

"We're here to pick up the parcel," answered Adam. "We're the guys from Philadelphia."

Silence.

Then the soft clanging sound of a door chain being unhooked.

Then the door opened.

Both Adam and Cherry recoiled, flinching from a fist of antiseptic odors thrusting out from Room 512. Had its occupants recently splashed the entire chamber in industrial-strength bleach? Did Room 512 house a conference of germophobes? Adam and Cherry covered their nostrils and braved entry into the hotel room, where they quickly discovered the source of the stink.

All the customary furniture—queen bed, night stand, lamp, a pair of cushy chairs—had been shoved to the walls, leaving the heart of the room available for a hospital gurney. On the gurney lay a slender blond gentleman in his mid forties. Naked. Greying hair receding. The tip of his nose as red as a rose petal. Ribcage clearly visible through papery skin. A brown face cloth covered his genitals. An IV ran from his left arm to a saline bag that hung from a portable wooden coat rack. His eyelids were shut. He was listening to a Walkman.

The beefy woman who had answered the door wore hospital scrubs. So did the room's other occupant, a freckle-faced man who sat on the queen bed and was clearing a hypodermic filled with pale yellow liquid of any possible air pockets.

"The couriers from Philadelphia!" he said. He sounded as if he were eight years old. "You've arrived at a most opportune time! Feel free to sit. Margaret, see if you can get our guests something to drink."

"Yes, Dr. Lansing."

Margaret fetched a pair of Coke cans from the mini-fridge and handed them to Adam and Cherry. They declined. They also remained standing.

"What … exactly is going on here?" Cherry asked.

"Euthanasia!" piped Dr. Lansing. "Peace for those in pain. The primary objective of all medicine. Margaret, if you would, fetch our friends the parcel. I need to administer the injection to Mr. Coe."

Margaret disappeared into the lavatory.

Dr. Lansing, needle ready, approached his calm, distracted patient.

Adam couldn't help his curiosity. "What's he dying of?" he asked.

"The most common affliction of them all: life!"

Adam glanced at Cherry, who appeared to be as clueless as he. "No, I mean, what does he have? Cancer? AIDS? He looks okay."

"He should. Mr. Coe here is in perfect health for a forty-four-year-old man. Exercises regularly. Eats conservatively. A little too conservatively. Has to do with an oppressive mother, I think, but psychology's not my specialty!"

"Then, wait, I'm confused. Then what is in that needle?"

"Nine grams of pentobarbital. I already administered a mild anti-epileptic before you arrived. What time is it now?"

Cherry glanced at the clock on the nightstand: "6:18."

"By 6:30 Mr. Coe will dead. It's what he wants. His wife just left him." Margaret reentered the room. In her arms she carried a cardboard box the size of a full-grown collie; by the way she was hefting, it must have weighed about as much too. The box was labeled "fragile." She placed it, with much relief, down by the door.

"Would you like to stay?" asked Dr. Lansing. "It's quite a spiritual experience."

"What a good question," replied Adam, trying very hard to keep from freaking. "I think I need to discuss it with my associate. Can you give us a minute?"

"Of course!"

Adam brought Cherry over to the room's lavatory. Before shutting the door, he turned to the good doctor and added, "Make sure you don't start without us."

"I won't!"

Adam shut the door.

"I thought I'd seen it all," he said, "but holy fucking shit."

"What's wrong?"

He stared at her. "Oh, I don't know. Murder?"

"That's not murder. It's suicide. Assisted suicide."

"The man's not dying!"

"We're all dying," replied Cherry. "He's just choosing his due date. But if this is bothering you so much, we'll just get the package and leave."

"Get the package? We're going to go back in there and get the needle!"

"It's none of our business."

"And that's fine with you? You can live that way?"

"I've lived that way all my life, Adam. That's why I'm alive and my brother's not. It's why you're alive. The man in that room, if he wants to die today, I say, let him die. Suicide is just as valid a life choice as any other."

Adam swiped his uninjured hand across the sink's tiny soaps and shampoos, scattering them into the nearby tub.

"Filbert robs the church coffers. You accept it because it helps you get closer to rescuing your sister. Filbert is decapitated and the man who swung the ax asks you to do an errand for him. You say, 'sure, why not' because it helps you get closer to rescuing your sister. The anarchists that John Ebbets ran with are selling nuclear bombs, putting potentially billions at risk. You don't care. You're just trying to save your sister. But now you put your foot down and say no? For a guy lying naked on a hospital gurney, a guy who wants to die? I don't mind a little hypocrisy now and then, but Jesus Christ. And why now? Huh? What is it about now that suddenly made your conscience kick into high gear?"

"My father committed suicide."

"Yeah, well, okay." Cherry wrapped her fingers around his. "That sucks. But the guy in there is not your father."

Adam wrenched his hand free. "Way to show compassion."

"Compassion for you? Yes. You want to talk about it? We'll talk about it. You want to talk about it here? Not the best idea. The clock's ticking. Maybe Bernard is still in the car. Maybe. What you're feeling is a sense of obligation to someone you've never met, someone you don't know, someone who—let me repeat it again—wants to die. You save him, and you have to save everyone. You didn't save your father and you never, ever will. Say goodbye to any notion of that. The best you can do in this life is save yourself, and maybe—maybe—in the process you'll accomplish something righteous. If you're lucky. Everything else is illusory. Trust me. I know illusions. Let's get the package and get out of here."

"Everything okay?" called Dr. Lansing.

"Everything's fine," replied Cherry. "We're coming out."

She opened the door.

After a moment, Adam followed her into the room. She was right. Once again, she was right.

"So," said Dr. Lansing, "are we ready?"

Adam stared at the man on the gurney. He appeared so content, listening to his music. He didn't even seem to mind exposing his shortcomings for all to see. He appeared so content ...

Like the Mennonite wife in her bed. And yes, like his father on the bathroom floor when Adam had discovered him ... so content ... The rest stop, the credit cards ... so easy ... The frat, Adam's friends, Adam's classes ... He was gliding through life, he was Bernard on the ice, he was Officer Neal on the highway, because the ends justify the means, but if you never make a choice, you never have to worry about the consequences, and the consequences, oh, the consequences, that inevitable rush ... Better to be John Ebbets and destroy the world than have to live in it, right? And after all, the package in here, the package, it's just a means, no harm will come, no harm will come, and even if someone gets hurt as a result, even if the contents of the package lead to five, ten more deaths—perhaps it's a grindstone for the Yogurt's ax, perhaps it's a ledger with the names of mob informants—their blood will be on Adam's hands but Anna's blood is redder than theirs, right— right—right?

No.

Adam walked over to where the man lay, gently lifted the headphones off his ears, and kissed him on the cheek.

Mr. Coe gazed up with sudden curiosity at this strange young fellow with the cast on his left hand.

"Adam," said Cherry nervously, "what are you doing?"

"The hard thing," he responded and waved at them all and promptly turned his back on Cherry, the package, Dr. Lansing, his assistant Margaret, the hotel room, Yogurt, Las Vegas and almost all hope of finding his sister alive.

Chapter Twenty-One

As they passed Philadelphia, cruising at a fixed twenty-five thousand feet, Adam peered out one of the airplane's face-sized windows and watched the City of Brotherly Love (final resting place for headless geriatric grumps and for broken promises made by desperate frat boys to yogurt-swilling mob bosses) twinkle into oblivion. "Well," he muttered, "that's that."

Bernard glanced up from his laptop game of hearts. "You say something?"

Adam shook his head and downed a sip from his cup of ginger ale. The liquid did little to irrigate his mouth, which was as dry as a bag of wood chips. He blamed it on his painkillers. Pointing the finger at a necessity helped keep the guilt at bay, at least for a few minutes.

The 757 jiggled.

Adam unbuckled his safety belt and squeezed past Bernard to the spacious aisle. They were flying first-class, purchased with a portion of the significant cash withdrawal Adam and Bernard had made on Yogurt's visa card before discarding it, and the cell phone, into a trash bin. Yes, Yogurt and his Swedish mafia would undoubtedly track him down eventually and probably separate his head from his torso, but without a credit card record of the plane fare, what were the odds they'd find him in Rhode Island?

Adam made his way to the cabin's lavatories. Both were occupied; already waiting in line was a lanky middle-aged Arab woman wearing a beige suit.

"I would use the facilities in the rear of the vehicle," said the Arab. Her accent was a harmony of Kabul and Dublin. "But I have never before flown first-class."

Adam nodded. The lady had a point.

"I am attending my daughter's wedding in Newport, Rhode Island. Have you ever been to Newport, Rhode Island?"

"When I was very little."

"My husband and I had to take a second mortgage on my home to pay for her wedding, but she is my only daughter, and I hope this will be her only wedding. I spent so much money on the wedding that I decided to buy a first-class ticket on an airplane. They offered wine. Now I need to use the facilities and the facilities are locked. The lengths we take for principle, yes?"

The lengths we take for principle. The lady had another point. Adam himself had learned this lesson only a few hours previous. He prayed that he and the Arab, bladders plump, were not just a pair of starry-eyed fools.

One of the two lavatories opened up. A statuesque stewardess and a diminutive, bearded man pushed out of the tiny space and quietly returned to coach. Adam and the Arab exchanged eye-rolls and then the mother-in-law-to-be took his place inside the lavatory.

The 757 jiggled again. This time, the jiggling did not abate. Adam reached for the back of a nearby seat to keep from falling.

"Ladies and gentlemen," crackled the pilot, "this is your captain. It appears we're encountering a patch of turbulence. For your safety, I am going to turn on the fasten seatbelt sign. I apologize for the inconvenience and will turn off the fasten seatbelt sign as soon as we have steadied out."

Sure enough, over every seat on the plane, occupied or not, the fasten seatbelt sign lit. Stewards and stewardesses immediately escorted all standing passengers back to their floatable chairs. The stewardess from before, the very tall brunette who had shared a few lavatory minutes with the bearded midget, approached Adam, offered him a solid, unabashed stare and suggested he return to his seat immediately.

"Sure," he replied, "I'm just waiting to use the—"

"Please wait in your seat, sir."

The other lavatory opened. A mother and infant child emerged and quickly returned to their row. Adam went to take her place at the latrine, but the stewardess positioned herself in his way and shook her painted head.

"Please wait in your seat. Sir."

Adam pointed at the latrine. "That's my seat."

"I'm afraid the toilet does not come with a seatbelt. Your safety is our concern. Let me escort you to your seat." She reached for her walkie-talkie.

Adam shuffled back to his row, turned around, and yelled back to her, for all the plane to hear:

"By the way, you have a very small pubic hair on your lower lip!"

Then he pushed past Bernard and took his seat. Regretfully, his remark reminded him of Cherry.

Cherry.

"Keep the noise down," mumbled Bernard, eyes still closed, "I'm trying to sleep."

Adam noticed the boy's fists were clenched over the armrests.

"You're afraid of flying," said Adam.

"Fuck you."

"It's okay to be afraid of flying."

"Really? Thanks. Fuck you."

"I'm afraid of clowns."

"Yeah? Many people die from a clown crash? Fuck you."

The 757 jiggled.

"I'd think it'd be hard to sleep with the plane shaking like it is."

Bernard replied with his middle finger.

"I hope it doesn't fall apart."

Bernard replied with his other middle finger.

Adam glanced out his window. Five miles below the gliding metal aircraft lay the great state of New Jersey. Home sweet home. The Sunday before Christmas. Parents and children and cousins and dogs watching *It's a Wonderful Life* for the umpteenth time. Between shots of rum-laced eggnog, the adults mouth the words of the film. The older kids, too cool for Jimmy Stewart, are instead eyeballing the swathed and swarthy Christmas tree. Later in the evening they will sneak downstairs and pick up their gifts and, to ascertain their secret identities, will hold the packages up to the light or will gently shake them to produce an identifiable rattling. Some packages are easy to determine—a CD in wrapping paper always looks like a CD in wrapping paper—but some packages were oblong, cockeyed, or just plain amorphous; no amount of examination offered the slightest clue for these deep-cover operatives.

In truth, Adam had no clue what occurred in those million homes concealed beneath clouds and snow and aluminum siding. He could only relate his own comfortable clichés and imagine the same for everyone else. Given his recent experiences, he felt foolish assuming anything. Most of the people he had met this past week had been nothing like him. Most of the situations in which he had found himself were as alien to his own expectations as a forest to a fish. He had been held up in a lavatory. He had been arrested, secured in the rear of a police cruiser and then almost died in a car accident. He was being pursued by the Pennsylvania State Police, the FBI and the Swedish mob. He had participated in a bank robbery. He had witnessed a beheading. He had been tasered—twice. His left hand had been shattered by a thug. He had hoodwinked both a cartel of nuclear anarchists and the vengeful boss of a lascivious casino. He had received a blowjob in an elevator at Caesars Palace from a woman he had first met on a highway when she had been dressed as a clown.

Still, some things never changed: Adam desperately needed to use the bathroom. He crossed one leg over another and hoped this turbulence would soon pass, the seat belt light would blink off and he would be able to unload his urine like a gentleman. They were expected to land in Providence in a half hour, but if this nasty weather forced them into a holding pattern over the Atlantic ... He stared at the near-empty cup of ginger ale on his tray table and wondered if he had the balls to unzip his fly and use the cup as a temporary repository for the hot liquid contents of his aching, aching bladder.

The 757 jiggled again, and this time the rocking did not abate. The gods shook the airplane to identify what rattling mysteries lay inside its metal wrapping.

"This isn't fair," muttered Bernard.

His shoulders convulsed. The boy sobbed. Adam reached out to comfort him, but Bernard slapped his hand away.

Then a white-haired matron sitting across the aisle leaned over and whispered to Bernard:

"Young man, we're not going to crash."

Her voice, though soft and light, so hummed with confidence that Bernard glanced up from his mournful reverie and offered her a quizzical look.

She replied with a grin. Her lips were all makeup and very little actual flesh. "We're not going to crash because I've already been in a plane crash once in my life. The odds of it happening twice to me are astronomical. You see, young man, because of my bad luck, I'm your good luck charm."

Her companion, an equally old man, added his own two cents with a throaty grumble.

"Oh, shut your pie hole, Adam," she shot back, "I'm telling the story."

"You always tell the story, Anna."

"We were part of an historical event. My brother has no sense of history."

"Your names are Adam and Anna?" inquired Adam (the younger).

The old couple nodded.

"My name is Adam. My sister's name is Anna."

"This life," observed Anna. Her painted eyebrows crinkled in amazement. "Coincidences and circles. My brother and I were part of an historical event. Have you ever heard of Flight 818?"

Adam and Bernard shook their heads.

"Of course they haven't heard of Flight 818, Anna. You think they teach about it in school?"

"Maybe they heard about it in the news."

"When they were in the womb?"

"Oh, shut your pie hole. So do you want to hear the story of Flight 818?"

Flight 2131 from Las Vegas to Providence bounced up and down like a racquetball. Bernard's grip on his laptop became iron-tight.

Anna slid her hand across Bernard's and told him the story of Flight 818:

"We were flying from Hawaii to San Francisco on TWA. TWA doesn't exist anymore, but when it did, it was very popular. TWA was founded by Howard Hughes. He was obsessive-compulsive. My grandson Jack may be obsessive-compulsive. They're giving him tests. He's four. Adam and I are flying there now to be with my son and his family. But back when we were flying from Hawaii to San Francisco, my son hadn't even been born yet. None of my kids had. We were flying from Hawaii to San Francisco for our honeymoon. Adam and I had a joint wedding. My husband and his wife are no longer with us.

"Most people honeymoon in Hawaii but we all grew up in Kaua'i and for us, California was the Promised Land. So close, so far. Our joint wedding took place at sunset in the shadow of Mount Waialeale. We had one hundred guests. Adam didn't want a luau but I insisted. I liked to get my way, when I was younger. We ate foot-long kabobs around a beachfront bonfire until the wee hours and then we went to bed.

"My husband's name was Iokua. I have a picture of him here. This was when he was in the Navy. He was an engineer. Look at those blue eyes. Aren't those the very eyes of integrity? He was a good man. Adam here married his sister Hekele. Adam doesn't keep any photos of her, but I do.

"This is Hekele. She's twenty-six in that picture. She died of breast cancer when she was thirty-three. Adam doesn't keep any photos of her. He used to, but one day he made up his mind and, well, I guess he likes to get his way too. I think it's sad. My husband died a few years ago. Heart attack. I still have hundreds of photos of him. Not that I need the photos. The last image in my mind on the day I die will be of him and his perfect blue eyes.

"But I'm going off track. I'm sorry. I do tend to do that, now and again. Bad habit of old age, I guess. Verbal sifting. What I was telling you about was the flight. Flight 818 from Honolulu to San Francisco, June twenty-first. First day of summer. We boarded the flight at 8:30 in the morning. All four of us were teetering from exhaustion and all four of us probably were still a little drunk but we behaved ourselves and took our seats in Row 18. Middle of the plane. Right by the wings. I had the window seat on my side and Adam had the window seat on his. There's a certain ease to window seats, isn't there? Not just to balance out the claustrophobia, although that helps, but being so close to the sky relaxes me. I've always gravitated toward the sky. My brother's always gravitated toward fire. Believe me, the day they banned cigarette smoking from airplanes was one of the worst days of his life. He travels a lot. He helped get us these first class seats for free thanks to his frequent flyer miles. He is a consultant for … oh, but there I go again with my verbal sifting. Please forgive me.

"We took off from the runway. Smooth sailing. Well, smooth flying. Not an ounce of turbulence. Unlike tonight. The flight from Honolulu to San Francisco was very long, so they showed a movie. They showed E.T. Well, I didn't much care for aliens, so I closed my eyes and drifted off to sleep.

"You know how sometimes you tend to wake up a few minutes before the alarm clock? How your body can sometimes anticipate something dramatic? Well, I woke up a few hours later for no apparent reason and lucky thing too, or I would never have seen what I saw. Everyone else was asleep. With the night we had, who can blame them? So I gazed out my window. What a sunny day it was, especially above the cloud line. I had to squint just to see. I stared out at the clouds and the sun and the silvery wing and the jet engine … and then suddenly the silvery wing and the jet engine weren't there. We heard a loud crash, as if someone had clanged together all the pots and pans in the whole world at the same time. Everyone woke up. The plane leaned to the left and very quickly lost altitude.

"We didn't know it at the time, but what had happened was that the wing had been hit by a falling satellite. A Chinese satellite had lost its orbit and plummeted to the Earth. These things happen all the time, apparently, and ninety-nine percent of the time the satellites fall harmlessly into the sea. After all, most of the Earth is water. Well, this satellite was heading for the water too. It just so happens that we were in its way and crash! Pots and pans. I looked out the window and I swear—I swear I could see pieces of the wing falling through the clouds and vanishing. I thought we were going to die. We all thought we were going to die. Everyone screamed and cried. Everyone except my Iokua, who just held my hand and looked me in the eye and I felt so reassured. Maybe he thought we were going to die, but I could tell that he was at least happy we were going to die together. And that's what did it for me. That's what kept me together through it all.

"We fell thousands of feet in minutes. The pilot radioed for help. Behind me I heard someone praying in Latin. In front of me I heard someone praying in Mandarin. I was an atheist. So I told Iokua I loved him and he told me he loved me and we waited for the big splash and the water to pour in and for the slow cold death in the Pacific Ocean.

"But there was no big splash. Are you sure you've never heard of this? It really made the news for many years. It was a miracle. A real miracle. A human miracle. The pilot and the co-pilot were able to right the plane just in time for us to slide across the surface of the ocean horizontally instead of nose first and we made it. Some windows cracked. A few bones were broken. But that was it. We made it. We survived. The Coast Guard showed up a few hours later and we survived. We never did get to San Francisco that day, but the airline gave us free tickets and we were able to fly to California the following month. Adam thought we were crazy. He never wanted to get on another plane again. Now he flies twice a month. His fear faded. Most things do. Most things.

"And I love to fly too. I fly every chance I can get. There's no risk involved, not for me. When it comes to flying, I'm a lucky charm. And it really is a great invention. Nevada to Rhode Island in only a few hours? A real human miracle. It's terrific, isn't it? Being alive? Fearlessly being alive? I wouldn't have it any other way."

Shortly thereafter, the plane steadied itself and soon prepared for its descent into Rhode Island.

Chapter Twenty-Two

Another foreign city, another cheap motel. This one lay across the street from the airport, snuggling tightly between a Kentucky Fried Chicken and an automated car wash. Unlike most urban airports, which were located on the outskirts of the city, Providence's T.F. Green Airport was not even in Providence itself. Instead, as Adam and Bernard soon discovered, they had landed in the nearby city of Warwick. The airport lived and breathed in the center of an overdeveloped commercial district bordered on one side by famous Route 1, that lollygagging stretch of pavement extending from the lobster traps of eastern Maine to the nude beaches of South Florida. It was here on Route 1, between the restaurant and car wash, that Adam and Bernard found shelter from the cold and soon fell aimlessly asleep.

When Adam awoke, at approximately 7:45 A.M., the ruined tendons and muscles in his left hand were painfully pulsating inside his fiber cast. He was more cognizant of that localized agony, and consumed by it, than he was of his heartbeat or his respiration. With his one good hand he reached down to the floor, where his clothes lay in a tumble, and found his painkillers. As he popped two into his mouth, not bothering with a water chaser, he noticed that Bernard was already awake, sitting up in his twin bed and typing away on his laptop.

"What are you working on?" Adam inquired.

"Nothing."

"It can't be nothing."

"It can be and it is," replied Bernard, "so go back to sleep."

Adam stumbled out of bed and stretched his tired limbs. "Computer game?"

"No."

"Chat room?"

"No."

Adam shrugged. "I'm just curious." He ambled toward the bathroom for his morning shower.

"If you must know," Bernard mumbled, "I'm working on my blog."

Adam closed the door behind him, turned on the shower, yawned, realized what Bernard had said, realized the ramifications of what Bernard had said and rushed back into the room.

"You're doing what?"

"You heard me. Got a problem with it? It's therapeutic."

"Bernard …" Adam slowly sat down at the corner of the boy's bed. "Just how explicit is your blog?"

"Explicit? Shit, man, it's nothing like that."

"No, by explicit, I mean, well, if someone were to read your blog, someone like, say, the FBI, would they be able to use that information to find us?"

Bernard frowned.

Adam frowned.

"It's not likely," said Bernard finally. "Nobody knows about my blog. Like I said, it's just therapeutic."

"Nobody else reads it?"

"No."

"Nobody from home? None of your friends from your home town, wondering how old Bernard is doing in the States?"

Bernard squared his gaze. "I didn't have any friends in my home town."

"Is that why you left?"

"Man, go take your shower."

Not wanting to push the kid, and at the same time not really knowing how to deal with him, Adam got up and went to the bathroom. He'd never had a little brother. All of his friends were underachieving alcoholics. And he had no gauge for his recent relationships with Filbert and Cherry. Bernard had sliced open his chest and twice electrocuted him. Still, to imagine what the boy had been through, what his father had done to him …

Fathers.

These were the thoughts that tumbled through Adam's head as he lathered, rinsed, and repeated. When it came Bernard's turn to wash up, the boy made sure to bring his laptop in with him and lock shut the bathroom door.

Adam, squeaky-clean and bemused, clicked on the TV and watched the Smurfs. When Bernard finally emerged from the bathroom, it was almost nine o'clock. He and Adam took advantage of the motel's continental breakfast (wheat toast and whole milk) and then hailed a cab.

"Providence Home for the Aged," said Bernard, and they were off.

Bernard whiled away the time with his laptop. Adam whiled away the time staring at the highway. Rhode Island had one: Interstate 95. Like its forefather Route 1, I95 ran the expanse of the East Coast. Just being on it, Adam felt connected to his mother in Newark, his cousins in Bethesda, his grandparents in Tampa. Maybe Ebbets and Anna were located somewhere on this lifeline. According to Bernard, Ebbets' mother knew.

Their speed slowed to a limp. They had entered morning rush hour. According to a sign by the side of the road, they were nearing Exit 14.

"What exit are we getting off at?" Adam inquired.

The swarthy cab driver, bedecked in Bruins swag, rolled down his window, spat out a chunk of chewed tobacco, rolled his window back up, glanced in the rearview and replied, "Twenty-three."

Adam sighed. Ebbets had promised Christmas Eve. Wednesday evening. Traffic moved in inches; the clock rolled on at a steady clip.

The driver picked up his cell phone and dialed his boyfriend. From Exits 15-18, they exchanged sweet nothings. From Exits 19-21, they argued about lasagna. By Exit 22, the conversation was over and the cabbie was once again chewing tobacco.

By then, it was 10:30.

Providence seemed an eclectic melding of traditional New England (understated downtown architecture, still more brick and mortar than steel and glass) and contemporary America (a march of billboards lined each side of the highway). On its cars, Adam noticed more than a few custom license plates and many quirky bumper stickers. And every few miles announced the turn-off for another exciting Dunkin' Donuts. All in all, thought Adam, this city's even weirder than Vegas.

Exit 23, where downtown became rundown. The cabbie navigated a series of one-way streets and landed them in the parking lot of a ten-story slab of concrete.

"This is the Providence Home for the Aged?" asked Adam. "All this?"

"Yes, sir. That'll be thirty bucks."

Adam and Bernard approached the building. Sure enough, right above the handicapped-accessible sliding front doors, hung the sign: PROVIDENCE HOME FOR THE AGED, EST. 1923.

"It's like a tenement," Adam said.

"Her name is Miriam," replied Bernard. "How do you want to do this? Are we long-lost cousins from Nevada? Children of friends? Students writing a term paper on old people?"

"Don't worry about it. I'll do the talking. I'll tell the truth."

"That plan is awful."

They entered the Providence Home for the Aged. The floors were partitioned (by colorful paper signage) into social areas and residential areas. The social areas consisted mainly of a TV Room (with many, many speakers) and a Game Room (billiards, mah-jongg, cards). The residential areas were divided into five-person suites (co-ed) and two-person bedrooms (single sex). This was no convalescence facility for people to whittle, wither and die. This was a frat house for the elderly.

Unlike the rest of the building, the first floor functioned mainly for administrative purposes: front desk, infirmary, etc. Adam and Bernard made their way to the C-shaped front desk (bookended by an itty-bitty Christmas tree on one end and an itty-bitty Hanukkah menorah on the other), where they were greeted by a spry geriatric wearing a seersucker suit and a well-oiled black toupee.

"Good morning," he said. "Welcome to the Providence Home for the Aged. My name is Giovanni. How may I be of service?"

"Um," replied Adam, "can we speak to someone who works here?"

"Oh, I work here." He flashed his pearly dentures. "Don't worry. I'm not offended. I'm also a resident. My name is Giovanni. Most residents volunteer. It helps keep our brains from turning to mashed potatoes. Mashed potatoes are the special of the day. How may I be of service?"

A dumpy nurse labeled MOREEN approached them. "Is everything okay here, Giovanni?" She carried a small cardboard box filled with assorted knickknacks.

"Oh, everything is five by five, ma'am. I'm just doing my job."

Adam glanced into the box. He spotted a wooden toy train, a half-eaten Nerf ball, and a black-and-white photograph in a cheap silver frame. Something about the photograph caught his eye.

Bernard cued in, "We're here to see Miriam Ebbets."

Adam stared closely at the photograph. Two adolescent boys standing by a pond. Nothing special there. But still ...

"Miriam has a pair of visitors?" piped Giovanni. "Oh, she will be excited. She so rarely gets visitors in person. I'll call her now. She'll want to put in her contacts."

As Giovanni dialed Miriam's extension, Nurse Moreen noticed Adam's fixation on the photograph. She did not like it. "Can I help you, sir?"

Adam reached into the box and took the picture out. In the light of the lobby, he could see the faces of the boys clearly now. The one on the right looked vaguely familiar, but the one on the left, with his hands in his pockets the smirk on his lips, was unmistakable.

Moreen snatched the photograph from Adam's grip and stuffed it back into the box. "Sir, it's best that you keep your hands to yourself. These belongings are not yours."

"Whose are they?" he asked. "Please, tell me."

Moreen huffed.

"Please. It's important."

"One of our residents passed away last week. These are what's left, what his family failed to claim."

Oh, God.

"Uncle Dexter," muttered Adam.

At that, the nurse transformed from dyspeptic to sympathetic. "You knew him?"

"He thought he was the king of Mars?"

She nodded. Her brown eyes welled. "He used to tell me when he returned to Mars, he'd take me with him. Because I could make him laugh."

"In that photograph ... that's him, and with him ... that's my father."

Nurse Moreen gently placed the box on the front desk. "If there's anything in here you'd like to take, you're welcome to it. Excuse me."

She swiftly walked away, sliding her hands across her moist cheeks.

"Adam," said Bernard, "you okay?"

Adam nodded.

"Mrs. Ebbets will see us now."

"She's on the sixth floor," added Giovanni. "Room 616."

"Thanks."

"I can keep an eye on the box if you want. I'll make sure no one takes it."

Adam smiled at the old man. "Thank you."

He and Bernard took the elevator up to the sixth floor.

"Sure you're okay?" asked Bernard.

"Just an unexpected surprise."

"Aren't all surprises unexpected?"

Adam chuckled. If any kid deserved a heartfelt wedgie, it was Bernard.

Room 616 lay near the end of a wide corridor. According to a plaque outside the door, it housed both Miriam Ebbets and a Gertrude Gaddis. Adam rapped on the door.

"It's unlocked." Mrs. Ebbets spoke in a reedy, quavering contralto. Adam wondered if she had Parkinson's disease. He pushed open the door and found her sitting on her made bed. She wore a brown dress two sizes too big for her body. Her makeup appeared slightly smeared, put on by trembling, unsteady hands. A Dixie cup of water and a bulky pair of glasses lay beside her on her nightstand. She had indeed, somehow, put in her contacts.

Gertrude Gaddis' side of the room was empty. She must have recently died.

"Good morning, Mrs. Ebbets," said Adam.

"Good morning, ma'am," echoed Bernard.

She smiled at them, indicated a nearby loveseat, waited for them to get comfortable and then slowly spoke:

"So, tell me ... what has my son done now?"

Adam shifted in his seat. "Mrs. Ebbets, what makes you think—?"

"Son, I don't know you. Christmas is three days away. Unless you're here bearing gifts from the North Pole, cut the crap. What has my son done now?"

Adam glanced at Bernard. Bernard responded with a shrug.

"Well," said Adam, "it's complicated."

"No, it's simple. My John is a fuck-up. Always has been, always will be. I love him to death, I swear I do, but I'd be a fool if I didn't see him for what he is. He's too smart for his own good and too impatient with the world to use his brains for anything decent." She fought off a tremor, glanced at Bernard and sighed. "You're Bernard."

Bernard stared down at his sneakers. "He mentioned me?"

"His protégé? Yes, he did. He says you remind him of himself at your age."

"Wow."

"That's not a compliment."

"Oh."

"So what has John done to bring you all the way from Las Vegas to Rhode Island in the middle of winter?"

Adam leaned forward in his seat, cleared his throat and told her the tale. All of it. Halfway through, Mrs. Ebbets took a pill to steady her Parkinson's. The telling took about fifteen minutes. By the end of it, the cold sun had risen above the view of the room's windows, lending curly shadows to the powder blue carpet.

"Well," said Mrs. Ebbets, "it sounds like you're selling me a box of bullshit, but I like to think I can tell the difference between the bold-faced truth and a bald-faced lie. I did live in Brooklyn most of my life. Don't ask me how I ended up here."

"What we need to know, ma'am, is where he might be." Adam absently rubbed his palms together. "I just want to get my sister back. I promise you, we'll do everything we can not to cause any harm to your son."

She smiled at them both, leaned back against her pillow and replied, "And stop the bombs."

"What?"

"You intend to stop him from detonating the bombs too, right?"

"Of course."

"Which is your priority?"

Adam frowned. "Does it matter?"

"I'm curious."

"We're going to try to do both. But first we need to know where he is. Do you know where he is?"

"No." She adjusted the bottom of her dress to cover her legs. "But I know where he will be on Christmas Eve. There's only one place he could be."

This was it.

"Where?" asked Adam.

"I'm not going to tell you," replied Mrs. Ebbets. "Not ever. Anyway, it's almost time for my walk. The orderly will be here soon. Have a nice day."

Chapter Twenty-Three

Adam and Bernard were speechless and powerless. Mrs. Ebbets slowly swigged her water. Her lipstick bloodied the rim of the tiny paper cup. She had to hold the cup with both hands to keep it steady.

"While I'm on my walk, they're going to freshen the air in my room. Since it's cold outside, they can't really open the windows so the way they freshen the air is with chemicals. Sprays. Why do you think they need to freshen the air in my room every day while I'm on my walk?"

She posed this question to Bernard.

The boy, still reeling from her refusal to assist, replied softly, "Germs."

"That's the superficial answer. That's the answer they give me when I ask. But the real reason is me. My organs. They're rotting inside my body and they're giving off a stink and they don't want their facility to smell like death. So they freshen the air in the rooms of those of us who … need our walks. Do you see that bed there?" She motioned with her thumb to the vacant half of the room. "Two days ago a woman lived there. This was her home. We were roommates. Her name was Gertie. She was a lesbian, but she never made a pass at me. She liked crossword puzzles. She had three sons and one daughter. Her children and grandchildren came to see her every weekend. I knew them all by name. Last month, they got a card for my birthday. They all signed it, the children and the grandchildren. You, there. The one whose sister got snatched."

"My name is Adam," replied Adam defiantly. "Her name is Anna."

"Whatever. Do you want me to tell you why I'm not going tell you what you need to know? How about you, Bernard? Do you want to know too?"

Their answers: stares of defiance.

Mrs. Ebbets positioned her glass back on her night table. "Bernard, what would happen if my son succeeded and twelve of these bombs went off Christmas Eve?"

"What would happen?"

"Yes. Take me through the aftermath. I'm curious."

Adam bounced to his feet and paced the room.

"The first effect," mumbled Bernard, "will be thermal. The bombs we produced … you have to understand, even though we knew what we were doing …"

"I don't want to hear your excuses, Bernard. I want to hear your results. Please."

"When your son recruited me, when I met Ebbets, he was the first person who'd ever understood what went on in my head."

Mrs. Ebbets tut-tutted. Adam sat back down, glared at her then stood back up.

As he had on the plane, Bernard clutched his laptop to his chest. "The first effect will be thermal. The blast radius will be much larger than Hiroshima."

"But that's just the beginning, right?"

"Yes."

"I grew up during the Cold War," said Mrs. Ebbets. "I remember hiding under my desk during air raid drills. I knew people who built fallout shelters. What will be the fallout of your bombs, Bernard?"

"It's … complicated."

"But you're bright. Like my John. You understand the process, don't you?"

"Yes."

"Please. Explain it."

Bernard wiped his wet cheeks and continued:

"A nuclear explosion is literally the explosion of the nucleus of an atom—enriched uranium—because enriched uranium is very good at splitting. When the atom splits, it releases energy. $E=mc^2$ and all that. One atom split becomes two atoms. Two atoms become four. The soot and smoke left over from the explosion is saturated with radiation from the fission process. The radiation spreads extremely quickly. Then evaporation. If these bombs detonate near-simultaneously, as Ebbets intends, the stratosphere becomes stained with dust and ash and the sun will be blacked out."

"Nuclear winter," said Mrs. Ebbets.

Bernard nodded.

"Thank you, Bernard." She offered him a shaky smile. It was the first time she had revealed her teeth. She had five. Unevenly spaced. Mrs. Ebbets had put in her contacts but had neglected to apply her dentures. "Thank you."

Adam punched his fist against her bed. "And you're going to let all that happen!"

"What can I do? I'm just an old woman in a used bed on her last legs. Either way, I'll be dead by springtime. And God knows, I don't believe in Heaven. Or the Greater Good, whatever the hell that means. I tried to do good in my life and now look at me. Do you see any Christmas gifts lying around? Did you have to wait in line to come to visit me? Ah, well. You really should get going. The orderly will be here any minute and if it's Todd, well, he doesn't take kindly to Negroes."

The shadows along the carpet stretched their many limbs across the walls and ceiling of the room. In his seat, Bernard wept.

But Adam was not finished.

"Then don't do it for yourself." He looked her in the eye. "You just asked Bernard to tell you what would happen. Why? You said it yourself. You grew up during the Cold War. You know what a nuclear holocaust will be like. You probably were shown filmstrips of it during science class! You asked Bernard to go through all that science and horror because you're proud of your son. 'Look what he will accomplish. Look how far he's come from bashing windshields in Brooklyn.' Or is it that he is all you have, him, this monster of a human being. Who kidnapped my sister. My sister. But none of that matters. None of what I went through to come here matters, because you are so full of bile and selfishness. When I walked through that door, I had no idea what to expect, meeting the mother of the man who has caused all this harm. Turns out the apple didn't fall too far from the tree. What a surprise. What a shock."

Adam touched Bernard on the shoulder and then helped the boy to his feet. As they ambled out of the room, Mrs. Ebbets suddenly called:

"Adam."

Expectations low, he turned around.

"In that story you told me, everything you've been through, have you had a chance to call your mother?"

Adam raised an eyebrow. "What?"

"I'll bet she's very worried about you," said Mrs. Ebbets. Her five teeth wobbled inside her red mouth. "I'll bet she's panicking. You should give her a call."

"Lady, you've got some nerve."

She shrugged. "I am what I am."

Adam joined Bernard in the corridor. On their slow walk to the elevator, they passed a wiry teenager with a shaved head. His scrubs bore the name of "Todd." Adam tapped the Down button by the elevator doors.

"So now what?" Bernard meekly asked. The lion had become a mouse. "What can we do now?"

Adam stuffed his good hand in his pants. It found his wad of bills, change, and pain pills … and the Mennonite cloth doll. Surprised he still had it, he took it out and examined its stitching; sure enough, they bore nary a scratch. Adam suddenly thought again about Filbert's reliable star. The perseverance of some things …

"Wait here," Adam said. "I'll be right back."

He headed for the nearby payphones, emptied the requisite coins into the slot and dialed Newark. The line rang twice before his mother picked up.

"Adam?" she said, as if she already knew. Or as if she just hoped every phone call over the past few days would be the one from her children.

"Anna?"

"Hi Mom," he replied. "I'm okay."

He heard her bawl. His mommy. The sound of her relief shredded his heart into tears.

"Mom ... I'm so sorry I haven't called. I've been ... selfish. As usual."

"Is Anna with you?" she asked, between sobs. "Are you both all right?"

Adam clutched the phone in his good hand, took a deep breath and replied, "Yeah, Mom. We're both fine. See, one of my friends got this great deal on this place in Tijuana ..."

"Oh ... okay ... wait ... Tijuana?"

"Yeah. It really was a once-in-a-lifetime opportunity. We really thought we'd be back by now but we just lost track of time and we've had trouble getting phone reception and, well, you know how it is."

"Tijuana?!"

"I promise you, both of us will be home by Thursday." One way or another. "I'm really sorry."

"You I can see doing this, you I'm not surprised, but your sister?"

"Her friends talked her into it. She really had a great time, Mom. She's happy. I want you to know that we're happy. And we'll be home soon."

"You better be." Her sobs had become less frequent. "Thursday is Christmas. You already missed your uncle's funeral."

"Yeah, I know," replied Adam. "I promise I'll end up in Rhode Island someday and pay my respects. Listen, Mom, I've got to go. You know how expensive long distance rates can be. But I'll see you on Thursday, all right?"

"Young man, be prepared for some major grounding. And chore work."

"I love you, Mom."

"I love you too."

End of call.

Adam ambled back to the bank of elevators. He took from his pocket the small cloth doll.

"Everything okay?" asked Bernard.

"Everything is far from okay," answered Adam, "but you already knew that. I'll be right back."

Adam walked into Mrs. Ebbets' room just as Todd was putting on her slippers.

"Can I help you?" growled Todd.

Mrs. Ebbets patted him on his forearm. "Leave us a minute, will you?"

Todd left them a minute.

"Come to yell at me some more?" she asked.

He sighed, clutched the doll in his hands. Saw her see it. Watched the confusion mount above her brow. Placed the doll on her nightstand, beside her Dixie cup and her bifocals.

"Now you have a Christmas gift," he said, and kissed her furrowed forehead.

She reached over with her quaking hands and picked up the doll. Slowly she turned it over and examined it. Adam had walked back toward the doorway, ready to silently leave her life, when she muttered something, almost under her breath. Almost, but not quite. She made sure Adam heard her.

Three syllables divided into two words.

Two words that indicated a specific location.

Where her son would be on Wednesday night.

Adam did not turn around, did not say thank you or ask why she had changed her mind. He just walked down the hallway, quietly shared his news with Bernard, and on the elevator ride down to the first floor of the rest home, the two of them methodically strategized their endgame.

Chapter Twenty-Four

However, one disagreement remained: how to get from where they were to where they needed to be; more specifically, the mode of transportation.

"An airplane is faster," said Adam.

"Airplanes have mechanical problems and crash," replied Bernard.

They bickered in a McDonald's across the street from the Providence Home.

"Do you know how unlikely it is," lobbed Adam, "for an airplane to have mechanical problems and crash?"

"Do you know how likely it is," volleyed Bernard, "for an airplane to have mechanical problems and crash during winter? Eighty-five percent of all air traffic accidents occur in the winter."

Adam filled his mouth with cheeseburger.

Then Bernard suggested, "We could go by bus."

Adam shook his head and washed down his food with a pint of vanilla shake. His feet tapped at his flimsy plastic bag on the floor, which contained, along with a copy of today's newspaper he had purchased at the rest home's gift shop, the framed photograph of his father.

"Why not?"

"Because." Adam took another bite. "It will take too long."

"You're spitting your food all over me."

"It's not intentional," replied Adam, spitting his food all over Bernard, somewhat intentionally.

Bernard fired up his laptop. "We've tried air, we've tried land. That leaves fire and water."

" 'Air, land, fire and water?' What is that, Bernard, some kind of Dungeons & Dragons thing?"

"Shut up."

He started surfing the net.

Adam finished his meal. He couldn't believe how famished he was. He even contemplated returning to the counter for another helping of fried McGoodness. Then again, when was the last time he had eaten a real meal? Had it been that misguided trip to Denny's with his sister?

Bernard tapped the screen of his laptop and declared, "Fire, of course. Fire." He swiveled his laptop to face Adam. The blue-tinted webpage displayed on the screen belonged to Amtrak.

"Amtrak?"

"It's perfect," said Bernard. "The speed of a plane and the safety of a bus. And there's a train leaving tonight at ten twenty-five that will get us where we need to be by ten Wednesday morning."

"Are you one of those kids obsessed with choo-choo trains?"

"Fuck you."

"Ten twenty-five tonight, ten Wednesday morning. Two days. A plane would get us there in three hours."

"Airplanes are off the table. This is perfect. Have you ever been on a train? They're terrific. They've got beds, food, wi-fi. Everything we could possibly need. And they're reliable. Do you know how many train accidents have occurred in the past ten years? Two."

"Maybe that's because no one rides the train anymore."

"We are," Bernard gloated.

Then Adam and Bernard split up. They agreed to meet up again at 9:30 at Amtrak's Providence Station but until then, they would engage in some "private time." For Adam, this meant, first and foremost, a trip to a bar.

The bar he found was a hole in the wall called The Still Toe. Its proprietors apparently had no concern for heating bills; the all-maple interior felt like a hot coal sauna. A Narragansett Indian with an unavoidable harelip and an inescapable Hawaiian shirt manned the bar. The only other occupant of the bar, a schoolmarm with a hacking cough, sat in a shadowy corner booth, applying a pen to the daily newspaper's personals in between bites from her cheesesteak.

Adam took a seat at the bar.

The bartender, engrossed in glass cleaning, didn't even turn around. "Can I see some ID?"

Adam sifted through his pocket for a good thirty seconds before remembering his ID was with the rest of his property down south, and his fake ID was gathering dust in a Las Vegas trash bin.

"Um," replied Adam.

Now the bartender turned around. His harelip stretched into a grotesque one-sided grin. "Beer?"

"Yes, please."

The bartender drafted him a full mug and returned to his cleaning.

"Thank you."

"Six bucks," grunted the bartender.

Adam nearly coughed on the froth. "Six bucks?!"

"No-ID surcharge." Now the other side of the bartender's face smiled. "Just in time for the lunchtime rush."

Adam glanced around the unpopulated sauna-pub. "Lunchtime rush. Right." He chuckled and sipped some more foam.

The front door swung open and in poured twenty-two uniformed postal workers. "Johnny," announced one of the mob to the bartender, "I just won the Santa lottery, the Santa lottery was just won by me! A round of drinks for everyone!" to which the mob responded with a series of hurrahs.

A bevy of waitresses suddenly appeared from a side door and as the postal workers took their seats at the tables and booths, the waitresses took their orders. Adam, more than a little bewildered, turned to Johnny the harelip Narragansett and inquired, "What's the Santa lottery?"

"What's the Santa lottery?!" This not from Johnny but from the lottery winner, who plopped down on the stool beside Adam. The middle-aged man's entire ruddy face was a smile; in fact, if Adam hadn't known better, he would have sworn the grin grew past the limits of the face, past the man's butterfly ears, and stretched all the way from one wall to the other. In his hands he clutched a burlap sack the size (and color) of an adult orangutan.

"My name's Dolan Wood," he said, frenetically pumping Adam's hand. "Dolan Wood's my name. And if anyone in this joint is fit to tell you what the Santa lottery is, it is I."

At that moment, Adam realized why The Still Toe was kept at such a balmy temperature. Its primary source of income was these postal workers who spent their working days exposed to the elements. He also realized that perhaps he had chosen the wrong bar at the wrong time in which to have a few beers.

"Dolan, you sperm sack, won't you leave this poor child alone?" This from another postal worker, her long white hair braided into a ponytail, who washed down her plea with a pint of Guinness.

"Am I bothering you, kid? Are you being bothered by me? I don't think he's being bothered by me, Karen."

Adam shrugged.

"See, now he's too shy to hurt your feelings. Dolan, be a dear and sit your bony Irish-American ass down at a table." Karen waited for a refill of her pint and then ambled back to her seat.

Then Dolan wrapped a friendly arm around Adam's shoulders. "What's your name, kid?"

"Adam."

"Adam! That's a fine, fine name. A fine, fine name it is. I don't suppose it's Irish now, is it?"

"No, sir."

"Ah well. Just the same." Dolan splashed a shot of seltzer water down his gullet. "So, you wanted to know about the Santa lottery! Of course you did. You're a curious fellow. I can see it in your eyes. How old are you? I've got a boy almost your age. He's curious about everything. 'Why' this and 'how' that. I love him to death. Beyond death. Want to see his picture?"

"No." Adam seized his beer mug for dear life. "Thank you."

The bartender slapped a hand down in front of Dolan. "Here's your tab, Santa Claus." He lifted his hands, revealing a slip of paper. The slip of paper displayed a dollar amount. It was not small.

But Dolan just kept on grinning, reached into his pants, removed a few twenties, and handed them up to Johnny. "Keep the change, my Indian pal. And fill me up a tall cranberry juice, if you would."

Adam checked the clock on the wall. He had nine hours to kill before he had to meet up with Bernard.

Nine hours.

Dolan hefted his sack onto his lap and said, "This, my young friend Adam, this is the Santa lottery."

"You won a bag?"

"Is a bag just a bag?" Dolan pointed at his sack, then at the flimsy plastic bag on Adam's lap. "Is our skin who we are? No, no, no! It's the contents! And inside this bag, inside this beautiful beautiful bag, oh my! You see, every year the post office receives thousands of letters—thousands—that are absolutely undeliverable. Every year between the months of October and December. I'm sure when you were younger you sent off letters to Santa Claus."

Adam hadn't. Aside from that brief childhood correspondence with his sister's ex-bff, Roxanne Banks (which had ended with a bus ticket to Philly and an unanswered door), Adam wasn't much of a writer. English class had always proved to be a great opportunity for him to catch up on missed sleep. Anna had written Santa, though. She had learned how to write in crayon at age two and in pencil at age three. She always made sure to write between the lines. She always made sure her spelling was impeccable before folding her letter and sealing it in an envelope and marking it with a stamp. She always made sure to accompany her mother to the post office. Mom would boost her up to the mail slot and she would deposit the letter herself.

Dolan picked out a handful of letters from the sack and placed them on the counter. They existed in all variations of rectangle (though mostly small), all colors (though mostly reds and greens), and on their surface all manner of scribble (though mostly crooked block print).

"All this undeliverable mail. Didn't you ever wonder what happened to it?"

"I guess I figured you just, you know, threw it away?"

Dolan laughed, patted Adam on the back, and bottomed-up his juice. "Many years ago, the local postmaster, he came up with the brilliant notion of what to do with all these wonderful heartfelt letters. He came up with the lottery. The day after Thanksgiving, all of us puts in a dollar. The money goes to the Hasbro Children's Charity. Hasbro's out of Rhode Island, you know? Anyway, the money isn't the point. Well, it is the point, but it's not what I'm getting at. Are you from New Jersey?"

Adam almost choked on his beer. "What?"

"You are, aren't you? I can always tell. My father could do it too. He could talk with a fellow for two minutes and tell him not only what state he was born in but sometimes what city. My father was a traveling salesman, so I guess that's not too unnatural. Me, I've never been out of New England. No, sir. And no desire to either. Well, I would like to go to Ireland some day. To retire. But that's a ways away, right? What was I talking about? I was talking about something."

"You were telling him about the lottery," replied Johnny, handing Dolan another stein of cranberry juice, "after you clear these letters off the bar."

"Sorry, sorry." Dolan delicately placed the letters back into his sack. "I am sorry."

Johnny nodded, snarled a bit with his harelip, and went back to filling drinks for his thirsty clientele.

"So," said Dolan to Adam, "the Santa lottery. Of which I am the winner. Me. Dolan Wood. It's quite an honor. It's an omen, really. Really, it's an omen. I should buy a Powerball ticket tonight. Johnny, do you know if they're having a Powerball drawing tonight? Eh, he's busy. Nice guy, Johnny. He lost his sister in the Gulf War. Friendly fire. Nothing friendly about fire, if you ask me. Fire's not my thing. No, sir. But as to the lottery, well, now you see, don't you?"

"You won the kids' letters."

"That's right! I won the letters. All of them. They all now belong to me. Today I am Santa Claus."

"But … I mean …" Adam slurped an inch of beer. He was beginning to feel a touch buzzed. "What are you going to do with them? Now that you have them?"

"What am I going to do with them? Well, now, there's the thing. What would you do with them, my lager-loving pal Adam?"

"I don't know." Adam didn't. "I honestly don't know." He honestly didn't.

"Don't worry, don't worry. It's not fair to ask you. Put you on the spot like that. You have my apologies. My apologies are to be had by you. But I've had years to ruminate on this very subject. Years of watching my colleagues win the lottery and take their sacks to their attics or basements and let them collect dust or worse, toss them away with the New Year's trash. Not I! I have a grand plan. Want to hear it?"

"Yes, I do." Adam did. He honestly did.

Johnny refilled his mug.

"I have some money saved up. Put aside for a day of rain … or for a day of sun like this. Like me winning the lottery. What I'm going to do is I'm going to open these envelopes, every one, and I'm going to do everything in my power to make sure these boys and girls get what they want from Old Saint Nick."

"Hrm?"

"I have their addresses. I have their list of toys and dolls. I will be their secret real Santa. Their secret real Santa will be me."

"But, wait—what if their parents have already gotten them what they write?"

Dolan frowned.

"What if, say, what if little Jimmy writes a letter to Santa asking for a tricycle and his mother helps him write a letter to Santa asking for a tricycle so his mother knows to get little Jimmy for Christmas a tricycle?"

Dolan frowned deeper.

"Am I wrong? Tell me if I'm wrong." Adam finished down another pint. "Because I'm wrong all the time. You have no idea."

Dolan stared down into his magical sack, then across the bar at his reflection in the mirror behind the stacked bottles. What he saw was a sad middle-aged postal worker holding a bag of undeliverable mail, and the drunken college kid who had set him right by proving him wrong.

"Dolan ... hey, Dolan, man, I didn't mean to rain down on your parade. Let me buy you a drink."

Dolan shook his head. "I'm fine."

"Dolan ..."

"This is what I've wanted for Christmas for fourteen years."

Adam sighed, patted the man on the back. Poor fellow. Poor fool.

Dolan groaned.

"Johnny," called Adam. "Pour my friend Dolan here a drink. Whatever he wants."

"Seltzer water," Dolan mumbled, as if cursing a misbehaving goat. "That's all I drink. I drink seltzer water. Seltzer water."

"Seltzer water, Johnny. Make it a double. On the rocks. Spare no expense."

Johnny rolled his eyes and followed orders. Dolan chugged down his drink in one fat gulp. Then he turned to Adam.

"Thank you," he said, without a hint of sarcasm, "for shattering my world."

"Uh ..."

"I have been so short-sighted, haven't I? I mean, haven't I? This is what a man gets for not going to college. You go to college, don't you? In New Jersey?"

"Michigan."

"Whatever. My point is, you see the sharks. The sharks are seen by you. Me? I didn't see the sharks. I only saw the pretty, sparkly ocean. I want to thank you, Adam. I want to give you a token of my respect."

"Uh ..."

So Dolan handed him the sack of letters.

"You are more deserving of this," swore Dolan, "than I will ever be.

Take good care of them. Each letter is someone's wish. Take good care of them. I know you will. Because I won't."

Dolan scratched behind his large ears, gave Adam a wet hug and then stumbled off to the men's room.

"What the hell am I supposed to do with this?" Adam asked no one in particular; no one in particular offered any particular help. He asked the question again an hour later, when the pub had been emptied and all the postmen returned to their posts and the waitresses had finished wiping down the tables and Johnny had served Adam his ninth, and last, pint of beer.

"It's time to go," said Johnny.

"You're closing?" asked Adam. He glanced up at the clock. The hands on it looked so funny, like long black worms. The worms waved at him: hello! Adam waved back.

"I'm not closing," said Johnny. "But you're going. I called you a cab. Should be here in five minutes."

"You called me a cab? That was so nice of you!" Adam wanted to hug the kind deformed bartender.

Five minutes later, Johnny escorted Adam to the curb in front of the bar. The cab escorted Adam to Providence Station. Adam escorted himself to a bench inside the train depot. He slipped his father's photograph into his bag of mail, used the bag of mail as a pillow, and let the clip-clopping footfalls of passing pedestrians lull him into soggy dreamland.

Chapter Twenty-Five

The kick in his thigh woke him from his sleep; the punch in his solar plexus opened his eyes. Bernard snarled down at him like a feral mutt.

"Ow," said Adam.

"You smell like a pisshole."

Adam sat up. His eyeballs swam in pain.

"The train's boarding. I took some money out of your pockets and bought us some tickets. Let's go, wino."

"I'd ask you why you attacked me, but that would be like asking a bear why he craps in the woods."

Adam followed Bernard to Gate 8, where a line of eighteen people had already formed.

"You haven't asked me why I have a bag of mail."

Bernard popped a piece of gum into his mouth. "Uh-huh."

"Aren't you curious?"

"I found you asleep and drunk in a train station. The fact that you have a mailbag ... well, I'm sure there's a funny story that goes along with it, but I'm also sure you come across in the story as a moron and I don't need any further proof that you're a moron."

Adam shrugged.

They moved up in line.

"So what did you do this afternoon?" Adam asked.

"I hacked into the website for the *New York Times* and changed every mention of the words 'New York' to 'Cock & Balls.'"

"Why?"

"I was bored."

They brandished their tickets, were given directions to their compartment, and then they followed those directions to their berth in Car D. Bernard had purchased them tickets for a "Superliner Bedroom."

One wall of the seven-by-eight-foot space was occupied by a green sofa. One was occupied by the window. One wall was occupied by, well, nothing really, except for a moderately comfortable green armchair. And one wall was occupied by two doors: one led to the corridor and one led to a private lavatory (and shower!) roughly the width of an oak tree.

Bernard immediately sat down in the armchair, plugged in his laptop, and commenced his evening net-activities. Adam plunked his mailbag down on the sofa and gazed out the window at starless darkness.

"I've never been on a train before," said Adam.

Bernard smiled.

Bernard smiled?

Yes, Bernard smiled. The glee of the train ride could not be contained, not even by his mask of snarl.

"Railroads created the modern world," he said. "Railroads enabled people who never in their lives would have left their cities, to go anywhere and see everything. Railroads made factories practical, which made science practical and profitable, which led to more scientific endeavors, which led to computers." The cabin shuddered, and then they were off.

Adam misspoke when he'd claimed to have never been on a train, and as the Amtrak clambered down its iron rails, he remembered, vividly, when last he had heard that distinctive rhythmic metal-upon-metal clanging and felt that unmistakable rocking in his joints and bones. Like millions of men, women and children, Adam had once been a passenger on the New York City subway system.

His hometown of Newark was not far from NYC. The famous Manhattan skyline was visible at night from Adam's bedroom window, but the relationship between New Jerseyans and New Yorkers was not amicable, especially since both of the city's football teams, the Jets and the Giants, had moved, by 1984, across the river to East Rutherford, New Jersey. The common prevailing wisdom was that all New Yorkers thought all New Jerseyans were white-collar prigs and all New Jerseyans thought all New Yorkers were blue-collar pigs. So when Adam and his family visited New York City (a trip which took twenty minutes), it always seemed very much out of the way, and only once had they deigned to travel underground; a cousin named Lucy who was attending Columbia University had insisted on showing the twins around the city "in the proper way." To Lucy's credit, she had purchased fares in advance for Adam and Anna (who were ten years old and already very, very different). Unfortunately, on their way from Columbia University to their first stop (South Street Seaport), Lucy and the twins ran into one of Lucy's many, many exs, (a furry vegan) who sidetracked them into spending the day at an anti-war protest across the street from Gracie Mansion (as if it were the mayor of New York who had declared war in the Middle East).

"I don't think I like trains," mumbled Adam.

About an hour later, as their locomotive shuttled through the bloodless countryside of Connecticut, Bernard finally put his laptop to bed and decided to do the same with himself. A twin-sized bunk folded down a few feet above the sofa; Adam and Bernard set up the bed and then Adam, who had not eaten a bite since McDonald's, left the cabin in search of the dining car. Instead of asking an Amtrak steward for directions, Adam wandered the span of the train, all eight cars, probing with his nose for the aroma of cooked food.

The reason he couldn't locate the dining car: there was no dining car. Not after eleven P.M. There was, however, a lounge car, set up for card games, board games, reading and snacking. Adam ordered a tuna fish sandwich and a Coke from a wandering stewardess; while waiting, he plunked down in a comfy armchair and picked up an issue of *Time*. The cover posed the question "Who was Saint Joseph of Nazareth?" Adam didn't care, but he thumbed through the magazine anyway.

The train made its first stop of the evening: New York City.

His tuna fish sandwich tasted great. His Coke tasted warm and dirty, as if it had been stored in the train's steamy furnace. If the train even had a coal furnace. So he gobbled up his sandwich and rinsed it down with a cup of water. By the time he was meandering back to his cabin in Car D, the train had left the station in New York and had entered the great Garden State.

His room was locked.

Grumbling nonsense syllables and completely indifferent to the lateness of the hour, Adam banged a fist against the locked door and demanded loudly for Bernard to open up.

And then he waited.

The train canted to the left, and Adam took a step back to balance himself. That was when the door opened, revealing Cherry Sundae in a sweater and jeans.

"Miss me?" she asked.

Adam lost his balance again. Not the train's fault this time. He gripped the wall for support, stared at Cherry for a whole minute and then finally responded with an emphatic:

"Huh?"

"Now that's the man I remember."

"What are you doing here?"

"How's your hand?"

"It itches."

"That's a good sign."

"What are you doing here?"

"It means the nerves are healing. Why don't we talk in my cabin?"

"You have a cabin?"

"Well, sure, silly. You don't think I snuck on, do you?"

Adam shrugged. Cherry smiled. He followed her to her cabin, two doors down. She butted the door behind her closed, slung her arms around Adam's neck, stared into his Nordic blue eyes and locked lips with him for 113 seconds.

"So I hear you had yourself a little drink," said Cherry. "Funny, all I taste on you is tuna fish."

"I had a bite to eat … in the lounge car."

"Ah."

They sat down on her sofa.

"So," she purred, "have you missed me?"

"I never thought I'd see you again."

She pawed his shirt. "Well, I've always liked surprises."

"No, I mean, I never thought I'd see you again. Ever. When I stormed out of that hotel room at Caesars Palace and you stayed, I really thought that was it."

"The hotel room. Yeah. Are you still mad at me about that?"

"Cherry, to be honest, right now I'm not mad or happy or anything … except extremely confused. How did you find us?"

"Bernard."

"Bernard?"

"We've been corresponding." She removed her hands from his shirt. "Back in Las Vegas, yesterday morning, really, you know, when we were trying to see if we could hack into the Black Gold, well, yesterday morning, Bernard showed me his blog. I think he has a little crush on me."

"That son of a bitch."

"Because he has a crush on me?"

"He showed you his blog!" Adam stood up and paced. "Who else did he show it to? Who did you show it to?"

"Nobody. I swear. But that's how we've been corresponding. I would go to a public terminal and read his blog and post comments to it, and that's how we came up with our plan. This plan. The plan to save the world."

"The plan to save the world."

"Yes."

"You and Bernard."

"Yes. Well, and you too."

"Why didn't anyone tell me about this?!"

"We're telling you now. Merry Christmas?"

Adam could not look at her—would not look at her—so instead his eyes fixated on the window in her cabin. Somewhere out there was Newark. Somewhere in the darkness, not many miles away, was his home, his bed, his mother. He tried to remember where exactly the train tracks were in Newark. He was sure he had crossed over them. Somewhere out there was Newark and he was in here. About to hear a plan concocted by an unstable vagabond clown of mysterious origins and vague morals, and a thirteen-year-old hacker/sadist from Canada. A plan which they had kept from him. How dare they! After all he had done ...

"I need air," said Adam.

He moved for the door.

"There's plenty of air in here. There are vents and everything."

Adam ignored her, yanked open the door, and staggered out into the wafer-thin corridor. He knew the train's layout from his quest for food. He knew where to go. He went. Cherry followed. They passed from car to car in screaming silence. End of the line: Car H. Passenger car. Those who couldn't afford berths spent the night here, in their seats. Some lay across two seats in an attempt to facsimile comfort. Adam walked beyond their rows and slid open the rear door. The icy wind assaulted him, sliced through his hair, invaded his bones, but he didn't care. He stepped out onto the short, railed balcony at the aft of the train and stared out at the dark past as it raced away, hundreds of miles an hour.

Cherry slid shut the door. Cold air roared around them.

"IS THIS BEST PLACE TO HAVE A CONVERSATION?" she observed.

"I DIDN'T COME OUT HERE TO HAVE A CONVERSATION!" he retorted.

"IT'S GOOD TO SEE YOU, ADAM!"

He stared down at the rolling tracks. The only part of his body not feeling the bitter frost was his left hand and wrist, encased as they were in a cast.

"ADAM, I SAID, IT'S GOOD TO SEE YOU!"

"I HEARD YOU!"

"YOU'RE SUPPOSED TO SAY 'IT'S GOOD TO SEE YOU TOO!'"

"I DIDN'T COME OUT HERE TO HAVE A CONVER-SATION!"

"AND YET HERE WE ARE, ADAM, YOU AND ME, HAVING A CONVERSATION!"

Finally he turned to her. "WHAT DO YOU WANT FROM ME?"

"YOU'RE GOING DOWN SOUTH TO STOP EBBETS AND RESCUE YOUR SISTER. I WANT THE SAME THING. I'M HERE TO HELP YOU!"

"I DON'T NEED YOUR HELP!"

"YOU MEAN YOU DON'T WANT MY HELP."

"I DON'T WANT YOUR HELP."

"BECAUSE I STAYED IN THE ROOM IN LAS VEGAS."

"YOU THINK THAT'S IT?" Adam waved his hands dramatically. "YOU THINK THAT'S ALL? I DON'T KNOW WHO YOU ARE! I DON'T TRUST YOU! YES, YOU STAYED IN THE ROOM IN LAS VEGAS! YOU SEEM TO HAVE NO PROBLEM DOING WHATEVER IT TAKES TO GET WHATEVER YOU WANT!"

"YOU DIDN'T SEEM TO HAVE A PROBLEM WITH IT UNTIL YESTERDAY!"

"AND I WAS WRONG! I KNOW THAT NOW! THE ENDS DON'T JUSTIFY THE MEANS! YOGURT ... EBBETS' MOTHER ... MY DAD ... GODDAMN IT, THERE IS SUCH A THING AS A GREATER GOOD!"

Facing aft, as they were, they hadn't seen the tunnel coming, so the sudden darkness took them both by great surprise. The rumbling of the engine continued but the howling of the wind had been muted, as nature was forbidden following them into the long dim tunnel.

As the train chugged on through, Adam and Cherry remained quiet. Neither could see the other, or anything for that matter. Was it this loss of sight that robbed them of their speech or was it some deeper, primal respect for the dark? Adam breathed slowly. His right hand wrapped itself tighter around the railing. That cold bar of iron felt so warmly comforting.

The train emerged from the tunnel, and from shadows to night. Now far from the city, Adam could see stars again in the sky. He immediately found Filbert's Pole Star, winking above him.

Cherry leaned into Adam's ear and whispered, "Let's go inside."

They returned to her cabin.

They sat on her sofa.

Adam sighed.

"You're right," she said. "Maybe. But your sister's still kidnapped and this lunatic has his finger on the trigger for Armageddon."

Adam glanced at her, then away. "This afternoon I think I convinced a guy in his fifties that there's no such thing as Santa Claus. Because there is no such thing as Santa Claus, right? As if that justified what I said. I broke the truth right over his head. Like a glass bottle. Whack! And now, for my troubles, I have a twenty-pound bag full of letters."

"You should hear my day."

"It can't be worse than mine."

They laughed.

Then Cherry said, "You know the bomb that was in the back of Ebbets' truck? Well, I figured the state police would hand it over to the FBI, and they did. The FBI brought it to their field office in Philadelphia. It didn't take me and Bernard long to confirm this information. Anyway, what I did today while you were beating the truth into some innocent ignorant man, what I did today was help our favorite ax-wielding Viking mob boss steal that atomic bomb."

Chapter Twenty-Six

He wasn't upset. He was too far in shock to be upset. He just asked her calmly, pleasantly, "And you gave him the bomb why?"

So Cherry told her story:

"When I got back to Philadelphia, I was met at baggage claim by two of the Viking's 'associates.' They were there to pick up the package. They asked where you were. I told them you had family business to take care of. Not a lie, really. I didn't want you to get in trouble. Not yet. Then I told them I needed to speak to the big man. I had another proposal for him. They dialed him up on the phone and that's when I informed him all about the bomb.

"Don't give me that look. We need to stop Ebbets. But how? Mug him from behind? Steal his radio detonator before he has a chance to set it off? What if we fail? What if we don't find him in time? We need a fallback. We need a failsafe. We need a bomb close enough to where he's going to be so we can be certain that will be the first bomb that is activated by his detonator. Bernard is certain—Bernard is pretty sure—that if someone cuts the circuit on that first bomb the moment the signal is sent, the signal will end and none of the bombs will go off.

"You think I'm devious and mercenary. That I go where the wind blows and have little regard for my actions. Maybe that's true. I don't know. A lot has happened to me in the past few years. A lot has happened to you in the past few days. You don't like me a lot right now and that's fine. Well, it isn't fine, but I'll have to accept it. I need you to see that what I did—what I'm doing—is for the greater good. The ends do justify the means. There's no way we could've stolen the bomb from the FBI. We needed to use the mob as our cat's-paw for that. But we can steal the bomb from the mob. And here's how."

"Wait." Adam reeled. He could barely digest all this information.

He could barely swallow it. Mob bosses and atomic bombs and double-crosses. "Please." He walked into her bathroom and poured himself a paper cup of water.

There was a knock on the door.

Adam heard Bernard enter.

"I forgot my toothpaste," he muttered. "Do you have some I could borrow?"

Cherry nodded, squeezed past Adam into the bathroom, grabbed her toothpaste, squeezed past Adam out of the bathroom and handed the toothpaste to Bernard.

"Thanks," said Bernard.

"No problem," replied Cherry.

Adam emerged from the bathroom. So much was already set in motion. Too late in the game to sit on the bench and quit. As if he really had a choice anyway. That decapitating Norse son of a bitch had the bomb.

"So how are we going to steal the bomb from the mob?" he asked Cherry and Bernard.

They told him.

An hour later, the train made its next stop on its coastline route. The locomotive pulled into Philadelphia's 30th Street Station, one block from progressive Drexel University and five from the fourth oldest institution of higher learning in the United States: the University of Pennsylvania. Normally this would have been a brief, quiet stop of the Metroliner, but the holidays filled every one of the country's airports, train stations and bus depots with gift-bearing relatives. As Adam, Cherry and Bernard disembarked, they passed a long line of cranky men and tired women bundled up in layers and waiting to board their steam-powered savior, bound as it was for one direction. Complain as they might in their day-to-day mulling about the "backward South," come December and January the most vocal critics would be yearning for the warmer climes of Georgia and Louisiana. They might be unsophisticated and old-fashioned and racist, but Southerners didn't have to dig out their cars every week from under hillocks of heavy snow.

A frown forced itself upon Adam's lips. Why was he becoming so distracted all of a sudden, and by these faceless, nameless passersby? He shrugged off his wandering thoughts and continued with Cherry and Bernard out of the station. Few walked the cracked black streets of this City of Brotherly Love during its witching hour. The only footsteps to be heard belonged to the three train travelers. No chirping, no buzzing. Not even a windy whisper from the air. Just footsteps, three pairs, clop-clop, clop-clop, clop-clop.

"Do you know how to get there?" Adam asked Cherry, but what he'd intended to come out as a soft question became, in contrast to the silent environment, a prodding bellow at which she flinched. "Sorry," he said. "Didn't mean to scare you."

"It's okay. And no, I don't. But Bernard does."

Bernard nodded. "I memorized the city map."

"When did you memorize the city map?"

"I don't know. One month, when I was bored. I memorized all the maps to all the major cities in the United States and Canada."

Adam stopped, stared at him.

"Don't look at me like that. Giving me a look like I just landed from outer space. I like to know where I'm going. That all right with you, or would you rather we wander about in the dark until we get frostbite and die?"

That caused Adam and Cherry to exchange glances. Bernard's comment had summoned in them the same memory: roaming last week with Filbert through the snowy woods; Adam and Cherry then reached the same conclusion: Filbert and Bernard, had they met, would have gotten along just fine. Lugging their bags and suitcases, they followed Bernard down dark city roads, barely wavering in their faith in the boy's certainty of data.

Until they ended up, forty-five minutes later, back at the 30th Street Station.

"Son of a bitch," mumbled Adam.

What had been plump with people and bright with electricity less than an hour ago was now vacant and closed. No establishment on the block was open, not at this hour, not so close to Christmas Eve.

"I don't understand it," Bernard confessed. "The map must have been wrong."

"The map must have been wrong?"

"Fuck you."

"Cherry, what time do we need to be there by?"

"I don't know, but I'm thinking it's got to be soon."

So Adam, Cherry and Bernard split up and canvassed the block for homeless people. The homeless had to know their way around the streets. And at this ungodly hour who else could be found for help? Unfortunately, the task proved more difficult than expected; apparently, the city's homeless did not spend their evenings near the glow of street lamps. Adam had to rely on colored illumination from strings of Christmas lights, which were tangled around awnings and rooftops like candy vines. Finally he found, sitting together near the door of a bakery, a raggedy family of orthodox Jews.

The daughter, maybe three years old, was asleep; she wore over her tiny body several polyester nightgowns of varying sizes and colors, long enough to cover her feet and hands but still leaving her face and ears exposed to the elements and bitterly red. The mother, maybe thirty years old, had long brown hair like her daughter; like her daughter she too wore several layers—a drab sweater over a black dress over another black dress, etc. The mother watched Adam approach, as did the father, who was maybe forty years old, had a thin black beard and wore a dark suit that appeared to be made out of construction paper.

"We're discussing music," said the man softly, so as not to wake his daughter. "We cannot settle the eternal debate. Perhaps you can assist? The debate, as I'm sure you know, goes like this: who is better, the Rolling Stones or the Beatles? Meryl—this is my wife, Meryl—believes there is an answer. I ... I am not sure."

"If a problem is broken down into its components," Meryl quietly explained, "and its components can be weighed, gauged, compared and contrasted, then it stands to reason that what is true for the pieces is true for the whole. Who is the better drummer, Ringo Starr or Charlie Watts? Who wrote the better songs, Jagger/Richards or Lennon/McCartney? Lists can be made. Answers can be found."

They stared up at Adam, waiting for him to contribute.

He stared back and didn't know what to say. So addled was he that he had even forgotten about his quest for directions.

"I think perhaps the boy is demonstrating the wisdom found in the sound of silence."

"So now you want to throw in Simon and Garfunkel and make our debate more complicated?"

Adam glanced down at their little girl then back up at them. "You're living on the streets," he said, simply. "How did you … I mean, I didn't think that people like you ever … you're homeless."

"So perceptive he is. Meryl, give the boy an apple."

Meryl reached into a pillowcase and removed a shiny red apple.

"No thanks," said Adam.

"Don't worry," she replied. "It's fresh. Not even a day old. Clean too. Been washed and everything."

Adam received the apple and took a bite. It tasted sweet. Its juice wet his lips and trickled a sugary stream down his chin.

"We'd offer you something to drink," replied the man, "but all of our water's frozen."

Water.

That reminded Adam of his task.

He asked them for directions to the docks.

Instead of prodding him for information—like what business he had at the docks at one o'clock in the morning—Meryl just smiled and assured him to follow Market Street east.

"But it's many blocks away," said her husband. "You would do better to get a taxi."

"Thank you. For that. And for, you know, the apple." He reached into his pocket and removed his wad of cash. "I'd like to give you something for—"

Meryl held up her hand in protest. "Kindness is free."

Then her husband held out his hand to receive the gift. "If kindness is free, Meryl, then this boy's kindness also is free. And to refuse free kindness is foolish. Thank you, young man."

Adam handed him quite a few bills. "Thank you."

He rounded up Cherry and Bernard and led them east on Market Street. They would walk until they found a taxi, and if they didn't find a taxi, they would walk until they found the docks.

But first they found a bridge.

"Here's the water," said Bernard. "I thought you said it'd be a long walk. Are we there already?"

"You tell me, map-boy."

Cherry pointed to a sign by the bridge. "We're trying to get to the Delaware River. That's where the pier is. This is the Schuylkill River."

Adam turned to Bernard. "See? This is the Schuylkill River."

As they crossed the bridge, they noticed a series of white, red and blue lights at the other side. About midpoint across, they were able to discern the source of the lights, and all three travelers immediately halted. Parked on the east end of the bridge were four black-and-whites, headlights on and roof domes flashing. Walking among the police were several men and women with yellow FBI insignias emblazoned on their blue coats.

"Wow," mumbled Adam. "We are tremendously screwed."

"We could head south and try to cross a different bridge."

But Cherry shook her head. "They'll have those bridges watched too."

"What's going on? Why are they doing this?"

Adam chuckled. "What's going on? You don't know? It's your plan! You had the mob take an atomic bomb! You didn't think the FBI would find out? They've probably shut down the city."

A strong wind suddenly gusted from the east, watering eyes and chilling flesh. Adam turned his back on the breeze and took a bite out of his apple. A few blocks west, not too far from this unexpected windstorm, sat Meryl, her husband and their little daughter.

"The key," said Cherry, "is confidence. We're not the ones who stole the atomic bomb."

"Yet," Adam added.

Cherry continued, "All we have to do is walk on by, confident that we have done nothing wrong."

"Yet," Adam added.

Cherry continued, "Or we can stand here and wait for a miracle."

They stood and waited.

Ten minutes passed.

Then they headed for the cops.

Adam and Bernard followed Cherry's lead. She walked slowly; they too walked slowly. Despite the blasting wind, she kept her head high; despite the blasting wind, they too kept their heads high. She waved at the police; they too waved at the police.

One of the uniforms, her nightstick already out, approached them.

"Can I help you folks?" she asked.

Adam and Bernard awaited Cherry's reply. She did not let them down:

"No, thank you, Officer. Me and my two brothers here are just heading home. We were on a trip."

The cop raised an eyebrow. Especially at Bernard.

"He's adopted," Cherry explained.

"I'm adopted," Bernard confirmed.

The policewoman frowned. "Whereabouts is home?"

"Oh, you know."

"No. I don't. Which is why I asked."

"Over by the docks," said Adam.

The policewoman's frown stretched to her chin.

Nonchalantly, Cherry poked Adam in the ribs.

"Gerry," bellowed the cop, "come over here."

A rotund policeman broke away from a conversation with the FBI agents and took his time strolling over.

"Yep?"

"These folks live over by the docks."

"Yep?"

"Why don't you give them a lift?"

"Yep."

He took out a chunky key ring and leisurely ambled over to his squad car. Distress had bloomed into blessing. They were going to be spared their long trek through the cold city.

So silly, thought Adam, to fear the police.

Cherry and Bernard scooted into the back seat of the car. As Adam bent down to join them, Gerry held up a hand and pointed at the half-eaten apple.

"No food in your car?" asked Adam.

"Yep."

"Okay. One sec."

Adam took three mouthfuls of fruit and then, to avoid an arrest for littering, he looked around for a trash bin. He found one several yards away, back by the lights and the cops and the bridge. Hoisting his mailbag over one shoulder, and balancing the apple core on the palm of his cast, he headed for the trash.

That was when Special Agent Epperson called out to the back of his head, "Hey. You. One sec."

Special Agent Epperson. Of course she was in Philadelphia. She and her partner, Special Agent Chang, were working British Fred's bombs and one of the bombs had turned up in FBI custody in Philadelphia. It made perfect sense she would be here. It was straight logic.

Adam loathed straight logic.

He let the apple core drop into the trash bin. He heard Special Agent Epperson's nearing footsteps. Clunky footsteps. Probably wearing designer boots. Probably wore designer boots every winter since she was six years old. Special Agent Elyse Epperson, ten feet and closing from the man she knew as Arvid Winkle, key witness in her case against British Fred and who had vanished from Las Vegas twenty-four hours ago and now, conveniently, was present at the scene of a major, and connected, robbery.

Adam glanced back at the squad car. He caught Cherry's nervous gaze through the rear windshield. There was no way Epperson was going to let them go. They would be grilled, they would be interrogated, they would be disbelieved, and at Thursday midnight GMT, the bombs would detonate.

Adam saw no choice. Someone had to complete their mission. He stared into Cherry's eyes and mouthed the word "Go." She understood. She did not wave goodbye, there was no time for pleasantries. She turned around in her seat and offered up to Gerry some convincing excuse and the squad car drove away, as Special Agent Epperson put a firm hand on Adam's right shoulder.

"Don't I know you?" she asked.

Adam sighed, spun around to surrender, and in doing so quite accidentally smacked Epperson in the skull with his mail bag.

She didn't fall to the ground, but she did stumble back a yard, slightly dazed and more than a little confused.

Adam saw his opening.

He bolted.

His mind went blank, so his legs took charge and carried him south, along the water. Federal agents and local law enforcement soon followed. They hadn't seen his inadvertent assault on Special Agent Epperson, but they all knew by heart one of the main rules of the street: if they run, they've got to be guilty of something.

Adam's knees bounced up and down like a pair of excited frogs. So far the cops hadn't taken a shot at him. So far. He whisked himself to the right, then turned another corner, then another, then another. He launched himself down shadowy side streets and soon could both hear and feel his heart and lungs pounding in his eardrums. Finally he just had to stop, lest his muscles and organs quit. He ducked into a cavernous doorway and sat down on cold cement.

Something about that cavernous doorway seemed to Adam strangely familiar, but he ignored his nagging *déjà vu* and concentrated on a plan. Any plan. Any plan that did not end with him perforated. If the plan included at the docks and on board the cargo ship, all the better.

The winter wind howled at his fate.

Adam shifted the weight of his mail bag onto his lap, but he never let it go, as if it were his security blanket. He leaned back against the locked door, glanced around the quiet urban space, realized why it all seemed strangely familiar, and let out a defeated giggle. He sat on the steps of the bank he and Filbert had robbed. His giggle grew into a chuckle. His chuckle rose into a hearty laugh and soon he couldn't contain himself. Of course it was the same bank. Of course he was here, with a sack of dead letters, in the middle of the night. Of course the police and FBI were moments away from shooting him down. How else, really, could his week end? His laughter filled the entire city block and even drowned out the thundering wind, and so it came as no surprise at all when Special Agent Epperson heard him and called out in true law enforcement fashion:

"Arvid Winkle! Come out with your hands up!"

Adam continued to laugh. Come out with his hands up? Sure, why not. He stood, stepped down from the stoop and faced Epperson in the middle of the street. Showdown in downtown Philly. She, armed with a .357 Magnum; he, armed with a bag of mail. The currents pressed against his back, as if wanting to push him even closer to the barrel of her pointed gun.

"Where's the bomb?" she demanded.

Adam shrugged.

"What's in the bag?"

Adam glanced at the bag then back at her.

"Put the bag down."

The wind intensified, and Adam slowly lowered the bag to the street. Then he smiled.

"What's so funny?" she asked.

"This," he replied and upended the bag.

The wind did the rest. Thousands of letters—red ones, green ones, long ones, small ones—were sucked out of the postal sack and swarmed toward Epperson. She held up a hand in defense, but twenty pounds of postage overtook her. They overtook the whole street, attacking lampposts and elm trees and, yes, even mailboxes.

And Adam ran. Reinvigorated, he ran east and did not look back. He ran and ran and never tired. Quite literally, a huge weight had been lifted from his shoulders. He ran and ran and before long could run no more, for he had reached the water's edge. It did not take him long to make his way up toward Pier 3. He had made it to the cargo ship after all. He had escaped the clutches of the …

But all he found at Pier 3 was water. A vast empty plot of water. The cargo ship had left.

Chapter Twenty-Seven

The river humped the pier. Mighty Atlantic waves—Norwegians, Spaniards, Liberians—thrust their wet masses against the dock's thick wooden posts. The posts groaned. Waves licked wood. Long blue tongues curling around old elephantine columns. Near it all, oblivious to it all, sat Adam, cross-legged, awaiting the arrival of the authorities.

Misery being rather insane, Adam dwelled not on the cargo ship, afloat and afar; nor on John Ebbets, carrying doom in his pocket; nor even Anna, possibly alive, probably not, either way his fault. Instead, Adam's mind focused on the small framed photograph of his father and Uncle Dexter. He had stored it in the mail sack. The mail sack was gone. The photograph was gone. Abandoned on some cobblestone-and-gravel Philadelphia street.

He stared down at his right hand. Then he concentrated on his left. Somewhere underneath that fiber cast, tattered flesh itched something fierce, as if an army of termites were excavating the remains of his palm. He knew his left hand would never completely heal. And Misery, beholding his encased hand (and being insane), unveiled for Adam a greater gloom and even pettier pain, than the lost photograph: with a crippled left hand, spat Misery, he would never be able to beat his Xbox baseball game. Adam almost laughed again, laughed like he had by the bank, but instead he wept.

"Oi! You there!"

Adam glanced up. A man slowly approached from the north. Limped, from the north. Harbor patrol? The limping man remained in shadows, so it was impossible to tell.

"What are you, deaf?" grunted the man. "Are you Adam Weiss or ain't you?"

Adam blinked. The man had called him Adam Weiss.

The police and FBI knew him as Arvid Winkle.

Adam rose and met the man by Pier 4. The fellow wore a squirrel fur hat, a tan duster, and, below the belt, honest-to-God black and white spats, as if he had just dipped his feet in a vat of Runyonland.

"Yeah, you're him," the man muttered. "I can tell by the look of you."

"Who are you?"

"I'm nobody. Let's go."

"Go where?"

"Nowhere." The man huffed with impatience. "Come on already."

Left with few alternatives, Adam followed the man. They strolled north along the water, passing pier after pier. Some docks were occupied by sleepy argosies, rocking to and fro on the busy waves. Some docks were occupied by nothing at all.

To make conversation, Adam asked his limping guide what happened to his leg. The man stopped walking. Reached into a pocket. Removed a tin of chewing tobacco. Dipped out a wad and coated his gums. Then he continued on his way.

Adam did not repeat the question.

Gradually, they neared Pier 8 and came upon a hulking orange mess. Adam could not tell if its general shape was round, square, or if its shipwright had simply decided to throw geometry to the wind and build the ugliest vessel ever to kiss water. Steel girders jutted every which way out of her superstructure. This thing answered the eternal question: yes, shit floats.

"What is it?" mumbled Adam.

"She's called the *Lusitania*."

"Didn't the *Lusitania* sink, like, a hundred years ago?"

The man shrugged and limped away. Adam was so busy watching him disappear into the shadows that he didn't see Cherry appear on the ship or hear her race down the gangplank, so when she jumped on him in a giddy embrace, her embrace became a tackle and they both ended up on the ground.

"Ow," Adam said.

"Ow," Cherry concurred.

They sat up.

She smiled at him. "I knew you'd escape."

"How did you know? And why aren't you at Pier 3?"

"Harbor patrol had them move the boat. Come on. Captain Hoock's getting antsy."

"Captain Hook?"

"Hoock. Hoock. Look, don't make fun of his name. He's very sensitive."

She tugged on his good hand and he got up and joined her on board the misshapen cargo ship *Lusitania*. They passed down one of the corridors (which were narrow, angled, and decidedly not fit for humans) and Cherry led him into their "stateroom," which consisted mainly of three throaty orange steam pipes. The pipes each bore the usual valves and rusted paint; unique to the stateroom, though, these pipes also each bore a down pillow.

"We're supposed to sleep on the pipes?"

Bernard, awkwardly akimbo on the middle pipe, sneered. "The captain assures us it's safe. The captain assures us the pipes won't get too fucking hot and melt the flesh from our bones. The captain is sleeping two decks below, on a bed."

Adam turned to Cherry. "We're supposed to sleep on the pipes?"

"It's just for a day or so. Just until we get to Miami."

"And once we get to Miami, how long is the car ride to—?"

Bernard answered that, all the while staring at his computer screen: "Trip will be three hours and thirty-five minutes. If we drive at a steady speed of sixty miles per hour. I've already arranged for a rental."

"And the bomb is on board?"

Bernard nodded at Cherry. Cherry nodded at Adam. Adam nodded at himself. Then the whole ship shook, as if jostled by God himself. Adam and Cherry fell back against the door. Bernard landed on one of the other pipes. His laptop hopped up and down. Bernard quickly examined it for damage.

"I guess we're underway," said Cherry.

And they were.

It did not take long for Bernard to turn green (thus proving the expression not only figurative but literal). Apparently, the boy's stomach did not fancy the constant swaying and pitching the *Lusitania* sustained on the high seas. The apex of concern from Adam and Cherry arose not from the noticeable color change in Bernard's face nor the intermittent gurgling which emitted from his midsection.

"Bernard," Adam said, "are you okay?"

"It's late," added Cherry. "Maybe you should try and sleep."

Bernard wordlessly agreed, lay down on his pipe, fidgeted for a minute, gurgled, fidgeted, gurgled, frowned, perspired, gurgled, turned over on his left side, quickly turned back to his right, fidgeted, frowned, and let off a keening, desperate yelp.

Cherry took him by the hand. "Let's go for a walk. Get some fresh air."

Not wanting to be alone, Adam joined them above deck. What he beheld astonished and awed every one of his senses. Not having traveled aboard a ship before, he hadn't really known what to expect, nor had he really cared to find out, but as he slowly walked toward the railing, he took it all in, the sights, the smells, the sounds, the tastes, like a child first stepping into Disneyland.

First, the stars. Real stars, bright stars, distinctly yellow and blue and green, glowing amid that featureless plain of black. And from the stars, snow. Sweet snow, sickly sweet, rock candy. Tumbling down through ionosphere and stratosphere and atmosphere, tumbling waywardly and carefree. Tumbling through beams of illumination, spotlights, the *Lusitania*'s roaming lamps, and tumbling, tumbling, humbly tumbling. Closing in on the dark surface of the sea and before impact, they vanish. Recycled, perhaps. Conveyed back up into the heavens by microscopic angels and left to tumble once more, waywardly, humbling, down down down, to the sea they will never touch. The dark and ravenous sea.

No fish could be seen. No sharks, no dolphins, no whales. They were there, to be sure, but they hid beneath the sweeping waves. Hid or cowered. Dared not meet the surface. The snowflakes feared to touch the surface, the ship's light did not pierce the surface, and as Adam stared down to the surface of the sea he wondered what would happen if he suddenly tipped over the railing and fell into the wet void. Would he be recycled like a piece of white snow or was he too scarred, too murky-hearted? No, the sea would swallow him up whole and he would never be found. He saw a certain solace in that release, a guaranteed unburdening, all this, all this, but still he gripped the ship's slender railing and did not let go. The tougher choice. Oh, his murky heart. Cherry curled a long slender arm along the small of his back and he felt loved.

Then Bernard puked. He let loose both lunch and dinner, mostly digested, over the stern; the goo splashed into the surface of the sea and was gobbled up.

"Oh …" he garbled. "Oh …"

Cherry rubbed the boy's back. "It's okay. It's okay."

He retched some more. He sounded like a whimpering dog.

"Leave me," he demanded. He spoke quickly, employing every sour breath. "I'll be fine. I want to be alone. Leave me alone. Go. Go. Go."

Adam and Cherry reluctantly acquiesced to his plea, left the sick child alone, and returned to their stateroom. They sat on the first and third pipes, respectively, with the middle acting as a buffer.

"Well," said Adam.

"Yeah," agreed Cherry.

"Poor kid. He doesn't like to fly either."

"A lot of people have motion sickness. We're all screwed up in our own way."

Adam glanced at her. Cherry had a strange lightness about her, as if the density of her molecules had begun to dwindle and at any time she could float up to the room's low orange ceiling.

"Why is everything in here orange?" asked Adam. "Do you know?"

"I think it has to do with floods. I think it has to do with what if the ship hit an iceberg and everything filled up. Orange would be easy to see underwater, I guess. I prefer grapefruit."

"Pink or white?"

"Pink." She smiled at him. All teeth. Hungry. "Pink."

Adam ran his fingertips across the smooth surface of his pipe. He had no idea what chemicals flushed through these cumbersome conduits (painted orange, like the poison warnings on bottles) and frankly, he didn't want to know.

"So this is quite an achievement," he said.

"What is?"

"Smuggling an atomic bomb on board. Hiding it from the FBI. I'm surprised the government didn't shut down the port."

"I think they did," replied Cherry. "But you-know-who has a lot of connections. We had to change piers, but we set sail. After all, he had to make sure the bomb could not be connected with him. He probably won't try to sell it for at least a year."

"And meanwhile it will be hiding in Miami. I would've thought he'd choose the first ship bound for home, like Iceland or Scandinavia."

"This ship is bound for Scandinavia. Stockholm, I think."

Adam blinked. "We're heading to Stockholm?"

"You have something against Stockholm? Relax, Adam. I'm just yanking your chain. The ship's manifest says we're headed for Stockholm. You-know-who thinks we're headed for Stockholm. But we're on our way to Miami. I promise."

"And how did you manage that?"

Cherry again showed her teeth. Her eyes twinkled like fresh-cut opals. "A magician never reveals her secrets."

"You have a lot of them. Secrets, I mean."

"I have my share. Are we going to have this chat again?"

"No." Adam looked away. "No."

"Good."

"I don't … I didn't … I'm sorry. About that. I shouldn't have judged you."

Cherry shrugged. "I don't mind being judged. I know who I am."

"You can know who you are and still want approval."

"I think you just want me to want your approval."

"I don't even know what that means."

"Want to see a magic trick?"

She scurried across the middle pipe and sat next to him. The cotton cloth covering their legs touched. Adam downed a pint of saliva.

"What's the trick?" he asked.

"Well," she replied, wryly cocking her head to one side, "do you want to see it? My trick, I mean."

"Sure."

Cherry cleared her throat and flourished her hands.

"Behold anyfing in m'palms?" she asked.

"Why are you talking like that?"

"I'm a Cockney illusionist, guv, remembah?"

"Oh. Right."

She once again flourished her hands.

"Behold anyfing, eh? Cards, coins, rabbits?"

Adam grinned and shook his head.

"Behold anyfing up m'sleeves?"

He snuck his right hand into each sleeve, tickling his fingers across her arms. She kicked him. Playfully.

"Anyfing up m'sleeves?"

He shook his head.

"Right then. Have a butcher's whilst I produce for your edification a loverly queen."

She clapped her hands together, closed her eyes, separated her hands, closed each into a fist, opened her eyes, winked and then sat back, staring at him.

"Where's the queen?" Adam asked.

"Check your right pants pocket," she replied, accent absent but wryness now abounding.

He slipped a hand into his right pants pocket but found nothing unexpected.

"Check your left pants pocket," she then said.

He did. Still no queen.

"Check your right pants pocket."

"I already did."

"That was over five seconds ago. I'm sure the queen's grown up by now. Check it again."

He slipped a hand into his right pants pocket ... and pulled out Cherry's queen-shaped salt shaker. His astonishment shifted from it to the girl.

"But I just ... I'm sure it wasn't ... how did you do that?"

She beamed. "I'm something else, huh?"

"Yes. You are."

Adam had never seen her so happy. He had a feeling that this here, this gleeful girl who somehow now danced without moving a muscle, he had a feeling that this was the real person. That underneath the miserable past and the disguises and laissez-faire attitude lay this beautiful, innocent soul who, despite comments to the contrary, did just want to be approvingly judged. He leaned in to touch his lips to her cheek and ended up kissing her on the mouth, and for no small amount of time.

The queen rolled into the valley between pipes. The king-shaped pepper shaker joined her shortly thereafter. A rocking motion on the pipes above rattled the tiny king and tiny queen against each other. Wood against wood. Tap-tap-tap-tap. Morse Code. Tap-tap-tap tap-tap tap-tap-tap-tap-tap. Wood against wood against orange metal against wood, queen and king, pepper and salt splashing into the valley between pipes.

Chapter Twenty-Eight

The next morning, somewhere in the Atlantic Ocean, Adam had breakfast with Captain Hoock. They ate with the rest of the deckhands; Adam and the captain occupied a small round orange table bolted to the orange floor in the center of the wide low-ceilinged orange space demarcated as the mess. They ate cantaloupe and sweet potato hash browns. While eating, Adam was reminded of the abortive breakfast David the Mennonite widower had prepared for him, Cherry and Filbert. The hash browns on the *Lusitania* were a little overcooked but much more edible.

Captain Hoock also had invited Bernard and Cherry for the morning meal, but Bernard, who spent the entirety of the evening dry-heaving on deck, probably didn't want to be around food and Cherry, apparently, didn't want to be around Adam. Upon waking up in Adam's arms, Cherry had gotten dressed, left to check on Bernard and never returned. When Adam received his invitation to breakfast and showed up, he had inquired for the whereabouts of his companions and Captain Hoock had simply told him that they had said no, thank you.

"But I'm glad," he added, patting Adam on his cast, "that I'm not eating alone."

Captain Hoock was baggy-eyed and bald. His accent sounded French, but he insisted he was Dutch-Portuguese and offered his thoughts on the French by spitting twice on the floor. He wore several layers of blue-striped cotton stretched tightly over a squat three hundred pounds. He ate his melon and potatoes with a flimsy plastic fork and a six-inch hunting knife.

"This is my father's" he said, referring to the knife. "He acquired it in Kyoto."

"What does your father do for a living?" asked Adam.

"He gets eaten. By worms." Captain Hoock splashed some tangerine juice (spiked with rum) down his gullet. "This is why I have his knife. It is a fine knife. Perfectly balanced. Let me show you."

He barked something in Portuguese and the twenty or so deckhands, calmly enjoying their morning feast, suddenly ceased all gobbling and chatter. The room became as quiet as a grave. Captain Hoock cleaned bits of hash browns off his blade, stood up, tossed the knife in the air like a tennis ball, caught it, then whisked it at high speed at a tin barrel by the wall, fifteen feet away. The knife sank tip-first into the barrel's chest and remained there, fixed at a perfect ninety degrees. That was one sharp knife.

The deckhands resumed their gobbling and chatter.

After retrieving his knife, Captain Hoock returned to his seat, stuffed another bite of fried potato into his mouth and said, "He acquired it in Kyoto. I sharpen it daily. I use it daily. It is a fine knife."

"I can see that."

"The Swede used it to gut my father."

Adam choked on his cantaloupe.

"The Swede prefers to use his ax. Your woman tells me you've seen him use his ax. My father had a shipping business. He owned fourteen ships, just like this. He started in Portugal, developing routes along the Mediterranean, and then shifted his attention to your country. The Great Superpower. Bah. You do not even have an adequate football team. You do not even call it football. You call it soccer. You call rugby football. Americans make me flatulent. Americans!"

The deckhands heard his cry and collectively spat on the floor. Twice.

"Juan will wonder why the floor is so wet," the captain mused. "So, to continue: my father's business prospered. Soon he owned twenty-five ships. We traveled all over the Atlantic. I grew up on Gibraltar, in Rio. I celebrated birthdays in Cape Town and Ramadan on Prince Edward Island. One day my father was approached by the Swede."

By now several of the sailors had finished their meals, bussed their trays and left the mess. Adam felt the room grow strangely colder as more and more of the *Lusitania*'s crew returned to their duties elsewhere on the ship. He sipped his chilled juice (sans vodka) and longed for a cup of coffee, but their supplies were strictly decaffeinated.

"The Swede wanted my father to run cargo from Philadelphia to Stockholm. 'What cargo?' my father asked. My father knew who the Swede was. My father knew what business the Swede performed. My father did not want to do business with the Swede. 'Jonas,' he would say to me, 'in life we must find our point of reference or we will get lost. When on the sea, we find our point of reference in the stars. In society, we find our point of reference in each other.' To him, the Swede was his point of reference, only in reverse. If the Swede said yes, my father said no. If the Swede liked the color green, my father suddenly hated the grass, leaves of spinach, lime jello. My father believed that any action he took or judgment he made that was in opposition to any action or judgment made by the Swede would be moral. Do you understand?"

Adam nodded. "I had a friend ... well, an acquaintance ... a friend ... he looked to the stars too. But in the end he did whatever he wanted anyway."

The mess was near-empty now, and frigid. Only Adam and Captain Hoock remained. Their plates were empty. Their glasses were near-drained. Adam exhaled a puff of nerves and watched his breath plume from his lips.

"Why is it so cold in here?" he asked.

Captain Hoock leaned back into his rickety chair, toyed with his knife and replied, staring into the reflective steel, "The ship is haunted. We'll leave soon. First I will finish my story. Unless you don't want to hear it."

"Please continue."

So he did:

"After my father rejected the Swede's offer, our ships began to have ... accidents. Pipes burst. Cargo spoiled. One ship, the *Braganza*, just vanished. All hands lost. By this time I was getting my apprenticeship here, aboard the *Lusitania*. There, even in naming the fleet, there you can see my father. *Braganza, Lusitania*. Moral superiority in the face of adversity. Who names a scow *O Navegador*? My father. He owned a five-hundred-year-old Indian chess set. He acquired this knife in Kyoto. He enjoyed fineness.

"I was captain of the *Lusitania*. While transferring cargo in Oslo, we were boarded by thugs led by the Swede personally. He rounded up all of my crew in here. He knew who I was. He offered me a choice. A man does not rise to the position he reached by being unreasonable or petty. He asked me what I wanted for the future of the company. I told him I wanted there to be a future for the company. I am not unreasonable or petty either. We recognized our common obstacle. 'If I do what needs to be done,' he said, 'which is not at all personal, will you retaliate? Will you carry your father's mantle or will you carry your own?' This is what he asked me in this room in front of my crew.

"The following day while my father was on his way home from a German opera, he was pulled into an alleyway and attacked by two men. Brothers, I am told. My father took out this knife and stabbed one of them in the eye. The other man, the younger brother, picked up the knife and used it to slice open my father's throat. I know these facts because they were relayed to me in person by the Swede. He made me the same business offer he had made my father. I accepted. Then he gave me the knife.

"Since that day, we have not had one accident. Financially, we are doing quite well. We never found the missing ship, the *Braganza*, but any sailor knows better than to chase ghosts on the water. Our main office is still in Lisbon. I was offered my father's position as head of the company but I refused. My place is here. My place will always be here.

"You want to know why. I can see it in your sad eyes. Why am I betraying the Swede? Can you trust me? I don't know. But we will find out when we get to Miami. Now please excuse me. This room has become far too cold with death."

Captain Hoock gradually lifted his bulky mass off his creaky chair and slowly made his way out of the mess. Adam followed; he didn't know where he needed to go, but he knew where he needn't stay.

He found Cherry and Bernard on deck. The outside temperature was barely warmer than that in the mess, but the crisp fresh air and vaguely sunny sky made all the difference. Adam sidled up to his friends and said hello.

"I have to go to the bathroom," replied Bernard, promptly leaving Adam and Cherry alone.

"Well," Adam said, "that was subtle."

Cherry looked away. The sea breeze caught her dark hair in its many fingers and splayed it about like spilt wheat.

"Man," he said, "you've got classic hair." He touched a hand to her shoulder. To his utter relief, she didn't flinch.

"I don't know what that means. I've got classic hair? I don't know what that means."

"You're upset."

"Yes."

"At me."

"Yes."

"Why?"

"Because you're an idiot."

Adam sighed.

"You are," she insisted.

"Am I arguing?"

"No, you're not." Then she turned around. "Why aren't you arguing? What's wrong with you? I call you an idiot and you just accept it?"

"Do you want me to argue?"

"No. Yes. I don't know."

"Cherry, you seem distracted."

"Yes. I am. Yes. You're distracting me."

"By being an idiot?"

"Yes!" She huffed and puffed. "I haven't had sex in three years!"

"Wow."

"Wow? That's your response? Wow?"

"Jesus."

"Now you're going with Jesus. I think I preferred wow."

"You haven't had sex in three years?"

"Think about it, Adam. When would I have had sex? I was hitchhiking across the country dressed like a clown."

"A Spanish clown."

"No, I think I was dressed like an American clown. I just spoke Spanish. I wasn't lonely. I made due. I'm very self-reliant."

"You can drive a stick shift and everything."

Cherry poked him in the ribs. "You're such a guy."

"Is that a compliment?"

"No, it's not."

"Okay."

"Bernard just showed me how to disarm the bomb. That's where we were. We were down below. He was showing me how to disarm the bomb. He wasn't hungry. I wasn't hungry. I'm hungry now, but that doesn't matter. You know what I learned?"

"How to disarm a bomb?"

"I have been away from society for so long and all this time I've been acting like everything's okay and pretending like everything's okay and everything is far from okay. I am far from okay. I have been away from society for so long! I haven't had sex in three years! I love sex! Vibrators are great, I really like them a lot, but there's no connection with a machine. You can't cuddle with a machine. You can't stand on the deck of a ship and argue with a machine."

"So what are you saying?"

"I'm not saying anything! Aren't you paying attention? I'm rambling. Why aren't you kissing me?"

"Because I'm an idiot?"

"You really are."

So they kissed. They necked. They fondled, petted, groped, galloped, prodded, inserted, infused, inlayed, squeezed, squashed, wedged, yapped, yawed, moaned, licked, nibbled, tasted, touched, smelt, peered, sweated, rubbed, bounced, stretched, irrigated, hardened, softened, hardened, wiggled, wriggled, and, yes o yes, fucked. By early Wednesday afternoon, when the *Lusitania* dragged its ugly physique into Miami's Biscayne Bay, Adam and Cherry had spent almost twenty-four hours in their stateroom; Bernard quickly relocated to a tiny bunk, sheeted in cheesecloth, located at the rear of the texas.

The city of Miami was draped in rain, so Adam, Cherry and Bernard observed the docking procedures through a porthole in the mess. Because of rain there was little to see, but they had been away from land for a day and a half; even a blurred skyline was a welcome relief. Each also wore a change of clothes (various shades and textures of genuine Iberian wool) provided to them by the crew.

"Midnight in Greenwich is seven P.M. here," said Bernard. "We'll have six hours to get to where we're going. Six hours. And the drive is three hours and thirty-five minutes. Give or take. It is Christmas Eve."

"I'll be here," Cherry said. She held Adam's hand. "I'll be here."

Bernard turned to her. "Are you sure you don't need me to go over those directions again?"

"I can do it, Bernard. I can deactivate the bomb."

"Remember, you have to wait until—"

"The red light comes on. I know. Otherwise the signal will just skip to the next nearest bomb. Wherever that is. Although you're going to try to stop him from activating the trigger anyway, right? Right?"

"Right." Then, reluctantly, he handed his laptop to her. "Take good care of it while I'm gone. I'll notice any scratches. And my taser is in the stateroom if any of these knuckleheads get frisky."

Now it was Adam's turn to interrogate Bernard: "And you're positive you'll be able to get to Ebbets. Get him to tell me where Anna is."

"As long as you keep your end of the bargain and he doesn't get hurt."

"Bernard, how could I hurt him? I have one hand."

"There's probably a lot you can do with one hand," he answered, eyeballing Cherry until she blushed.

With a violent tremor, the ship docked.

"All right," said Adam. "Now we wait for the captain to get us and we'll be on our way."

"Why's it so cold in here?"

"It's December," Cherry responded.

Adam didn't elaborate.

"So how's it feel?" she asked him.

"How's what feel?"

"To be near the end. After all this time."

"It's not over yet."

"Just message me when it is. Please."

Bernard nodded. "We'll go to the nearest payphone and call the laptop. Just make sure it's up and running."

"And I turn it on how?"

"Fuck you both," grumbled Bernard, and then, despite his best intentions, he grinned.

So did Cherry.

So did Adam.

Then the pressurized door to the mess hissed open. The crew of the *Lusitania* filed in one at a time. They did not appear too happy. After the crew came Captain Hoock. He refused to even look Adam in the eye. After the captain came two giant men who had to slouch just to clear the doorframe. Adam didn't recognize either of them, but their pinstripe suits looked eerily familiar.

After them came Yogurt.

"I believe you have something of mine," he said. "I'd like it back now please."

Chapter Twenty-Nine

To which Bernard loudly replied: "Who the fuck is this?"

"That's him," Adam murmured. "The guy from Philadelphia."

"The psychopath?" Bernard, again very loudly. "With the ax?"

Cherry nudged the boy in his ribs.

"Psychopathology implies mental disease," said the Swede. "I have met psychopaths. I have even had to employ a few. Psychopaths are reckless. Psychopaths are unpredictable. I am quite predictable. A thief absconds with one of my belongings and I track that thief down. The captain's insubordination will be dealt with in due time, but first: hello, Adam. Hello, Cherry."

Cherry half-heartedly waved back.

"These are my associates: Sven and Dix. They are professional gentlemen. Someone is going to escort Sven to my cargo. Show him everything is in order. Now."

Glances were exchanged. Silent miseries were shared. Adam could feel, literally feel, any hope of a happy ending dissolve inside him into a puddle of organic goo.

Then Bernard stepped forward.

"Yeah, okay, whatever. I know where the bomb is. Let's go, fuckhead."

"Bernard," muttered Cherry.

The boy led Sven out of the mess.

A long, anguished minute passed.

"Mr. Weiss," said Yogurt, "I assume I paid for your cast. It looks sturdy. I haven't seen my statement yet but I assume I paid for many expenses in Las Vegas. A man offers you his generosity and you rob him blind. That is not kindness."

"You don't understand! Ebbets has a trigger. He's going to

detonate—"

Dix removed a sizable handgun from his vest and fired two shots; the bullets came within inches of obliterating Adam's toes.

"Jesus!" he cried.

"I think what my associate is trying to say, Mr. Weiss, is that I am not here for rhetoric. I am here for my property."

Then another shot: BAM! All eyes turned to Dix. Dix, confused, examined his gun. But his gun had not fired the shot.

The door to the mess swung open and into the room staggered Sven, suddenly in quite a foul mood. He growled several Swedish sentences to Yogurt.

"Bernard attacked Sven," translated Captain Hoock for Adam and Cherry's benefit. "He went into the stateroom. He had a stun gun. Sven shot him."

Cherry muttered, "Oh, God."

"Is he dead?" Adam asked Yogurt. His voice sizzled with fury. "Did your professional gentleman kill the thirteen-year-old who 'attacked' him?"

Adam stared the mob boss down. According to logic, he should've been worried about his own health. According to reason, he should've been trembling in awe and fear of this Thor wannabe and his trigger-happy pals. But Bernard had been shot. That irascible, foul-mouthed, ice-skate-wielding, taser-happy innocent child. Logic and reason were irrelevant. Adam stared the mob boss down.

If only looks could kill. Pistols could kill, however, and Sven and Dix, unnerved by that look in Adam's eyes, aimed theirs at the soft space between Adam's eyes.

Adam did not flinch.

Then Captain Hoock spoke up.

"I'll take you to the bomb," he said. "I'll check on the boy."

Yogurt quietly nodded and instructed Dix to follow the captain.

Another long, anguished minute of silence, save for the sound of pelting rain from outside. Adam's right hand suddenly ached; he glanced down and noticed it was clenched in a fist. He had to will his fingers to uncurl. The fury inside him did not abate.

Bernard had been shot. Bernard had been shot. Bernard had been shot.

"I love this time of the year," the mob boss spoke. He appeared unnerved. Perhaps it was the relentless quietude. Perhaps something else. "The weather forces us to stay indoors and confront each other. We are pushed into reflection. The air may be cold but the human heart during the winter months remains heated. It's all very natural."

The door opened. Captain Hoock reentered. His gaze remained low.

The self-centered, untrustworthy son of a—

Then Adam caught a glimpse of the Kyoto knife, held blade up by the captain's side. Sven, however, still carefully watching Adam, did not see the knife. Sven would never see the knife; in one swift motion, Captain Hoock flipped the knife into throwing position and shot it blade-first into the back of the thug's skull.

That was one sharp knife.

His puppet strings severed, Sven collapsed to the floor. His pose— arms askew, legs criss-crossed—appeared quite uncomfortable, as weirdly angled in fact as the *Lusitania* herself, but the thug did not seem to mind, being that he was quite undeniably dead. Yogurt reached down to get his associate's pistol.

"Don't," warned the captain, Dix's pistol at the ready.

Yogurt stood back up and slowly raised his large pale hands.

Captain Hoock turned to Adam and Cherry. "Bernard's all right. He was shot in the leg. I gave him a tourniquet but he will need medical attention. He's in his stateroom."

"Thank you," said Adam.

"Thank you," said Cherry.

Captain Hoock shrugged.

Adam and Cherry rushed out of the room. From the mess they heard Yogurt say:

"This is a surprise and a mistake." And the captain reply: "I don't have any answers. But I do have the gun. And a knife. And a taser. And an old rusty blender in the kitchen."

They found Bernard in the stateroom, lying topless on all three pillows. His shirt, wound around his left thigh, had become a bloody rag.

"Bernard," said Adam, "are you okay?"

"The fucker shot me!"

"He's fine," replied Cherry. "I'll call 911. You need to go."

"Go? I can't go without Bernard."

"He can't go without me!" the boy echoed.

"You have no choice, Adam. And you don't have a lot of time. Right now, we know where he'll be but after tonight, he could go anywhere. And he has your sister."

Adam didn't need reminding of that. Nor did he need convincing. Cherry was correct. He had to go. He had to go alone. He had to go alone and try and talk down an armed madman who had nothing to lose.

All things considered: typical day.

He and Cherry wanted their farewell kiss to last for days. They had to settle for ninety seconds. Adam promised her he would call. He waved goodbye to Bernard. Bernard flourished a middle finger, and instructed Adam on how to reach his destination.

"Do you need me to write that down?"

"I'll remember it."

"Uh-huh. Cherry, get me a fucking pen."

Yogurt and his goons had a black Saab sedan (automatic transmission, thank heaven for small miracles) parked near the dock. Adam found the car's keys in Dix's pockets. Before long, the *Lusitania* was nothing more than a dwindling image in the rearview mirror.

By the time he reached Fort Lauderdale, following the turnpike north along the Sunshine State's Atlantic coast, the rain had tapered off, although the slate-shaded clouds made the hour seem much later than it was. The drive ahead was scheduled to take three hours and thirty-five minutes, but that did not take into account the vast and varied turnpike traffic on Christmas Eve. Adam's sedan teetered north at a laborious forty miles per hour, trapped behind a leprous hatchback towing a U-Haul twice its size, sputtering up the high speed lane.

Then they reached the road construction. What had been a steady crawl became a jerking stagger, braking and speeding and braking all the way through the clay-laden counties of Broward and Palm Beach, America's most popular retirement destinations. Impatient and frustrated, Adam flipped through the radio stations. Christmas standards … Christmas standards … country Christmas standards … smooth jazz … Christmas standards interpreted by smooth jazz artists … Latin pop … Christmas standards … Christmas standards … classical … reggae … reggae Christmas. Adam clicked off the dial. He longed to have his sister back, if only for the arguments.

Once the turnpike angled away from the coast, both the traffic and the construction dwindled. Not many, it seemed, had family in central Florida. The sky darkened at an alarming pace. He still had a few hours left before midnight in Greenwich, but he also still had over a hundred miles to travel. And his stomach bitched about food.

For a half-second, he considered pulling into a rest stop.

Thirty miles outside Orlando, traffic once again started to glut. Even now, as day evolved into evening, people lined up on the freeway to get into Disney World.

And suddenly Adam realized the huge and obvious hole in his plan.

"Disney World." That was what Ebbets' mother had said. On Christmas Eve, her son would be in Disney World. Not once in the days since that visit in Rhode Island, not once had Adam or Bernard or Cherry stopped to ask themselves where in Disney World Ebbets might be located. It was not as if Disney World was a fifteen-by-fifteen foot corner store and all Adam had to do was check the aisles. Disney World was four massive theme parks. Disney World was forty-seven square miles. Ebbets could be anywhere.

Adam pulled over to the side of the road. Without care, he opened his door and stepped out. Cars and trucks zipped past. Several honked. One or two displayed rude gestures. Adam sat on the hood of the Saab and stared into space.

Ebbets could be anywhere.

He would never reach Ebbets in time. Even if Cherry were able to deactivate the trigger signal, there was still Anna, somewhere in Disney World, until 12:01 A.M.

Faintly, he heard the grumbling of car horns. Somewhere above, a traffic copter circled. Adam watched the gravel at his feet sparkle in the dusk. Sparkle like stars. Adam glanced up. Maybe even down here he could see Filbert's star.

The helicopter's spotlight blinded him. He raised his injured left wrist to block out the phosphorescent glare. The whirr-whirr of the helicopter's rotating blades grew louder. Adam turned away from the light and noticed, with mild confusion, that the highway was empty. A fifty-yard span had been cleared, with police cars blockading either end. A fifty-yard span, with him right in the middle of it.

The helicopter touched down on the highway. Shielding his eyes from a sudden hurricane of dust, Adam noticed two well-dressed women emerge from the copter. They walked toward him. Neither seemed to be holding a gun, which was good.

Then Adam recognized them. Which was bad.

He waved to Special Agents Chang and Epperson.

To which they scowled. As happy to see him as he was to see them.

"Mr. Weiss," said Chang, "we don't have much time. You need to come with us."

Weiss? She called him Weiss? But they only knew him as Arvid Winkle, didn't they?

Special Agent Epperson added, "You need to join us on the helicopter, Mr. Weiss. Now."

In no position to argue, and frankly at a complete loss of options, Adam followed them into the helicopter, which quickly lifted off the ground. Strangely, his first thoughts were of Bernard, and how the copter ride would be making him hurl.

Special Agent Chang smacked him in the jaw.

"Ow! Jesus!"

"Like you didn't have it coming."

"By the way," growled her blonde partner, "do you know it's a federal crime to steal other people's mail?"

The Christmas letters. Damn it. He just couldn't win.

"Yeah, I can explain that."

"Later. Right now, you listen."

Chang took over:

"We've been tracking the warhead. We wanted to know where it was headed, who else was involved, et cetera. We showed up at the ship about twenty minutes after you left. Your friend Bernard's going to be fine. Your friend Cherry told us everything. Everything. Listen, she's not going to be able to intercept the signal. Bernard found a failsafe built into the bomb. Built into this specific bomb. Ebbets' idea of a joke, I guess. We can't intercept the signal. He pushes the trigger and the bomb goes off. This bomb, and all the others. That could be why he stole the bomb in the first place when he left Las Vegas, as some kind of contingency. I don't know. And then we got his call."

They approached EPCOT. The massive geosphere of Spaceship Earth, the park's "giant silver golf ball," was unmistakable. Oddly enough, the helicopter seemed to be heading straight for it. Soon, Adam saw why. Perched atop the geosphere, sipping a can of Pepsi, was a man in a long coat.

"He won't talk to anyone," said Epperson.

"We think he'll talk to you," added Chang.

"Yeah." Adam stared at Ebbets, for the first time seeing the man's face. Wet purple splotches had deformed his skin into a swampy wasteland. This was Adam's nemesis. This small sick man. "He'll talk to me."

Epperson lowered a rope ladder. Chang handed him a megaphone.

"Go ahead, Weiss," she said to him. "Here's your big moment to save the world. Talk."

Chapter Thirty

The megaphone proved ineffective; with the constant din of the helicopter's rotors, no one could hear Ebbets' replies. So the FBI decided that Adam had to descend the rope ladder and conduct his negotiations atop the shiny globe, almost two hundred feet above pavement.

Adam did not approve of this plan of action. Not that it mattered. With the clock ticking, he had little choice. Taking a deep breath, and refusing to look down at the mass of tiny tourists staring up at him from the faraway ground, Adam began his descent. One-handed. He maintained eye contact with Special Agent Chang. Supposedly, the bottom of the rope ladder dangled half a foot above one of the silver geosphere's topmost panels. Once down, Adam had no intention of letting go of the ladder.

Surprisingly, the racket provided by the rotors' whirring helped, overwhelming his senses and providing just enough distraction to keep his heart from launching itself up his throat. Step, step. He had no idea how long the ladder was or how many rungs it contained, but he was certain he had to be nearing his destination. Step, step. He peered into Chang's face for any indication but all he beheld in her dark eyes was apprehension. Step, step. Then a pair of thick black serpents slid across his waist, and Adam panicked. His grip on the ladder loosened and he fell—

Half an inch. The snakes had been Ebbets' arms, spotting him, helping him balance. Adam quickly reached for the ladder, found it with his right hand, and held it very, very tightly. Then he looked at Ebbets.

The man was short, maybe five foot five, and up close his face, emaciated by disease, really did appear skeletal. Adam could trace outlines of cheekbones and jawbones, hollowed pockets of thin white skin, rheumy blue eyes. Atop his skull, random crops of long grey hair, like an ancient, depleted rain forest. His lips and hands palsied. Ebbets opened his mouth to speak and instead launched a series of barking coughs.

Finally, he was able to speak:

"You look better (WHEEZE) on your driver's license."

"Where's the button?"

"It's a switch."

"What?"

Ebbets reached into the deep pockets of his coat and removed a small black square. He showed it to Adam. The trigger indeed was a flat switch, best operated by sliding one's thumb.

"Very cool. Mind if I see it for a second and, you know, accidentally drop it?"

Ebbets chuckled himself into a moist coughing fit. "You're funnier now."

"It's remarkable what stress can do to a guy. Can I have my sister back now, please?"

"You want the trigger (WHEEZE) and you want your sister." Ebbets placed the device back into his coat. "That's greedy."

"It's Christmas."

"That's why I came here to Disney World. I've never been to Disney World but all these people come here for their Christmas vacations. Now that I'm here, up here, seeing it all, you know what I think? I think (WHEEZE) it would've been better (WHEEZE) to come here when I was younger. How about that?"

"Woulda shoulda coulda. Where's Anna?"

A beep emitted from Ebbets' wristwatch. "Five-minute warning," he said, "so I'll make you a deal; I'll offer you a present. Because it's Christmas. Because it's Disney World. I'll give you the trigger or I'll give you Anna. One or the other. Choose."

"Fuck you."

"Fuck me? You sound just like my protégé Bernard! My mother said she had two visitors. Why (WHEEZE) isn't he here with you?"

"He got shot."

Ebbets looked away.

"Don't worry. He's okay. For the next five minutes."

Ebbets thought for a moment, wiped away some blood he had coughed up then nodded. "He's with the bomb?"

"A couple hundred miles southeast of here. Still, an explosion of that magnitude, we should be able to see it from up here, don't you think? We've got great seats."

"The choice is yours now. Not mine. The bomb (WHEEZE) or (WHEEZE) the girl. Four minutes."

Perhaps it was the halo provided by the helicopter's spotlight, perhaps it was the realization that a week's worth of misery had been provided by such a small, pathetic man, perhaps it was something in the way Ebbets fidgeted his trembling fingers up and down the lip of his coat, but in that moment, for Adam, everything clicked. The grieving Mennonite, the man on the table in Las Vegas. Miriam Ebbets. Adam's father. Captain Hoock. Everyone. Adam could see now what was driving this man sitting inches away and understood how to stop him.

"The choice is mine because you're too much of a coward to make it yourself," said Adam. "You want me to stop you. You're begging me to stop you."

"I was right. You are funnier now."

"Your mother could never stop you, could she? Even though you wanted her to? First time we met, all you did was babble on about what a rough childhood you had. Pointing a gun at a stranger in a restroom, all you need are his car keys, and you babble on about what a rough childhood you had?"

"Keep talking." Ebbets turned away. "You've got three minutes."

"My father needed help but he didn't know how to ask so he hurt himself. You need help and you hurt others. You're both fucked up. You think finding you was easy? You know who I had to ask for help? A bank robber. A mob boss. I had to fleece the FBI in order to find you. But I did it."

"Two minutes," whispered Ebbets.

"What do you think, Ebbets? On the phone, you called me an immature twit. Well, this immature twit is twice the man you are. What do you think about that? Huh? What's that make you?"

"I built (WHEEZE) a dozen atomic bombs out of little more than wire hangers and goat cheese. I'm (WHEEZE) a fucking genius."

"Then you know I'm right." Adam touched the man on his bony shoulder. "You know I'm right."

They sat there. Time passed. Rotors whirred and lungs wheezed and Adam kept his hand on Ebbets' arm, near his jutting elbow. Down below, the crowd was corralled by security guards and local PD. Not too far away, in the Magic Kingdom, a train of Christmas floats paraded down Main Street. The onlookers sang carols. Soon there would be fireworks.

Ebbets' wristwatch beeped again.

It was time.

He reached a shaking hand into his pocket.

He frowned. Turned around.

Adam had the trigger in his hand.

"About a minute ago, I stole it out of your pocket," said Adam. "It's a trick I learned from a friend named Cherry."

Adam opened his hand and let the small black square drop several hundred feet.

It did not survive the fall.

"You're not going to jump," Adam asked him, "are you?"

Ebbets let his head hang low. He was dying, but he wasn't suicidal. As Adam had suspected, he was a man who hurt others but never himself. Still, as they approached the rope ladder, Adam insisted Ebbets climb first.

That was when Ebbets told him where he could find Anna; he was helpless not to. Fifteen minutes later, the chopper had touched ground near the base of the giant silver golf ball and Adam rushed past security and into the closest restroom.

"Anna!" he called. "Anna!"

He kicked open a stall door. Empty.

"Anna!"

He kicked open a second. Empty.

"Anna! Anna!"

He kicked a third. It didn't budge. Then he stepped back, took a deep breath, and rushed forward. The lock broke and the door swung wide.

His twin sister, bound and gagged with duct tape, sat on the toilet. She stared up at him with disbelieving blue eyes. Adam hugged her in his arms for a good two minutes and by the end they were both weeping. Then he took to removing the duct tape, carefully, from her mouth and wrists.

"Are you okay?" he asked her. "Did he hurt you? Did he—?"

"Is he gone?"

Adam nodded.

"Then I'm okay."

"I'm so sorry," Adam muttered.

"It's not your fault. How can it be your fault? Neanderthal."

They walked out of the restroom, brother and sister, hands held. Like bees to honey, the press had arrived and already snapped pictures. Special Agent Chang rescued them from the flashbulbs and escorted them into a makeshift operations tent. A cadre of medics immediately treated Anna for assorted cuts and bruises.

Chang handed Adam her phone.

"Hello?" said Adam.

To which Cherry replied, "We didn't go boom."

"No." Adam smiled. "No boom."

"And Anna?"

"She's fine. Thank God. So if it's okay with the Feds, how do you feel about heading up with us tomorrow to Newark?"

"Newark, huh? So tempting. What's tomorrow?"

"It's Christmas."

"Christmas. I hear that's a pretty special holiday. Sure you want me with you and your sister?"

"And my mother. You're going to love her."

"Yeah, I need to go run away now."

Adam laughed. "I'll see you in a little bit."

Adam handed back the phone to the FBI agent, who then browbeat him with a very long speech about civic responsibility, the consequences of lying to a federal officer, etc. She then thanked him for aiding in the capture of British Fred and Yogurt, and assured him that any erroneous warrants issued by the Pennsylvania State Police would be expunged, if he agreed to be debriefed at length on Thursday in Washington and didn't suddenly try to disappear, which would be foolish anyway, she underlined, because the FBI had all of his contact information.

By the time Adam and Anna had emerged from the tent, the crowds and press had been dispersed. The man on top of Spaceship Earth had been arrested and that was that. Besides, it was Christmas Eve. Even members of the press had in-laws to tend. Adam and Anna joined the slow-walking throng strolling out to the parking lot just as EPCOT closed its gates. A vast sea of sedans, compacts, hatchbacks, trucks and minivans lay before them.

"Great," mumbled Adam.

"Yeah," agreed Anna.

And they searched one of the world's largest parking lots for Adam's beat-up green car.

About the author

Joshua Corin,

an accomplished and award-winning

screenwriter and playwright,

is a member of the

Mystery Writers of America

and the Dramatists Guild.

This is his first novel.

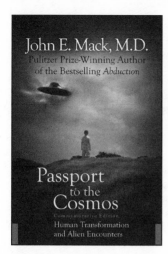

Passport to the Cosmos
Commemorative Edition: Human Transformation and Alien Encounters
■ John E. Mack M.D.

In this edition, with photos and new forewords, Pulitzer Prize–winner John E. Mack M.D. powerfully demonstrates how the alien abduction phenomenon calls for a revolutionary new way of examining the nature of reality and our place in the cosmos. "Fascinating foray into an exotic world. From Harvard psychiatry professor and Pulitzer Prize-winning author … based on accounts of abductions." —*Publishers Weekly*

US$ 14.95 | Pages 368 | Trade Paper 6x9"
ISBN 9781601641618

Hide & Seek
How I Laughed At Depression, Conquered My Fears and Found Happiness
■ Wendy Aron

Hide & Seek shows how to tackle important issues such as letting go of blame and resentment and battling negative thinking. Instructive without being preachy, it is filled with humor and pathos, and a healthy dose of eye-opening insight for the millions who suffer from depression and low self-esteem. "Learning how to cope with hopelessness has never been so fun." —*ForeWord*

US$ 14.95 | Pages 256 | Trade Paper 6x9"
ISBN 9781601641588

Mothering Mother
An unflinchingly honest look at family caregiving
■ Carol D. O'Dell

Mothering Mother is an authentic, "in-the-room" view of a daughter's struggle to care for a dying parent. It will touch you and never leave you.

"O'Dell portrays the experience of looking after a mother suffering from Alzheimer's and Parkinson's with brutal honesty and refreshing grace."—*Booklist*

US$ 12.95 | Pages 208 | Trade Paper 6x9"
ISBN 9781601640468

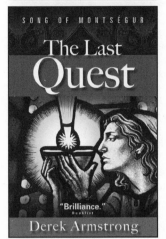

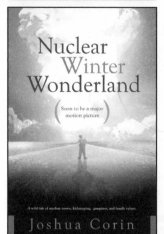
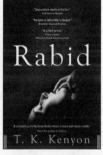
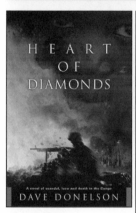

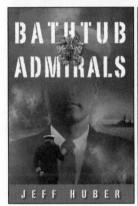

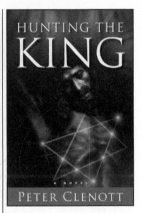